CW00545058

SKEIN AND BONE

Also by V.H. Leslie

Bodies of Water (Salt Publishing, 2015)

Praise for *Skein and Bone*

"The strange and vivid worlds in V.H. Leslie's stories have a nightmarish fairy tale quality to them - a pantry full of secrets, nursery wallpaper whose pattern resembles 'a forest of umbilical cords,' a crinoline petticoat 'like an enormous birdcage.' An absorbing and gorgeously unsettling collection."
- Alison Moore, Author of *The Lighthouse* (Short-Listed for the Man Booker Prize)

"A delicate and considered approach to richly imaginative stories."
- Adam Nevill, Author of *No One Gets Out Alive*

"Tales of quiet unease, enigmatic, beautifully told, varied and darkly poetic. Your trepidation with a V.H. Leslie story is not that you might be disappointed but rather the thrill of just how good it is going to be."
- Stephen Volk, Author of *Whitstable*

"V.H. Leslie's fiction builds in intensity, but at the same time possesses a strange, silky kind of calm. Like a spider, she constructs delicate webs, and she lures you in with elegant, oblique writing. There is an almost unbearable patience to her stories, and, in the best possible sense, a horrible inevitability that shivers within them."
- Conrad Williams, Author of *The Unblemished*

For my mother

"weaveth steadily"

SKEIN AND BONE

V. H. LESLIE

Dear David
Thank you for
befriending me at
breakfast!
Thread & Thrum
V.H. Leslie

UNDERTOW
PUBLICATIONS

Table of Contents

Namesake

Her name was Burden. Cecelia J. Burden. Her parents had at least tried to compensate by giving her a pretty first name, hoping no doubt to disguise the surname behind flowery sibilance. Yet neither name was really quite right. The J stood for Joan or Jan or Jane, a legacy of some distant aunt. Whichever name, it had been forgotten and mislaid long ago with her birth certificate in a loft full of paper. J was happy just to have retained the initial, whatever it stood for. Jane, most probably, on account of how plain she was. Its mystery appealed to her, so that's what she went by J.

J had liked her surname once. Before she really understood what the word meant. She liked the sound of it and would break it into syllables and imagine her name was a place where birds lived. *Bird-den*. Burden. She even decorated her textbooks with scribbles of robins and owls, and dotted her i's with curved silhouettes of birds in flight. It would have been the perfect name for a life a crime, she often thought, or a serial killer. She read a lot about serial killers; they often had hard childhoods, unrealistic responsibilities forced upon them at a young age, a huge emotional chip on their shoulders weighing them down until they finally reacted with violence.

V. H. Leslie

She'd thought about changing her name—she even had the forms at home, ready and signed—but she worried about how her parents would react. Did they like being Burdens? She'd never asked her mother how she felt about taking on her father's name. A test of love, perhaps, a declaration of her devotion, taking on such a heavy toll. But her mother was attracted to suffering—she'd prolong a cold, or walk instead of taking the bus. She probably should have married a Martyr instead.

No, J was resigned to waiting it out. She looked forward to her wedding day for reasons different to most young women; it wasn't the fairy-tale castle or the princess dress that she fantasized about, it was about finally being shot of her name.

But finding a husband was no easy feat. It wasn't like you were going to run into Mr Rochester or Mr Darcy at your local greeting card shop, where J worked stacking shelves. To make matters worse, J wasn't exactly brimming with self-confidence. The weight of her surname accompanied her through her adolescence and into her twenties and had lived up to its meaning, a constant pressure on her neck and shoulders that made her feel like she was hunched.

At least Internet dating allowed you to disguise your projected defects as well as your name. J's mother said only freaks and perverts used the Internet. J thought a hunchback like herself would fit right in. She described herself as busty and bubbly, avoiding the obvious B word on her mind, and issued herself instead a nice humdrum surname—Bentley. She avoided all the potential matches the computer spat at her. She had her own method of selection. When she saw the name, she knew he was the one.

Blithe.

൴

The bar had changed. It hadn't been much to look at back when J knew it, but there'd been something reassuring about the shabby décor, the sticky floor. It had character. You knew what to expect. It was called Frank's or Ed's then, something suitably proprietary and ordinary. Now it was Bar None and J wondered how many drunken men had appealed to the bar's signage as they were manhandled out the door by bouncers. Inside was modern, the tables high, surrounded by bar stools which gave you a strange feeling of vertigo when you managed to get up there. Red lights shone from behind the bar in regimented unison, the glow refracted in the chrome and glass surfaces like the beams of sniper rifles. Sitting by the bar felt like an ambush.

She sat near a large spiral staircase, an artistic showpiece of metal and wire that allowed the men gaping at the bottom to look up women's skirts as they descended. With mock confidence the women negotiated the chrome stairs in their three-inch heels, gripping the banister desperately to prevent themselves falling into the pit of testosterone below.

J scanned the men lining the bar, trying to remember the picture of Andrew on his profile. She hadn't really cared what he looked like, it was the name she was interested in. The bar's clientele had changed as well, which made it harder to spot him. All the men wore suits as if they'd just come from work and the women were as groomed and as glossy as their surroundings, sipping expensive cocktails from martini glasses. *Bar None* seemed pretty apt; there was no individuality here, everyone looked the same. J felt adrift on her bar stool, she glanced at the cocktail menu: *Adonis, Tom Collins, Harvey Wallbanger, Scarlett O'Hara*. Good names. She ordered herself a *Bloody Mary* and waited.

"J?" a man in a red jumper asked.

"Yes. Hello." She held out her hand and he shook it.

"Andrew," he said. "I'm sorry I'm late. Parking was a nightmare."

"You won't be drinking then?" J regretted the two glasses she'd had at home and the cocktail in front of her.

"I might. I can leave my car here, pick it up in the morning if..." he trailed off, hoping not to have sounded presumptuous.

Andrew sat down on the barstool opposite. J had already learnt it wasn't easy to do elegantly and a puff of air dispersed as he made contact with the upholstery. His face reddened.

"The stool..." he began,

J laughed. "Mine's the same. But there is one cool thing about them."

She pressed the lever on her chair and suddenly disappeared under the table. She reappeared with a hydraulic hiss.

"That *does* look cool." Andrew found the lever and began to disappear from view.

Behind them the barman shook his head at the newcomers bobbing up and down like fish caught in a net.

The chrome spiral staircase must have been an architect's joke or a test of sobriety. How many people had fallen down, J wondered, trying her best to concentrate on each step. It didn't help that her vision was blurred.

Andrew was waiting at the bottom, holding her coat. She hoped he was gentlemanly enough not to glance up through the rails. She'd allowed herself to get ridiculously drunk on the first date; there would be no coming back from this, she thought. She'd be ruined in his eyes forever as wife material.

"I'll walk you home," Andrew said, helping her with her coat.

"I'm a Burden," she spluttered in reply.

"It's no hassle."

"No, that's my name. Burden. Not Bentley."

Andrew looked at her for a moment, weighing up whether to make a joke or not, wondering whether she'd be able to make light of it.

"It's not funny. *You* try being a Burden?"

"It could be worse."

"Could it?"

"I went to school with a girl called Paige Turner. Seriously."

J smiled.

"Anything else I should know?" he asked. "What does the J stand for?"

Plain Jane. But buoyed up with alcohol, on Andrew's arm, she didn't feel plain at all. She felt blithe.

"Nothing at all," she replied.

"What's in a name anyway?" Andrew asked later as they lay in bed.

J shrugged, content and satisfied, sleep weighing heavier on her than her name ever had. Andrew's flat was small and comfortable, surprisingly decorative for a bachelor. Not that she'd seen a great deal, led almost straight away to the bedroom. It was a small room but felt bigger because of the high ceiling, with mezzanine at the far end, which Andrew said led to the attic, though J couldn't see a ladder. From where she lay, she could watch the shadows gathering up there, black shapes converging behind the rails. She blinked and the shadows dispersed.

"It's a hard name to live up to," Andrew continued, "Blithe. People expect you to be constantly happy."

J hadn't intended to be so easy on the first date, but he'd been so understanding about her name, her initial deceit. If he'd noticed the way she hunched over he hadn't mentioned it, he made her feel beautiful and he was so much more attractive than she'd hoped. Naked in his arms, she thought of other names for herself, taunting herself with the insults her mother threw at the TV when celebrities wore too few clothes. *Whore, Slut, Slag.* She didn't want to think about that right now, but the words repeated themselves over and over in her mind until they became a litany. Blithe's voice in her ear couldn't compete.

"People don't imagine that you'd have troubles and strife with a name like mine. J? J?"

But J was fast asleep, dreaming of any name but her own.

Burden and Blithe went well together. J hadn't expected Andrew to call after such a drunken first date but he did, the very next day. And he'd surprised her further by asking to see her that night. Three weeks later, they'd spent every available minute in each other's company. J had even acquired a drawer and a cabinet in the bathroom and her stuff was slowly creeping in, cluttering up Andrew's small flat.

"Maybe I could store some stuff up there," J asked

one day, pointing at the mezzanine. "You don't seem to use it."

It was the only area in the flat that gave the impression of space. Andrew hadn't said as much, but without a ladder it was clearly off limits.

He shook his head. "I'm in the process of decorating. I'll clear out the cupboard in the hallway instead, how about that?"

J smiled, happy that he was making space for her in his life. She looked up at the mezzanine all the same and for a brief moment had the curious feeling of being watched.

To change the name but not the letter is to marry for worse and not for better. Such was her mother's response to the news that they'd set a date. It was typical of her mother to kill her enthusiasm, to lace her mood with a little bit of the misery that she enjoyed so much. J didn't care about old wives' tales; changing her name was her priority and she wanted to be blithe more than anything.

Yet it wasn't just her mother cautioning her whirlwind romance. J had moved in entirely now with Andrew, yet she was far from settled. *Cold feet* she told herself, though she knew that wasn't true. The negativity wasn't of an emotional kind, it was more tangible and it stemmed, she was certain, from the mezzanine.

"Maybe we could move," J asked one night in bed. Andrew had always regaled her with his stories of foreign travel yet he looked uncomfortable at the suggestion.

"I can't, J, I'm tied here."

"Why?" she asked. He wasn't particularly enthused about his job, though it allowed him to work from home. He'd never introduced her to friends or family, in fact he was frustratingly vague about all family ties. What was keeping him here?

"I'd never get out of this mortgage," he said, taking her hand. "I'm up to the hilt in debt I'm afraid."

Marry for worse and not for better sprang to mind, but she swept it away with *for better or worse.*

J woke in the middle of the night, conscious that someone was watching her. Andrew was asleep at her side, his snoring obscuring the sound of something above. She wanted to reach for the bedside lamp but she couldn't move. She stared back in the blackness and listened hard.

She heard footsteps on the mezzanine.

She lay still, willing the noise to repeat itself, wondering if she had heard it at all. She waited, gripping Andrew in readiness.

A creeping movement this time. Unmistakable now. Something was up on the mezzanine. Her mind conjured the image of a person walking up there, sneaking about in the dark.

She shook Andrew awake.

"There's someone up there," she whispered, pointing in the darkness.

Andrew looked about, barely comprehending. He switched on the bedside lamp, flooding the room with light. "What?"

"I heard a noise," she repeated, "up there."

Andrew sighed. "Oh. That. Sometimes birds get into the attic. It's happened before. They're protected, would you believe. Allowed to nest up there."

"It didn't sound like birds," J said.

"Listen, J, there's nothing to worry about."

12

"But Andrew-"

"I'll check it out in the morning if you like." And with that he turned off the light.

Burden.

Bird-den.

She imagined a room full of birds in flight. She watched them orbiting an attic space, circling it again and again and again, until she drifted back to sleep.

J was in the wedding aisle again, stacking the shelves with images of happy couples, garters, and wedding cakes. Since her engagement she spent longer in this part of the shop than any other, arranging the cello-phane-wrapped cards in order of preference instead of price codes. The manager, Sharon, a girl barely out of college, was more interested in her mobile phone than what J did. She barely noticed that J had neglected the birthday and bereavement aisles, along with the balloons and silly string display.

J looked around the shop. It expressed every senti-ment but the one she felt. She couldn't stop thinking about the birds in the attic. Andrew's conviction that there was nothing to worry about had been enough for her to go to sleep. But the birds had swooped into her dreams instead and flown around and around her mind like an inky whirlwind. It wasn't just the birds; J hadn't liked the way Andrew had cut her off, refusing to listen to her as if she hadn't said anything at all. Was that what she was expected to do? To accept Andrew's word on the subject despite her misgivings, to honour and obey him?

Yet he'd been so considerate before she left for work that day. He'd made her breakfast in bed and promised to check the attic when she left. He said that maybe the wedding stress was getting to her. He'd help more with organising the venue and the caterers. He added that he didn't expect her to take his name if she didn't want to. They were a modern couple after all. He'd happily be a Burden.

J knocked the cards from their stand and they fell like confetti. What were a few birds in the attic compared to the albatross about her neck?

J stooped to pick up the cards from the floor. *Warm Wedding Wishes, To the Happy Couple, May Your Nest Be Filled With Joy.* J slipped the last card into her apron pocket.

J went home sick that afternoon but sat in the café opposite Andrew's flat instead, watching for him to leave. She felt like a criminal casing the joint. She sipped her second tea and considered what she really knew about the man she was marrying. *Freaks and perverts*, her mother's voice chimed.

Andrew emerged an hour later, his Bag-For-Life folded neatly under his arm, presumably on his way to the supermarket. J would have adequate time; she could be in and out without him ever knowing. It was only when she stood in the bedroom, staring up at the mezzanine, that she wondered whether she was breaking some moral law, committing some breach of trust. He hadn't exactly forbidden her to go up there, but then why the need for such secrecy? Maybe she should just leave it be.

Just a peek.

So she hauled the bedside drawers across the room, stacked a table on top and a chair from the living room. She stood back, assessing her crude ladder, then began her ascent.

The mezzanine was more spacious than she imagined, unfurnished and bare, with no signs of decorating. It had a perfect view of the room below and the bed in the centre. J imagined something monstrous watching them sleep, like a gargoyle on a Gothic façade, looking down while they made love.

She turned her attention back to the mezzanine and saw a small door in the wall that presumably led into the loft, though something closer drew her eye. Coiled up at the edge of the platform was a rope ladder. But what was the point of it being up here, J thought? Unless someone could throw it down?

J moved towards the door, trying not to think of the fairy-tale she'd been told as a child, of the princess with the extraordinarily long hair. The princess who was locked away from the world with her unusual name: Rapunzel.

The door opened onto a dark and musty space. J moved through the darkness, through a rank and pungent smell. She followed it while her eyes adjusted and began to discern shapes.

A stained mattress lay in the middle of a room, amid a scattering of black feathers. It was a nest, but not for birds. Someone lived up here.

J looked around in alarm. A squatter? But the ladder implied that Andrew knew.

J stepped backwards, the smell suddenly stronger. Something was close. Something was watching her. She scanned the room and saw the whites of wild eyes staring back at her from a blackened face in the dark.

The figure was filthy, hunched over in the gloom. J could make out a tangle of hair, a ripped and tattered nightdress, a strong abhorrent feminine smell. And at her feet, a coil of rope tied at her ankle.

Why would she be tied here? Why wouldn't

she scream? And then she saw. She nearly screamed herself.

The woman had no mouth.

J moved closer—it was a trick of the light, surely, but the woman's face was oddly smooth where her mouth should have been and her face was expressionless and vacant, except for her eyes which blazed with rage at J's intrusion.

The wild woman moved so fast that J barely had time to react. She managed to stumble back, through the impossibly small door, back onto the mezzanine. Crouching, she tried desperately to unroll the ladder but her hands were shaking and the figure was at the door, rushing towards her, hands clawing at the air.

J remembered the night she met Andrew. The ridiculous chrome staircase in the trendy bar. *Bar None*. How she had to concentrate on each step.

And J was falling, landing on the tower she'd made, scattering the furniture like a house of cards. She landed hard against the floor, knocking the breath from her chest so she had nothing with which to scream.

Burden-Blithe did have a ring to it. Double barrels were the trend nowadays but she'd always thought it cruel forcing someone else to share her Burden. Tempting as it was to let someone else carry it with her, she'd rather simply be rid of the whole thing.

Just Blithe, she thought. How did the song go? *Be you blithe and bonnie*. Bonnie and Clyde. *Blithe and Bonnie, Bonnie and Clyde, Jekyll and Hyde*. Some partnerships were destined for infamy.

J shook her head clear and she looked up at the mezzanine, remembering what she'd seen. She put her hand to her temple and was surprised to find she was bleeding.

Some couples amalgamated their surnames. A stab at gender equality, no doubt, merging parts of their names to make something wholly original. Smith and Jones became Smones or Jith. J smiled but felt a stabbing sensation behind her eyes. Burden-Blithe would be Burthe or Blurden. *Bludgeon*, she thought, looking up at the mezzanine.

Andrew deposited the groceries in the kitchen and walked through to the bedroom. The rope ladder was down and he smiled, undoing his shirt and pulling off his trousers. In just his underpants, he climbed up.

"Honey, I'm home," he called.

He moved through the darkness with familiarity. "Where are you, Mary?" he said.

He smiled more broadly when he saw Mary lying face down on the mattress, her nightdress pulled up, waiting for him.

"So you want your turn do you?" he said. "Happy to see me?"

"Ecstatic," said a voice behind him.

Andrew turned and saw J hunched in the dark, a bloodied gash on her brow.

"What are *you* doing here?"

"I could ask the same of you. Checking for birds?"

He looked at his feet.

"I found your little secret."

Andrew made to object but J merely glanced toward the figure on the mattress. Andrew could see that J had tied her down with the rope.

"There shouldn't be any secrets between a husband and wife."

Andrew sighed. "I tried to tell you that very first

night. I tried to tell you about my trouble and strife. My-"

"Wife."

J had seen the gold band on the wild woman's finger as she'd lunged at her, pushing her back down to earth.

"I was too young," Andrew said. "She was so different. I didn't notice that she wasn't quite right."

"You didn't notice? You would have *married me*," J said. There was a name for what he was. Her mind struggled over the syllables—a polygamist. There was a name for what she was, too, though she wasn't ready to say it.

Andrew wiped the tears from his eyes. "I *still* want to marry you. I'd do anything for you, J. Just name it."

For a moment J saw the Blithe she'd met on the first night. But he'd lured her with false promises and a name that was already taken.

"I should have divorced her," he said, "but I'm all she has. She needs me."

More likely the other way around, J thought. "You're still making the most of your conjugal rights, I see."

Andrew covered himself with his hands. "I know it's hard to understand, but I'm bound here. I'm tied."

Mrs Blithe—the name was already occupied. That made her the other woman. She wasn't wife material at all.

She'd wanted so much to be blithe. *Blithe and Bonnie. Bonnie and Clyde. Jekyll and Hyde.* A life a crime. She would have done anything for him. She had. She'd done it for his name's sake. But names ache.

"You need to untie her, J," Andrew said, walking towards the mattress. J thought it was a bit rich considering that he was the one who'd tied Mary up in the

18

first place. The old ball and chain. J didn't like his tone but she let it go because of what she had done.

As Andrew edged closer he saw it too.

"J?" he whispered.

"I finished the decorating," she said evenly, pointing at the blood on the walls.

There had been a lot of it, more than J had expected. So much that it had drenched the wild woman's face, obscuring her features. J wondered whether she had imagined the absence of lips, the pink slip of a tongue. Either way, Mary was his silent partner now.

Andrew collapsed onto the mattress, taking Mary's limp hand in his. He sobbed into the bloodied sheets.

There couldn't be any lawful impediment in the way of their happiness but J saw now that Andrew would always be tethered. A memory was stronger than a name.

Blithe and Bonnie, Bonnie and Clyde, Jekyll and Hyde.

The names soared around and around in her mind like birds in flight. J flew with them, barely noticing that she'd forced the rope around Andrew's neck. That she'd pushed him down onto the marital bed, that she'd made him stare into what was left of the face he'd made his vows to.

Afterward, J climbed back down the rope ladder. The pressure on her neck and shoulders had eased and she walked into the world standing tall, ready to make a name for herself.

Skein and Bone

They parted company at Paris Gare Montparnasse, Laura and Libby waving goodbye to Jess who stood with her coterie of male admirers. Laura was only pretending to wave goodbye to Jess and the boys; it was Paris that she was really bidding farewell. Libby, on the other hand, waved enthusiastically to her friends on the platform, regretting already that she had agreed to leave. As if to confirm her misgivings, Luc kissed Jess on the cheek and the other boys jostled around, eager to impress her now that Libby was gone. They didn't look back. And as the train pulled out of the station, Libby wished for a moment that she didn't have a sister.

Laura sat at her side, a book already open on her lap.

"Happy now?" Libby said.

"You didn't have to come. I'm quite capable of going on my own."

"Yeah, and Mum would be really happy about that."

"Your choice."

Laura always had to have the last word so Libby responded by switching on her iPod and crossing her arms. "Wake me up when we're there."

Laura nodded but didn't take her eyes off her guide-

21

book. She was used to her sister's moods and wasn't going to allow it to affect the trip. She hadn't allowed it to affect things so far, though her sister had been particularly obstinate since their arrival in Paris. When Libby teamed up with her best friend Jess, trouble usually followed and Laura was under no illusions that their mother had insisted on Laura's going as a way of restraining them. Laura was bookish and dependable, the sobering presence in their trio. And though Libby was quite free-spirited, as the older sibling she maintained an iota of responsibility with her sister in tow.

But the boys they'd met in Paris had proven a challenge. Jess had been smitten with Luc straight away and Libby enjoyed being surrounded by male admirers. They'd already extended their time in Paris. Laura didn't mind at first, as it allowed her time to peruse the art galleries at her leisure (while her sister and Jess sat in cafés drinking and smoking their student loans away) but it didn't leave a lot of time to see the rest of France.

When Luc had suggested that they leave the youth hostel to stay in his apartment in the Latin Quarter Laura thought it really was time to go. What she couldn't understand was that her sister had actually considered the offer and that without Laura's voice of reason, Libby would now be shacked up with Jess and a load of Parisian boys.

Perhaps that was why her sister was so pissed at her.

They had never been very alike. People always talk about unbreakable bonds between sisters but Libby and Laura had always just tolerated each other. Libby was beautiful and very aware of it, with naturally golden hair that fell in waves to her shoulders. Laura was happy to admit that she was fairly plain, as if all the beauty in her parent's genetic recipe had been exhausted in the creation of their firstborn, but she prided herself on her intellect. A far greater asset, she reasoned, viewing the attainments of the mind more pressing than the pursuits of the flesh. Laura poured over books while Libby chased boys. Even their mother looked at them quizzically sometimes, as if she couldn't believe they had both come from the same space in her womb.

Jess however wasn't bound by sibling duty so she opted to stay in Paris until the end of the week and then meet the girls in La Rochelle. Laura didn't like Jess. She was a constant reminder of what her sister could become if left to cultivate her vanity and arrogance. But perhaps Libby wasn't beyond saving.

"Votre billet, s'il vous plaît."

Libby woke with a start to a young conductor waiting. The seat beside her was empty.

"Um. Sorry. *Excusez-moi.*" She looked through her sister's backpack. Laura was always in charge of the documents and paperwork. It was one of the perks of having her along on the trip, plus she had the best French. She was the reliable one.

The conductor looked at his watch.

Laura returned and handed the conductor the tickets from her pocket. He punched them and gave them back.

"Where have you been?" Libby asked.

"To get some food. Want some?" She dropped a cellophane wrapped baguette into her lap.

"Why didn't you wake me?"

"You said not to wake you until we got there."

"You're so pedantic. Don't sneak off, ok?"

"I've been on my own in Paris for nearly three

V. H. Leslie

weeks, I think I can manage."

"Whatever." Libby stretched. "You were in art galleries. You're not as worldly wise as me."

"Clearly."

"Hey!" She raised an eyebrow at her sister, an expression she used occasionally to remind Laura that she was the eldest and therefore in charge. If she knew how it furrowed her forehead she probably wouldn't do it. She opened the baguette and took a bite. Then she pulled a magazine out of her bag and flicked through the pages. She folded back the corners, a habit she had for when she saw an outfit she liked. Not that she could afford the price tag of many of the garments gracing the glossy pages. Or, for that matter, the clothes that adorned the shop windows in all those little Parisian boutiques that had mercilessly lured her. She'd decided that when she got home she was going to uncover her mother's sewing machine in the loft, perhaps take some lessons at the local college. After all, imitation is the highest form of flattery.

"What are you reading?" Laura asked.

"Vogue."

"It's in French."

"So? The language of fashion is universal."

Laura rolled her eyes but peered at the double-page spread anyway. It featured a group of anorexic models in animal print. "What's she wearing?"

"Dior."

"Looks more like a zebra."

"It's the fashion."

"Well she looks more like a fashion victim," Laura observed, "but not as much as the zebra." She chuckled at her own joke, only stopping when she saw her sister's eyebrow rise again. She returned to her guidebook instead. "I didn't realise but we're passing through a

24

small village that has a really awesome château."

"Uh huh." Libby didn't look up from her magazine.

"It says, "The house is a resplendent example of Renaissance architecture, notable for it's association with the Court of Louis XV and for playing host to some of the most lavish balls of the eighteenth century.""

Libby turned the pages of her magazine but Laura could tell the lavish balls had her attention.

"Why don't we get off there, take a look around and pick up the train later?"

Libby shifted in her seat. "It's getting late. If it's a small place there might not be a later train."

"We could catch one tomorrow. We could always stay in a hotel. There's bound to be one if the château is mentioned in here." She held up the guidebook to support her point.

Libby closed her magazine with a sigh. "It could be deserted."

"Aren't you always saying I should be more spontaneous?" Laura insisted. "You know, like you?"

Libby shook her head.

"It also has." Laura traced the text with her finger, skim reading, "a library, an ornamental garden, an aviary and er... an "unsurpassed collection of period costume.""

"Ok, ok. Just a few hours. Then we'll carry on to La Rochelle."

"Fine."

When the train pulled into the next station they were the only two to get off.

"There has to be a mistake," Laura said as she thumped the pages of her guidebook once more.

25

"Brilliant," Libby said, taking the last warm swig of mineral water. She had made a seat for herself from their luggage and was watching her sister with increasing irritation. They were camped in front of large wrought iron gates. A sign reading "*Fermé*" in large red lettering hung from the bars. Laura peered through to the château beyond.

The road to the château had been difficult; there were few signposts and the château itself was hardly mentioned. They'd followed a sketchy map in the guidebook but the book was old and many of the street names were omitted. Added to this, the village seemed pretty deserted. They passed derelict buildings, run down farmland and neglected vineyards, seeing only the occasional inhabitant whose directions to the château had been likewise vague. On top of this, the day had been unexpectedly humid. Even now, in the gathering dusk, the heat remained like a heady, suffocating weight. Their clothes clung to them and the dust from the road had seemed somehow to stick to their skin, getting between their toes and on their lips. They licked it away but could taste the red earth.

It became clear that there was no hotel or bed and breakfast and it was looking increasingly likely that they would be spending the night sleeping on a bench in the railway station.

"What do we do now?" Laura asked.

"I don't know. You're the one with all the answers."

"I thought it would be open. I thought there would be a later train or at least somewhere to stay." She sat on the ground beside her sister. She thought back to the train station. To the tourist information and accommodation guides in the revolving bookstand next to the ticket office. That she hadn't picked up.

"Usually I plan things a bit more."

"Spontaneous doesn't suit everyone," Libby replied. "Ok, here's what we'll do, we'll head back to the station and on the way we'll knock on a few doors and see if anyone knows of a hotel or something."

"I feel funny about knocking on people's doors."

"You're the one who made us get off the train."

"Ok. Ok."

"It's starting to rain," Libby announced as she began to gather her things.

"No it's not," Laura replied. But as she reached out her arm for her backpack she felt it. It was replenishing at first but within the space of a few minutes it fell in floods, intent on washing away the humidity.

"Let's go," Libby called.

Laura nodded but gripped the railings. "It's just so annoying. We came all this way." She rattled the bars in frustration and was surprised when the latch gave way. The gate opened ever so slightly, though still secured by the chain. It was wide enough for a person to squeeze through.

Libby looked at Laura.

"No way," Laura began, "it *says* it's closed."

"I'm only going to have a quick look."

And with that she slid between the gap.

Even in the diminishing light, and even with in rain, it was clear to see that the garden was overgrown and neglected. Laura could make out a variety of topiary shapes lining the path, their forms vaguely familiar. They looked like birds. Some seemed to lean over, their beaks in the ground as if rummaging for food. Others seemed to stand upright, pushing out their chests, perched high on their circular platforms. And finally, at the front of the house, two peacocks perched either side of the entrance. They guarded the entrance like beautiful gargoyles, their fan of feathers spread out like a hand of playing cards, their eyes ever watchful.

The château was a grand, impressive building. It was built in the Renaissance style, comprised of pilasters and large windows and topped with cylindrical turrets. In the dusk, the slate roof, illuminated by the moon, appeared almost blue. The château looked like a smaller version of the Château de Chenonceau they had visited in the Loire Valley when they first arrived; back when Laura still had some influence over the places they visited as a group. Laura had wanted to see it because it was created by women and designed for the sole purpose of producing aesthetic pleasure. A castle where female aristocrats could play architect, where beauty as opposed to war had governed its construction. Even Libby, not one for heritage sites, had appreciated its grandeur. And here they stood, soaking wet, at the entrance of a building that rivalled it.

Libby took the large brass knocker in her hand.

"What are you doing?"

Libby knocked in response. There was no answer. The rain continued. Libby went to the windows and peered through.

"What can you see?"

"Not much. It's dark."

"Is anyone there?"

"I don't think so."

Libby returned and knocked again. She waited a while longer then tried the doorknob. It turned in her hand.

"Wait," Laura cautioned. "Wait! We can't go in."

"Why not? I thought you wanted to see this place?"

"I do, but-"

"C'mon, just for a moment, until the rain stops." She pushed the door open and stepped inside.

Laura stood a moment longer on the dark veranda then hurried in after her sister.

Libby felt the walls, looking for a light switch. "Guess there's no electricity then."

"It's probably abandoned."

"We don't know that."

Laura followed Libby. The diminishing light shone through the large windows, illuminating the passages. They rounded a corner and found themselves in a large drawing room. It was decorated with high panelled walls, ornate cornicing spiralling out onto the ceiling toward a huge chandelier that refracted the light in glittering pools.

"It's like a castle," Libby exclaimed. She turned on her heel and darted back into the corridors, swept away on her own tour. She was like a magpie uncovering a nest of shiny treasures. Laura followed steadily behind.

"Wait, hold on, you're going too fast."

The corridors snaked further into the building, away from the light of the windows. Libby followed the sound of her sister's footsteps. She heard her climb a staircase.

"Wait."

When she reached the dark landing Laura didn't know which way to go. The house was quiet.

"Libby? Where are you?"

She walked slowly now, a sense of isolation making her cautious. She looked into each room that she passed, hoping she wouldn't find the owner sitting in the darkness. She felt a tightness in her chest, a fluttering anxiety, aware that this was an act of trespass.

She needed to get her sister and get out.

She found Libby standing in a room full of people. Laura was so shocked to find the place inhabited that she nearly cried out. But as her eyes became accustomed to the dark she saw that they weren't people but mannequins, dressmaker's dummies donned in the most elaborate costumes.

"Isn't this place amazing?" said Libby.

Laura, intending to reprimand her sister, found instead that she was drawn into the strange room. The mannequins converged around Libby, as if they were gossiping at a grand soirée. Each wore a dress more extravagant than the next. They wore gowns with full skirts scaffolded by panniers and copious petticoats that pushed the fabric out in a billowing mass. They had low, scooped necklines and fitted bodices that emphasized the hourglass figures that had once been so fashionable. They were different by degrees; some had pleated underskirts revealed by decorative loops, whilst others exhibited sleeves that, at the elbows, swelled into layers of frills. One even flaunted a sacque, a loose fold that fell from the shoulder of the garment to the hem, resembling a cape. Each was made of the finest materials. Brocade and silk, voile and velvet, ribbons and lace, tassels and pearls and feathers, all in an array of muted pastels and silvers that glittered in the moonlight.

"They must be so old," Laura said, reaching out to touch the fabric. She expected it to be paper-thin but all the gowns shone with fresh lustre, as if they had just been made.

"It's like the dressing room of Marie Antoinette," Libby exclaimed. "Look on the dressing table, you can see the powdered wigs. And there's a selection of hats in the boxes over there."

"I don't think we should be snooping around."

"How can we not? This place is amazing. Look in the wardrobe."

Laura didn't want to, but she opened the door. A crinoline petticoat hung inside like an enormous bird-cage. Laura touched one of the hoops; it was strong, reinforced with whalebone, the kind used in the nineteenth century before steel hoops were favoured. But to Laura it reminded her of a medieval torture device she'd seen in a museum in Carcassonne, a gibbet used to detain prisoners as they perished slowly from starvation. The skirt hanging on its railing looked just as torturous.

"This one's my favourite," Libby declared as Laura closed the wardrobe door. She moved aside to reveal another mannequin. Until now it had been concealed behind her.

It wore a gown of red. The skirt, not quite as full as the others, was topped with a corset in burgundy brocade, the edges of which were scalloped into sharp points. It was fastened at the back with a bright red ribbon that tied into a bow at the lower back. It was a fairly simple design compared to the other gowns but there was something devastatingly beautiful about it. Then Laura noticed the waist.

Libby had noticed it too and was caressing the bodice enviously. She liked the way it drew the body in, the way it coerced the shape into such a beautiful silhouette. An impossible waistline.

"Do you know, Scarlett O'Hara's waist was seventeen inches," Libby said clutching her hands around the mannequin's waistline.

"Scarlett O'Hara was fictional."

"Still, it was typical of the age."

"No wonder everyone died so young. Probably of

31

collapsed ribs and compressed internal organs."

"I think it's beautiful."

"It's unrealistic and we shouldn't be here."

"I wonder what it would look like on?"

"No way. What if someone finds us? How would we explain what we're doing?"

"There's no one here," Libby said, untying the ribbon. She turned to a gilt mirror above a fireplace and stood behind the mannequin, imagining what the corset would look like on. "Don't you think it would suit me?"

Laura looked in the mirror and met the eyes of her sister's reflection. The red gown seemed to draw out her colour, as if her blood was draining into the gown. Her pallor, now white, made her features strangely cruel.

A blurring at the corner of Laura's eye distracted her from the curious image of her sister. She could make out a shadow in the corner of the room by the door. She looked deeper into the mirror. Had there been a mannequin there? She turned slowly.

A woman stood in the doorway, her face illuminated by the light of a candelabra she held in her hand. Laura jumped and Libby shrieked, releasing the mannequin and the red gown.

"Um, *excusez-moi*," Laura stuttered. She drew her phrase book from her pocket and rifled through the pages to disguise her reddening cheeks. Eventually she explained in convoluted French that they were lost.

The woman looked at them both for a moment, as if considering the words. Laura wondered if she'd made a mistake with the pronunciation and after a few more moments, considered that maybe she hadn't uttered a sentence at all. That maybe fear had taken her voice.

Finally the woman moved. She walked towards the

red gown, picked up a large sheet that lay discarded on the floor and threw it over the dress. Then she held out an arm and directed them to follow her. They retraced their steps back through the house, the dark corridors brightened now from the light of the candelabra, revealing dozens of portraits on the walls. Staunch-faced relics from a bygone time, left to reside over the labyrinthine passages of the house, watched their departure, for Laura fully expected to be shown the front door. She wouldn't have been surprised if the woman had called the police and she wondered how she would explain the whole episode.

Instead they were directed to a library.

Laura gasped.

It was a large room and each of the four walls, from the floor to the ceiling was filled with books. Even the inside of the door was papered with their image, like a secret doorway, so that when closed you would be literally immersed. In the centre of the room were four large armchairs arranged around a circular table on which more books were piled, small towers that clearly couldn't fit anywhere else.

The lady instructed them to sit and lit the sconces on the wall and a grand chandelier overhead with a taper. She then busied herself lighting a fire in the stone hearth. All the light emerging allowed Laura and Libby to take in her appearance. She wore a long black dress with a high neck. It looked like the kind of attire a maid or a housekeeper would wear in the nineteenth century. Even her face seemed to bear a strange sense of age, though her body belied it. In fact, there was something curious about her face, not unattractiveness exactly but a kind of emptiness. Perhaps it was merely the mask of servitude, but it was undoubtedly not a face you wanted to look at for very long. With the room now providing an inviting glow the woman withdrew, leaving the girls alone among the leather-bound relics.

"What the hell is going on?" Libby asked in a whisper.

"I'm not sure."

"Maybe we should go."

"We can't go now. We've trespassed. There will be consequences."

"Even more reason to go."

The woman returned with a silver tray and two small crystal glasses filled with an amber liquid. She offered them.

"*Merci,*" the girls said in unison.

Laura winced at the taste but it warmed her as much as the fire.

"*Asseyez-vous près du feu et je prépare le repas et une chambre pour la nuit,*" the housekeeper said softly. Again, Laura had the same strange reluctance to make eye contact. The housekeeper began to leave but paused by the door and turned. "*Excusez la vieille maison, il a beaucoup de souvenirs.*" Then she bowed and exited.

"What did she say?" Libby asked once the door was closed, "I heard something about beds."

"I think she said that she will prepare us a meal and a room for the night." They exchanged glances. "We are to wait here by the fire. Then she said to excuse the house and its memories. I think. Her accent was very strong."

Libby smiled broadly. "We've hit the jackpot here."

Laura frowned. "It's very hospitable, considering she found us snooping around her house."

"Perhaps it isn't her house. Did you see the way

she was dressed? She looks more like a servant." Libby leaned forward in her chair. "Maybe she's being so nice to us because she doesn't want to get into trouble with her master."

"And why would she get into trouble?"

"Negligence. She left the door open. And the gate wasn't much of an obstacle. Surely it's her job to keep this place secure? It's asking for trouble."

"And we're the trouble."

Libby smiled. "You bet."

Laura stood and perused the shelves, running her finger along the spines. There were the classic authors one would expect of a library of this kind—Proust and Flaubert, Zola—but there was also an array of non-fiction and political treatises. There was a wealth of knowledge at her fingertips but Laura felt strangely uneasy at the discovery.

Laura reached for a leather-bound copy of Proust's *Le Temp Retrouvé* and in doing so glimpsed the garden outside. She put the book down and walked to the window. The rain had stopped as if it had merely conspired to get them to inside. A thought that unsettled Laura more than it should have. She could see now how overgrown and neglected the garden was, a sad testament to the spirit of the house. All except for the topiary birds, whose shapes were concrete and precise, the only order amid the confusion. Peering closer, Laura saw that many of the birds were surrounded by willow cloches; constructions designed to shape and curtail their growth. They looked appropriately enough like large birdcages, fashioned to prevent their beautiful captives from taking flight.

"Laura? Why do you think she covered up the red gown?"

Laura could have reasoned that perhaps it was the

most expensive, or the oldest, but as with everything about this place Laura was not sure.

Dinner was a lavish affair. The housekeeper spoke very little. She instructed the girls to eat, then marched back and forth to the kitchen bringing out a variety of courses on silver platters. Her movements were controlled and considered, graceful despite carrying dishes and plates, a feat perhaps even more noteworthy because of her small frame. She was slight in build and had a wasp-like waist; drawn in by the corset she was undoubtedly wearing underneath her black dress.

The table was laid as if the house were expecting important dignitaries. Silver candelabras ran the length of the tale, interspersed by arrangements of wild flowers. Even the crockery was decorated with delicate illustrations of birds of paradise that seemed to flutter eagerly in anticipation of meal to come. There was more cutlery than they knew what to do with but as soon as the housekeeper placed each meal down, she withdrew, closing the door softly behind her, and so the girls dispensed with manners to grapple at the feast before them.

"Isn't she going to join us?" Laura asked with her mouth full.

"She's clearly a maid. That's what she does. She waits on people. Maybe she thinks we're royalty."

"It's a bit archaic, don't you think?" But Laura saw that her sister was having no problem at all stomaching their sudden elevation of status.

They feasted on the finest food; *cèpes à la Bordelaise*—mushrooms sautéed with garlic and parsley—before a generous serving of *moules marinières*, which arrived steaming in white wine with shallots. This was followed by *blanquette de veau*—a rich and creamy veal stew—and was concluded with *clafoutis*. For each course, the housekeeper served a different wine. The meal became a heady, fragrant experience, a gastronomic banquet of tastes and flavours. Libby's lips were stained with merlot.

"What if it's been poisoned," Laura asked holding up the crystal goblet. They looked at each other a moment before bursting into laughter, the wine making them light-headed and high-spirited.

"I wouldn't care, it tastes too delicious."

Laura pushed a cherry around her plate with a fork. "I don't think I can eat another bite."

"Give it here," Libby said, "it's too good to waste."

They leaned back, nursing their engorged stomachs and licking their lips to recapture the memory of the meal.

"How did they do it?" Laura asked.

"What?"

"Wear corsets like that. Every day." She undid the top button of her jeans.

"Discipline, I suppose."

"You wouldn't be able to eat meals like this," Laura continued, pointing at the empty plates and bowls and glasses strewn before them.

"Unless you were laced in really tight."

Laura put her hand to her mouth. "Don't, I'll be sick."

The housekeeper returned with a tray of strong smelling coffee and a cake stand full of small pastries and chocolates before leaving with yet more empty plates.

"She must have a master," Laura said when she had gone. "Where do you suppose they are?"

"Probably away. In Paris, maybe," said Libby. Laura

sensed no resentment, though normally she'd have expected some. "What does it matter? We're the only ones that count right now."

The housekeeper led the girls back along dark corridors to a bedroom. The rain had renewed its efforts, as if it too had only paused for some supper, and it hammered now against the side of the château, creeping in through the cracks and crevices around the windows and doors, echoing wildly in the belly of the old house.

The bedroom the housekeeper had prepared was an opulent refuge from the storm. The walls were covered with large tapestries that portrayed the Garden of Eden. The weave, in lustrous colours, depicted nature's abundance; fruit in all its wondrous variety hung temptingly from the canvas, ready to be picked. In one, a curvaceous Eve, offered the apple enticingly to the viewer. The snake had entwined itself around her, its serpentine body clinging to her waist, emphasising the curve of her hips, and it draped off one shoulder, like an elegantly hung garment, tantalisingly concealing her full nakedness. Below the tapestry, a fire already raged in the stone hearth and a large four-poster bed stood in the centre of the room, adorned with hanging panels of fabric that closed around the bed like a curtain.

"This is awesome," Libby whispered to Laura.

The housekeeper pointed to an urn and a bowl on the dresser, bowed, and withdrew. Libby dived on the bed.

"I've always wanted to sleep in one of these," Libby said, "though I'd never imagined sharing with you."

Laura wasn't as enthusiastic. She tried to accept

the evening as good old-fashioned hospitality but everything had been so extravagant, so superfluous. After what Libby had said about the housekeeper's negligence she had watched her closely. Laura wasn't as concerned about why the house was unlocked as to why it was closed in the first place. It seemed to lack all the features so typical of a tourist hotspot. From what Laura had seen she was beginning to think this place hadn't seen visitors for many years.

The girls dressed for bed and snuggled beneath the covers. The rain against the windowpane only served to make them feel more content in the warm bed.

"Well, this is better than sleeping on a bench at the station," Libby said merrily. She sat up and began untying a ribbon attached to one of the bedposts.

"Don't pull the curtain down," Laura said, "I don't want to feel trapped in here."

"Don't be silly."

"Please, I don't like the idea of not seeing a way out."

Libby shrugged and lay back down.

"It's been a good day," Libby announced, facing her sister. The coffee had sobered them a degree but Laura wondered if the wine was still exerting its influence on her sister's mood.

"We haven't had a meal like that, just us I mean, for ages."

Laura nodded.

"I had fun."

"Me too."

"And we haven't shared a bed since we were little," she continued. "Do you remember?"

Laura nodded, remembering her sister traipsing out of bed in the early hours to sneak into her parents' bed; taking any opportunity to monopolise their parents' love without Laura around. But Laura was woken by the absence of her sister more effectively than any alarm clock. She'd follow her sister into the parents' bed and through the course of the night their fidgeting would force their parents out and up early, leaving the two girls alone in the bed, lingering in the warmth of their parents' bodies.

"I wonder what Jess is up to," Libby said, breaking her reverie.

"Why do you like her so much?"

Libby thought for a moment. "She's fun to be around. I know you don't like her, but she's ok."

"I wish it could be just us sometimes."

"I know."

Laura recalled all her lonely meanderings around Paris. The times she *had* spent with her sister were while she waited outside changing rooms, separated by a curtain as Libby tried on countless outfits. Libby's relationship with her reflection was perhaps more significant than any sisterly bond. "We've grown so different."

"C'est la vie," Libby smiled. "We're still sisters. We'll always be sisters."

They looked at each other for a while longer, their faces glowing from the warmth of the fire. The bed was incredibly comfortable and the rain outside a strange lullaby. Laura felt her eyes closing.

"Wouldn't it be great to go back to the dressing room before we leave," Libby whispered.

Laura stirred. She thought of her lonely tours of the Louvre and the Musée d'Orsay. She'd described the beauty to her sister at dinner but they had been just words to Libby. She couldn't imagine it, and even if she had, she wouldn't have appreciated the aesthetic merit of a group of old paintings anyway.

But how her face had lit up in the dressing room. In the moonlight everything had shimmered like a Moreau painting, misty and iridescent, twinkling as if glimpsed underwater or in a dream. To her sister it was a siren song.

"Promise me you won't go back to that room?" Laura said.

"Why not?"

Laura thought that the contents of that room should be torched. That all those things perpetuated an image of women that was artificial and unrealistic. Those fashions were designed by men to reflect the moral rigidity of the age, to keep women laced in, confined and shackled. The corset signified restraint and conformity, going out of fashion when women's rights were à la mode. Not that things were much different today, in an age of tanning salons and plastic surgery. Society's concept of beauty had always been governed by impossible ideals, usually at the expense of the female body. But she couldn't tell Libby any of that. Her sister hated it when she voiced her feminist leanings. Besides, she was too sleepy and didn't want to spoil the evening's magic.

"Just promise," was all she said.

"Ok," Libby conceded. "Goodnight"

"Goodnight."

Laura found herself in the library. She was sitting in one of the enormous armchairs and the fire smouldered in the grate. In her lap was a copy of Rousseau's *Du contrat social*. She flicked through the pages, marvelling that the house existed long before such enlightened thinking, when social roles were so clearly delineated.

She put the book down and looked around the room. From her seat, the shelves loomed above her; a vastness of knowledge that was far from liberating. It was intimidating in fact. She stood up and made her way to the door.

Except there was no door. She scanned the room. The door, she remembered, had been papered over with the image of books. She made her way to the corners of the room and felt along the walls, searching for the mystery door. But her hands only touched leather spines. She began to pull them out in frustration. Their paper insides fluttered as they fell to the ground. She ran her hands along the entire length of wall, unable to accept that the door had disappeared. She tried to suppress the alarm mounting inside her. There had to be a way out.

She began pulling greater quantities of books from the shelves, casting them into a growing pile in the centre of the room, an enormous unlit bonfire. She ignored the titles as they flew from shelves, titles that would have ignited her interest at any other time, and she ignored how the books tossed and turned on the ground, flapping and flailing like dying animals. That was when she realised she was dreaming.

With the room stripped of its beauty, all that remained was the skeletal structure of the bookcases, resembling the bars of the crinoline petticoat she'd glimpsed in the dressing room. She ran her hand along the smooth surface and realised they weren't constructed from wood. The shelves were stone, or something else, pale and hard and calcified.

Beyond the bookcases, Laura could make out a door. She stepped between the bars of the bookcase frames and opened it.

She was in the dining room. The table was laid as it had been earlier that day. The cutlery and crockery gleamed and the crystal goblets sparkled. In the centre of the table stood a number of enormous cake-stands, topped with an array of dainty iced cakes and plates of cheeses and fruits crammed every available space. It was a tempting feast. But as she approached she discerned small darting movements. Something rested on her hand and she looked in bewilderment at a tiny bird.

As suddenly as it appeared, it flew from the perch she provided and re-joined the others dancing over the table. There were a dozen or so, darting over the porcelain crockery. Others were nestled on the display of fruit, an edible nest, nimbly feeding as if they were in a garden, leaving small tell-tale trails of juice and cream and sugar on the white tablecloth. Some darted between the cakes and others perched on the edges of exquisite teacups, dipping their beaks into the tea.

Each of the birds was more beautiful than the next. A parade of plumage. For some their feathers formed skirt-like layers, while others had wings tipped with extraordinary colours, or the most beautiful patterns emblazoned on their chests.

Laura wanted to touch one again.

A shadow moved across the table and the startled birds flew in fright. But they stopped short before they could get far. Their wings beat frantically but they seemed unable to get beyond the orbit of the table.

Laura recoiled as she saw what had frightened them. Between the cake-stand and a teapot, a snake, fat and silver, crept along the table's expanse, knocking against the crockery, causing cakes and pastries to fall from their podiums.

The birds continued to beat their wings but they

couldn't fly away. A tangle of red threads covered the feast as fine as cobwebs. She followed a single skein and saw that it was tethered to the foot of a bird. In fact, all the birds were bound by red thread.

The snake coiled around the cake-stand, climbing elegantly despite its heavy body, hauling itself higher and higher. With its jaw distended it made a series of jerking movements in its throat, as if calling to the birds so desperate to flee. A green bird suddenly crashed to the table. It flapped its wings meekly but seemed wounded from the force of its landing. Laura followed the thread and saw it ended, they all ended, in the mouth of the snake, like small arteries. The bird continued to fight and flutter but its attempts became more sporadic and then the snake was suddenly upon it. In one swift movement it swallowed the bird whole.

Laura turned away from the scene in shock and when she turned back the shape of the bird bulged within the reptile's scaly skin, coursing its way down into the body of the beast.

Laura watched with horror as the snake returned to its platform. It opened its jaws, not yet satisfied and the other birds flapped their frenzy.

Laura woke up flailing in the bed-sheets. The drapery must have fallen in the night, as she couldn't see beyond the fabric of the bed. She pulled it aside and saw the space beside her empty.

"Libby?"

She looked out into the dark room. Shadows had gathered in the corners, creeping out from behind the tapestries, but otherwise it appeared empty. She knew where her sister would be. Like the birds in her dream, she felt an invisible thread connecting them.

She walked softly but swiftly along the corridors, but the château was vast and she was beginning to think the housekeeper had taken them up a different staircase after dinner. She came to a central stairwell and followed the balustrade, reasoning that if the house were symmetrical this would lead her to all the rooms. Her progress was surveyed by the portraits of the dead, and she wondered how many of them had met their end violently, kneeling at the guillotine or in some other horrible fashion.

She heard a rustle up ahead and quickened her pace. They had trespassed and tested the hospitality of the housekeeper enough already; Laura wanted to retrieve her sister and leave.

In the dressing room, Laura couldn't see her sister at first. She had the same strange impression she was witnessing an extravagant party, the mannequins arranged as if conspiring in the midst of a grand ball. Then Libby stepped out of the crowd, resplendent in the red gown.

"How do I look?"

She looked stunning. The corset drew her body in, her silhouette willowy and delicate. As before, the red of the gown seemed to draw her colour, her skin the sickly, anaemic pallor that was once so fashionable.

Laura couldn't reply but Libby didn't really need an answer. She addressed her reflection and danced in front of the glass as if it were an imaginary dance partner. She twirled, enjoying the feeling of the taffeta as it moved.

"We need to go," Laura said.

"Ok, ok." But she continued twirling.

"I'm leaving."

Libby sighed. It was no fun playing dress up with her sister here. "Untie me then."

Laura stood behind her sister and faced the mirror. Beside Libby she appeared so plain. Yet in the glow of the red dress, she noticed that there was a similarity; the arch of her eyebrows, her high cheekbones, her full lips. She was a poor imitation but not without a beauty of her own.

She fumbled with the laces but they were knotted tight.

"How did you do this?"

Libby shrugged. "I just slipped it on and it settled into place. I only tied it loosely."

Laura persevered but the laces were taut.

"I don't know what you've done but I can't undo it."

"Don't pull."

"I didn't."

"Stop tugging."

Laura stepped away. "I'm not. I didn't touch you."

Libby shoved her. "Sure, then why—Ow!" This time she doubled with pain as the laces around her waist tightened. Laura watched as Libby's diaphragm contracted with the force of the material, heard her breath escape in a rush.

"Get it off me!" she gasped.

Laura groped at the laces but they were steadfast. She watched as the ribbon, pulled by invisible hands, tightened further. She tried to stop it but the force was too strong.

"It's tightening on its own!"

Libby clutched her chest, her breath coming in short gasps now. She scratched at the material, trying to rip the corset from her skin. Laura pulled the bodice roughly but it was stiff and unrelenting.

Libby tried to speak but there wasn't enough air in her lungs for words. Her waist contracted again, impossibly sylphlike. She began coughing, only slight sounds, and even in the dim light Laura could see the blood.

Laura looked around the room. Mirror. Dressing table. Wardrobe. She needed something with which to cleave the gown off Libby.

"I'll be right back."

She made a run for the door but tripped on the hem of a gown and went sprawling. She scrambled on the floor, crawling through layers of fallen silk and taffeta, brushing aside the excessive petticoats of a hundred dressmaker's dummies, layer after layer until she found herself confronted by the bars of a crinoline petticoat. She made to pull it aside-

But couldn't lift it. She tried to turn, to crawl out the other side, but she was enclosed within it, as if it had been lowered over her. She shook the bars of her cage. They didn't feel like the whalebone struts she had touched in the wardrobe. These were not covered in fabric and they were thicker, much thicker, the calcified yellow of bone many centuries old.

Libby's coughing, feeble as it was, suddenly ceased and she collapsed to the floor. She could hear the pop and crunch of her ribs breaking. Laura could see her panting, tiny breaths that gave her nothing. Her eyes were wide. Her chest was stained with blood and it ran down onto the gown. Her waist, impossibly small now, continued to shrink before Laura's eyes.

Laura heard footsteps on the threshold and turned to face the door. The housekeeper stood in the doorway, dressed in a high-necked dressing gown, a candle illuminating her face as she took in the scene before her.

Laura grasped the bars of her tiny prison. "Help us!"

The housekeeper entered the room slowly, closing

the door behind her. She walked toward the dressing table and sat down. Laura watched her movements, reflected in the vanity mirror.

"What are you doing?" Laura called. "Help us!"

But the housekeeper didn't respond. Instead she began applying white powder to her face, matching her pallor to become the same unnatural shade as Libby's.

"Hey!" Laura called again. "You have to help us!"

The housekeeper still didn't respond. She removed one of the powdered wigs from its stand and put it on. She was no longer the housekeeper who had welcomed them. She undid her dressing gown and let it slip from her shoulders.

Laura gasped.

Her neck had been slashed open. The flesh parted in a wide gash, a laceration that had long since ceased to bleed but offered instead red threads that unravelled to the floor, each one a degenerate bloodline.

The housekeeper's reflection stared at Laura, her eyebrow raised in displeasure. There was a moment of eye contact, then the housekeeper merely turned away to resume her routine. As if she was dressing for an important occasion.

The housekeeper examined her features in the mirror and ran a finger along the fleshy crevice of her throat, playing the threads like a silent instrument. Her other hand reached into one of the drawers, and withdrew a feather boa of vibrant, exotic feathers. She cast it around her neck and her transformation was complete.

Laura looked around the room in desperation. But the room was changed. Dusty, ruined, the clothes on the mannequins were merely the tattered remains of gowns from a bygone era, cast over the models like shrouds. The paper-thin fabric was frayed at the edges, moth-eaten and yellowing. It was all a masquerade. All but the red gown.

It clung to her sister in her last moments, contracting still.

Laura screamed. She shook the bars of her cage in desperation, stopping only when she felt a sharp tug and a fleeting sensation of pain. She looked down and saw, around her ankle, a single skein of red thread.

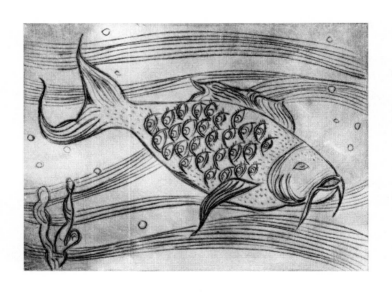

Ghost

The water hadn't been clean since Fergus died. The pond filter had stalled that very week, its rotary apparatus refusing to turn as if in silent protest for Fergus' passing. Annette had been far too busy arranging the funeral to be concerned with the small matter of a defective motor. And afterward she had to contend with the solicitors, the bills, the pension scheme, on top of her three daughters—all grown but somehow children again since the loss of their father—crying into her apron as if they were smaller than her and not the other way around. Annette envied the faulty filter, wishing that she could just stop dead as Fergus had. But she had to keep going, getting up each morning to propel their lives forward, ensuring that their little world continued to turn.

Only much later, when she'd cast off her mourning duties, did she notice how murky the water had become. The pond was little more than a large begonia-rimmed smudge across the lawn. She peered into the gloomy depths wondering if her neglect had affected any of the pond's inhabitants. But the muddied surface gave nothing away. If life existed at all it was in the dark. She reached for the net that was balanced across the back of a ceramic tortoise; left there from the last time

Fergus had used it. Long idle judging from the accretion of leaves lining the mesh. She shook it clean and plunged it deep.

It was like a lucky dip, these blind sweeping motions through the water, only to be rewarded with a brimful of algae. She picked out the woolly clumps and drove the net in deeper. The only thing that was clear was that nothing could live in such a stagnant pool.

A flick of silver and the brief shimmer of fish scales contradicted her. And then it was gone. The bobbing water as the ripples receded were the only clue that something had been there at all. So there was life in the old gal yet. Annette waited until the water settled and returned indoors.

Every one agreed that the pond was in an alarming state. Her daughters complained of the dank smell and they ushered their children away from it as if it were contagious. *Why don't you pave it over, Mum*, they said. *It would make a lovely patio area. You could get that hammock you always wanted.*

The pond had been Fergus' province. Annette didn't know the first thing about maintaining it. She had no understanding or desire to understand the specialist equipment, the maintenance regimes and checks, the disease prevention measures which Fergus had detailed so meticulously in various notebooks and manuals. It would be too much upkeep for a woman of her age. Her daughters had all married partners as ineffectual as they were. None of them wanted to take on Fergus' legacy. None of them were prepared to get their hands dirty. It was easier to cover it over and start again.

She didn't tell them about the fish she'd seen, the one she'd glimpsed numerous times since. It would only complicate matters. People were overly sentimental about pets. Let them believe nothing existed in those dark depths. The pond had become so congested with silt and leaves, clogged with blanketweed, that it was easy to think that life within had just given up. Preferable in fact, than the idea that something dwelled in those black and putrid waters.

But life subsisted. Annette watched a solitary fin skirt the surface, hovering there as if to afford a better view, its milky, almost translucent colouring vaguely familiar. She recalled the times spent at pet shops and leisure centres where koi enthusiasts would display their fish in the shallow confines of paddling pools or tanks. She could see Fergus immersed in this exotic world of colour, selecting the best on offer, the babies mostly—cheaper and more likely to be disease free—to be netted and bagged. On the journey home, the girls, children then, would each clutch a plastic bag, relishing the spongy weight in their laps as the fish turned circles in their transparent worlds. And they'd christen them with silly names, *Gill-ian, Fishfinger, Jaws*, which they forgot as they got older, as they became more interested in life beyond the back garden.

Annette found carp pretty unmemorable too, all except one, on account of its cloudy anaemic colouring, the shadowy patterning along its belly and sides so that its dorsal fin stood out white and skeletal. A ghost koi, which the girls had rather un-inspiringly named *Ghost*.

It was Ghost that remained now, Annette was sure of it. Solitarily haunting what was left of the pond.

The possibility of moving it to another pond wasn't an option. She had a vague memory of it having contracted some kind of carp disease. A disease that had made its body swell, forcing its eyes to bulge outwards. Its skin developed a milky film of mucus that seemed to encircle it like ectoplasm, making its name even more appropriate. Perhaps she remembered the fish so well because of her husband's repeated attempts to treat it. It had been relegated to the children's paddling pool more than once, in makeshift quarantine while he administered homemade remedies or drugs recommended by other fanatics. She'd found Ghost once, floating lifeless on its side, as if dead. And she'd been somewhat relieved that this sickly fish had finally kicked the bucket, freeing her husband from further toil, only for it suddenly revive and dart off into the depths. Perhaps it wasn't sick at all, just indolent.

Ghost rose now to the surface. His huge suction mouth gulping at the air. The barbels either side resembling a drooping moustache. He looked whiter, strangely more translucent, visible only because the water was so dark, so murky. Had the water been as clean as Fergus would have liked, Ghost may have disappeared altogether. That was what she wanted. Why couldn't he have just died in the paddling pool all those years ago? Annette felt a stab of guilt, but let it swim free with thoughts of her new patio. She'd already selected the hammock she wanted from the catalogue, complete with stripy awning and drinks holder. Her dreams were finally becoming more concrete and she wasn't going to let some ailing phantom get in her way.

So she'd tried in her subtle way to engineer his death. She removed the plastic heron, which stood sentinel-like from the top of the shed and even sprinkled bird feed next to the pond—an open invitation for nature to attack tooth and claw. But the birds refused to make a meal of it, as did the neighbour's cats, which avoided the pond as if sensing Ghost's unnatural existence, his strange abnormal longevity. If only something could finish him off. She'd begun to feed him less and less, and now she'd stopped altogether, hoping that she could starve him out. She tried to think of it as a kindness. To live in such darkness could only mean to suffer. She knew that in time, without clean, properly oxygenated water, the pond would become ripe with disease. Wouldn't it be better to hasten it along, than to draw it out any longer than was necessary?

Fergus had hung on as well. Much longer than anyone had expected. When he was brought home it was because everyone knew there was no hope. The treatments and drugs had all failed; they couldn't stop his inevitable decline. So he was tucked up in his own bed, to live out his final days with his family. But Fergus didn't seem to get the memo. He refused to comply with the doctors and nurses, the specialists and their expert prognoses. He just wouldn't roll over and die. Instead, the bedroom became a stagnant holding pen, Annette's linen took on the odour of death and she and the girls became as pallid and ashen as Fergus was. Living ghosts, while Fergus kept his head above water and swelled and burgeoned, fed with drugs and fluids by matronly carers. Initially, he tried to haul himself out of bed, but his arms were too frail. She'd watch as her daughters clasped his hands, hands that had once relished the handiwork around the bungalow, hands that had served the pond so diligently, now swollen and ineffectual. Near the end he couldn't speak. Communication was reduced to the most basic of exchanges. *Blink once for yes, twice for no.* His lashes would flutter lightly in obedience, while he lay there day after day, immobile, listless.

That night Ghost swam into Annette's dreams. The pond was a dark shadow illuminated by the solar powered spotlights Fergus had installed around its periphery. A deep black hollow, an open sore across their otherwise perfect lawn. Surely nothing could live in such a place. A cluster of white buds, translucent like frogspawn, broke the surface. They floated there a moment but then reared upwards like mushroom stalks, reaching into the dark night, until they stopped suddenly and drooped forward as if exhausted by the enterprise. Then Annette realised what she was seeing. Fingers. Long, anaemic fingers which groped at the paving slabs, and pushed against them to haul the rest of it—whatever it was—from the depths. Amid the dark and the splashing, she could see flashes of white, the metallic shimmer of fish scales and long wiry barbels licked the air.

She watched the strange hybrid scurry out of the pond, with hands where its dorsal fins should be, walking on fingertips across the lawn, towards the house. In her dream, she saw herself sleeping soundly, while the strange white spectre crept towards the bed, gripping the sheets with its long ghostly fingers, pulling its scaly wet bulk up onto the pillow beside her. She watched as the long fingers curled over the top of the bed sheets, reaching out towards her, with its gulping fish mouth, those snaking barbels, moving closer and closer.

The bed was soaked through when she finally woke up. Her body was still clammy and feverish as she pulled off the sheets and carried them through to the washing machine. She was relieved when her daughters arrived later that day, a large cardboard box in tow. Whilst Annette made the tea, the girls opened it, strewing the contents across the lawn. Annette glimpsed the stripy upholstery, green like the algae that festered along the rim of the pond. While her daughters argued over the self—assembly instructions, Annette encouraged the children to throw stones into the pond. *There's nothing in there*, she told them as she filled their palms with pebbles.

Maybe that was the truth. In her dream, Ghost had pulled himself out of the water and left the pond behind. Was that how it had been all those millions of years ago, when our piscine antecedents had pulled themselves out onto land. Had we all emerged from a form of pond life? And did those creatures have hands too, or had they just dragged themselves upon fat fins, tossing and rolling themselves forward because it was better than staying where they were.

Annette could understand that. Why would anything want to stay in such a dark place? She remembered how upset Fergus had been a few years before, when a couple of koi had leapt from the pond. The nitrate levels had been too high, inducing suicidal tendencies. Of course the fish didn't know it was suicide, Annette had argued. To them, the unknown was a better option than a long, drawn out death. It was actually a leap of faith. What she couldn't understand though, was why they hadn't all jumped, why some stayed behind and tolerated those toxic levels. Why some would always linger at the bottom of the pond and persist in the darkness.

The children had made a game of throwing stones and now ran at the pond like shot-putters with larger slabs they'd acquired from the rockery. If Ghost hadn't left on his own accord, they were actively prompting his exorcism. Her unknowing assassins. Annette heard her daughters cheer as they lifted the hammock upright, one of them gently pushing the swing seat. Her attention was only away from the pond for a moment but when she turned back her grandson was at the pond's edge, and a white fin was cutting through the black water.

She saw it all as she rushed towards her grandson, the milky hand rising up out of the water as it had in her dream, clasping his little ankle and pulling him down into the murky depths, where he'd remain forever, turning circles and blowing bubbles that would break pitifully on the surface. She said as much to her daughters, who led her inside with alarmed looks, guiding her towards her bed and fetching aspirin. The grandchildren, bewildered but unharmed, continued with their game, filling the pond with rocks.

The hammock sat on the lawn beside the pond. The upholstery was darker, saturated from the rain. Annette hadn't been outside to place the tarpaulin cover over it. In fact, she'd hardly been out at all, confined to the house since her strange episode in the garden. She tried to keep herself busy, but the housework only took so long. She couldn't bear idle hands so she made her way to the bedroom and sat down on the freshly laundered sheets. She picked up a pillow and held it to her face. She thought she'd gotten rid of it, but it was still there, lingering in the background. The smell of death. She stripped the linen and carried the bundle to the washing machine. Kneeling on the floor, she watched the sheets go round in the drum. A white blur. She had to keep her world turning, she reasoned. Her bright, sanitary world.

After she'd tumble-dried the sheets, she ironed them. There was something enjoyable about prolonging these small tasks. She never had the time when the girls were young. How they would interrupt her chores, get under her feet as she made the beds, placing the sheets over their heads with warbling cries, *Woooo, woooo,* playing ghosts.

She'd had her fill of ghosts. The one that disturbed her most haunted a little over four feet of water. They'd existed in this strange stalemate for too long already. She moved to the window and looked out at the pond. The water was dark, motionless. Perhaps she was finally free of Ghost.

She made her way out into the garden, surprised at the alarming growth of her wisteria, the rebellious borders. The pond's surface was covered in a sickly crust of algae and pondweed like the membrane of a scab. She reached for the net, still balanced on the back of the ceramic tortoise and drove it into the water.

There was nothing but pond debris and leaves. At first she was cautious but then she swept the net through the water blindly, without hesitation. It couldn't do more damage than the rocks the grandchildren had deposited so violently into the water. She was beginning to sense victory, when the net pulled and she felt a weight at the end of the stick.

As she lifted Ghost from the water, she was reminded of Fergus, without his dentures, gulping air from his wide toothless mouth. The drugs had given his skin a translucent quality, a wet slickness, though the skin itself had dried, making his eczema more pronounced, the skin flaking off into the bed sheets where it accumulated in clumps like shavings of parmesan. *Blink once for yes, twice for no,* the girls had chorused, encouraging him to answer their inane questions.

When they were alone, Annette didn't engage in any form of communication. She was sick of his inert body, lifeless except for his eyes, which followed her around the room, blinking hard to get her attention. She wanted to close them. She wanted her bed back, the sheets clean, free of disease. She ran her hand on the pillow beside him, recalling the children beneath the white sheets. Ghosts.

She lifted Ghost free of the water, his body curled within the net like a white flag. She watched him unfurl and loll against the mesh, struggling for breath, his gills labouring. She saw the scaly, metallic surface of his skin, the patina of mucus, interrupted by numerous ulcerous cavities, inflicted probably from the barrage of stones and pebbles. She could identify the onset of disease—recalling images from Fergus' books—in the curvature of Ghost's spine, the pine-coning of his tail. His scales fanned outwards, his fins rotten and torn, trailing behind him like ribbons.

Now will you die? Annette thought, turning the net towards her, looking into the face of her adversary. But there, above his bulging eyes, two fleshy flaps hung loose. Was this some strange new growth, a leprous protuberance? If Annette didn't know better, she'd have said they were eyelids. Holding him aloft, she saw her reflection in his black pupils, could sense him regarding her from behind white-lidded eyes. And he blinked twice.

Making Room

⎯⎯⎯⎯ ৩৯৫ ⎯⎯⎯⎯

The rain kept Julie awake. It always did. It drummed against the window in a persistent patter as rhythmically as Rob's breathing next to her. Neither lulled her. They only served to disturb the thing under the bed.

Julie curled herself into a foetal position and backed herself into Rob's warm body. The blanket was tucked tightly around them both, its weight reassuring and restrictive, preventing limbs from escaping and dangling out.

Still she could sense that the thing was lurking.

"Rob," she said, shaking him awake, "under the bed."

Rob groaned, switching on the bedside lamp and clambering out mechanically.

"Well?"

"Nothing. As usual," he said, climbing back under the sheets.

He was less obliging these days. At first he thought it was adorable. Indulging her childish fancies, he would check inside the wardrobe as well and even bought her a ladybird nightlight, which glowed red. Over time though it became tedious. Sleep deprivation was *serious*, he'd said, and he had to be up early for *work*.

Julie had work *too* she wanted to remind him. What about *her* sleep deprivation? The creature under her bed didn't care about all that, about the havoc it was wreaking on her relationships. And Rob would soon tire of playing the rescuer each night.

With the approach of daylight, Julie faced the space under the bed. It had become a haven for forgotten things. Space was a premium in her one-bed flat but under the bed was unclaimed territory, a refuge for miscellany. Everything that didn't belong belonged here.

There was no indication of the thing. Julie half expected there to be tell-tale signs; a nest of valentines cards and photos, teeth marks on the corners of shoe boxes, maybe beastly hoof-prints in the dust. But there was nothing.

Instead Julie pulled out a pair of dusty trainers. It was about time to begin jogging again, she reasoned. About time to exorcise those extra pounds she'd put on, which she inevitably did at the beginning of a new relationship. When everything was good. Before her secret reared its ugly head.

Rob was waiting for her when she returned from her jog that evening. He wanted to *talk*. Rob was much better at it, since he was clinically trained. Perhaps that was why she'd been attracted to him: that he had the potential to fix her.

"We've got to do something about that junk under the bed," he began, "it's unhealthy. The stuff juts out and trips you up, plus the dust upsets my sinuses. Also, I really think you could do with letting a few things go," he said.

"You mean have a car boot sale or something?"

"Maybe. But you're obviously holding onto that stuff for a reason. You should confront it, put it away, or get rid of it."

Julie didn't really want to confront it. Who knew what she would find? Plus the stuff was a kind of buffer between her and...

"I don't know."

"You're clearly fabricating monsters because of the negative associations you've accumulated under there. It's time you accommodated me in your life and until you do this, I just don't think there's room."

Julie hated it when he spoke in psychobabble and even more when it was directed at her. Still, he'd laid his cards down. It was him or her stuff.

It took Julie the rest of the evening. She hauled out cardboard boxes containing keepsakes and mementoes; teddy bears won at the fairground by old boyfriends, school books etched with love hearts and photo albums of loves lost. Some boxes were labelled, *Sam 2001*, *Pete xmas 1998*, *Dan 2005-6*, others were not, and she was ambushed by dead relationships preserved beneath bubble wrap and tissue paper.

There was no room anywhere else in her tiny flat, so she pushed everything to the periphery of the bedroom, ready to take out with the bins the next day.

Rob was impressed, though he had to step over the debris to reach the bed in the middle. Julie cast one last look under the bed at the vacuous space she'd created. A huge, hollow emptiness. There was no thing.

Content at having faced her demons, she fell almost instantly asleep.

Rob, on the other hand, couldn't quite unwind; perhaps it was being surrounded by Julie's baggage, both literal and emotional, or maybe it was the sense of something close by.

And then he heard it. A sound so faint it was almost a whisper, so soft that he doubted whether he'd heard anything at all. It sounded like a muffled scream. Coming unmistakably from under the bed.

Rob thought about waking Julie but, illuminated by the glow of the nightlight, she looked so peaceful. Besides, he was the man of the house, at the frontline to protect Julie from fears real or imagined. It was a bedtime ritual he'd hoped to have vanquished but he found himself pulling aside the covers and kneeling in the dark.

He looked tentatively underneath.

Crouching in the darkness, the thing stared back at him.

Rob wanted to move but his body didn't react. Only when the creature scurried towards him did he manage to retreat but by then it had grasped his ankle and was pulling him under.

"Julie!" Rob called. "Jul—"

He hit his head as his other leg was whipped out from under him. From the floor the world above seemed hazy and the wall of junk engulfed him. He was concussed. *The boxes couldn't do that*, he told himself. The room could not close in on itself. Yet he was being dragged along the floor, under the bed, followed by cardboard boxes, teddy bears and photo albums.

"Julie!" he called again. "Julie!"

But muffled by the remains of Julie's failed relationships all that emerged was a murmur too soft to be heard. And above, Julie rolled over, sleeping soundly.

Family Tree

———— ✣✣ ————

Tyler's mum was wearing the horrendous bobble hat again. It was so poorly constructed with looping loose stitches and gaping holes that she might as well have wound the yarn around her head like a turban. The worst of it was the enormous green pompom, which toppled back and forward as she crossed the playground. Tyler winched on seeing her and hoped Kevin and Phil hadn't noticed.

"Nice hat, Mrs. Burrows."

"Oh, thanks Kevin." She smiled. "I made it myself."

"Really? Wow."

Tyler thought Kevin's incredulity was a bit overdone and would have elbowed him if he'd been closer but his mum didn't seem to notice. In fact she patted her hat proudly. Tyler and Phil fell in step behind them as they continued to discuss the creative potential of knitting all the way to the car.

"Nice day at school boys?" she asked when they were seated in the old camper. With its cheap paintjob failing to disguise the rust it was almost as embarrassing as his mum's hat.

"You know, Mrs Burrows, another day another dollar," Kevin said, buckling himself in. He'd made a habit of using "grown-up" expressions around adults, which essentially meant mimicking his old man's clichés. Tyler hoped it wouldn't lead his mother into another rant about capitalism but Kevin could do no wrong today. He'd claimed the front seat as usual, his prize for making small talk. Tyler and Phil, on the other hand, were squashed into the back, sitting amongst boxes of cardboard and paper from the recycling bank, the materials from which Tyler's mum would fashion mini works of art in Papier-mâché.

"And what about you two?" his mother asked, shouting over the rumble of the engine.

Phil maintained his stare out of the window making it clear he wouldn't be participating in any chitchat. It fell to Tyler.

"It was ok," he managed, hoping she would leave it there.

"Details, sweetheart?" she pressed, and Tyler knew she wouldn't be appeased until he'd mentioned at least one salient feature of his day.

"Um, well, we've been planning our experiments."

"And what experiments are those?"

"For the science fair, Mrs Burrows," Kevin chipped in.

"The science fair?" She adjusted the rear view mirror and Tyler met her eyes in the glass. "And I presume you were going to tell me about this eventually?"

Tyler hoped the question was rhetorical and shifted to look out of the window.

"What's it about?"

"We're analysing blood cells," said Kevin.

Tyler's mum screwed up her face, the many ethical objections that came to mind visible on her brow. She was vegan in spirit if not in appetite.

"*And*," Kevin continued, "Tyler's been paired *with a girl!*" He laughed but it was exaggerated and Tyler suspected it contained a degree of envy. Because it wasn't just any girl he'd been paired with but Janie Tailor. Blonde and slim and beautiful Janie Tailor. The only girl in school with the unmistakeable budding of breasts, with the exception of tubby Shanice Bolton, whose obese rolls provided cleavage to rival any surgically enhanced celebrity.

But Tyler wasn't feeling lucky. Science was his favourite subject and having a new partner, and a girl at that, was proving a distraction. It didn't help that she had lots of opinions. He'd been used to working with Phil and Kevin, whose apathetic involvement usually allowed him to work entirely on his own. Just as he preferred.

"Ohhhh. What's she like, sweetie?" his mother asked.

It was for this reason that Tyler preferred reticence. He didn't want to face a barrage of questions on a subject he vaguely understood himself. Girls were a mysterious species, communicating with eyes full of giggles and shyness and knowing. And later they'd turn into creatures that in some ways resembled his mother. That was the most perplexing part of all.

It was easier to act the part of a typical adolescent; he shrugged. "She's alright."

"My goodness, Tyler, you'd think I'd brought you up without any refinement," she sighed, pulling into the driveway. "Are you like this at home, Kevin?"

Kevin cast a superior glance into the back of the camper and smiled.

"Certainly not, Mrs Burrows."

෨

Tyler opened the fridge and grabbed three cartons of pomegranate juice. His mum was setting the table, sweeping sketches, palette knives and paintbrushes onto chairs. She laid the table slowly with an artistic eye. Plates laden with pita bread and falafel, bean salad, hummus and olives were arranged as if they were part of an exhibition. Tyler looked at the spread and rolled his eyes. Why couldn't they have chicken nuggets and spaghetti hoops like other children?

Not that he would dare tell his mum how many chicken nuggets he consumed at Phil's house. He knew she'd call the whole thing off if she found out he was living on a diet of junk food. Whenever Tyler returned from Phil's he'd tell her he'd eaten cottage pie again, something bland and wholesome, too dull to raise suspicions. No doubt Phil did the same, substituting tajine for toad-in-the-hole when quizzed. Phil's mum was as fearful of the spice being stirred into her son's life as Tyler's mum was of the absence of it. He realised that the whole arrangement pivoted on a delicate foundation of wilful deception.

The arrangement was part of the imaginatively named "Parent Share", an ingenious plan to parcel out their parental responsibility once a week in exchange for one blissful night off. Of course if Tyler's mum could rely on Tyler's dad there wouldn't have been any need for the arrangement. But as it was, Tyler liked going to Kevin and Phil's and getting as close to normalcy as possible.

Tyler's mum liked it too. It was marked on the calendar as "Marian's Time Out" though Tyler objected to the insinuation that he was something she needed time out from. When Tyler returned home from either Kevin's or Phil's, the house would be littered with trinkets to attain inner calm—candles, crystals, incense. The drawback was that two nights a week her inner-calm was countered by the presence of three raucous boys instead of one.

At least they could play in the garden.

"Tell the boys to stay near the house," Tyler's mum called as Tyler bounded out of the back door cradling three cartons of juice.

"It's nearly dinner time."

Tyler ran across the lawn to Kevin and Phil. They were kicking a football back and forth. Kevin, slightly over-weight for his age and without any aptitude for sport, was putting a great deal more effort in than Phil who returned the ball lazily with his hands in his pockets.

Tyler liked the garden. There were elements that weren't to his taste—a half finished mosaic mural by the shed, a spattering of lanterns along the path and a pergola that sat snugly and slightly off kilter on the lawn—but luckily Tyler's mother flitted from project to project like an insect to nectar and her attempts to beautify and tame the garden were short-lived. The vegetation had precedence now; the shrubbery was overgrown, concealing a wealth of wildlife, the hedge-rows were neglected and wild, and thick foliage at the bottom of garden formed a towering, impenetrable wall.

Kevin passed the ball and Tyler returned it. At what height did a lawn stop being a lawn Tyler pondered as the long grass tickled his shins. Tyler wasn't interested in football but it was an enjoyable challenge in the long grass. The ball compressed the grass it rolled over, forming a series of interlacing paths like an exposed mole tunnel.

"Why doesn't your mum cut the grass?" Phil asked when his shot swerved off centre.

Tyler sipped his juice thoughtfully. Cutting grass was a job for dads.

"Why don't you?" Kevin replied as he retrieved the ball.

"Oi butt-nugget, who asked *you*?" Phil responded. He didn't speak much but when he did he made a point of creating obscene combinations. And he didn't shy away from the hard stuff either. Tyler remembered when he had called Ben Walker the C-word in P.E. The word had swum in Tyler's stomach for days afterwards; it's semantic weight indigestible.

"*You* should cut it since you love Mrs Burrows so much," Phil continued.

"Whatever," replied Kevin, though he kicked the ball as hard as he could. The long grass brought it to a sluggish stop just before Phil's feet.

"Why do you always have to suck-up to her so much anyway?" Phil asked.

"It's called being polite, you should try it some time."

Tyler watched their exchange, emphasized by the kicking of the ball. Kevin broke the monotony with an ungainly punt, which bounced in the long grass and approached Phil mid-air. Phil took the opportunity with enthusiasm and volleyed the ball as hard as he could. It flew into the pergola, rebounding off the canvas, which propelled it further down the garden. It cleared the trees and they heard it crash into the wild grass at the bottom.

"Well done," Kevin said.

Phil smiled. "Come on," he called running for the ball.

"It's alright," Tyler said, "I've got another one in the

shed."

"Stop being a wimp," Phil replied, "you scared of spiders or something?"

Tyler found himself running to catch up with Phil. Kevin trudged on behind. Tyler wasn't really bothered about spiders but now, delving further into the undergrowth, he saw there were a lot of them. Their speckled bodies rocked precariously on webs as three lumbering boys darted through their terrain.

"Listen, Phil. Let's go back," Tyler panted.

Before he knew it Phil had disappeared into the wall of green. Tyler and Kevin exchanged glances before Kevin, too, vanished. Tyler followed reluctantly behind, wondering how he was going to explain.

As he emerged he saw his friends staring in disbelief. An enormous tree house stood three metres or so off the ground. An impressive veranda surrounded it with a ladder that ran up to the entrance. Above the door a lopsided sign read, "Tyler's Place."

"It's just the old tree house," Tyler explained.

Kevin and Phil turned to him with raised eyebrows, shocked at the breech of trust.

"Why haven't you shown us it before?"

"It's dangerous," Tyler continued, "we're not supposed to play down this end of the garden."

Phil and Kevin looked at him in bewilderment and burst out laughing.

Tyler picked up the ball, "Why don't we go back to the house now?"

"Fuck that," Phil replied.

"Seriously, Mum said dinner was ready."

"Who made you the boss?" Phil challenged.

"Shh," Kevin said.

"Me, it's my house, you have to-"

"Shh!" Kevin repeated, "I think there's something

in there."

Kevin and Phil crouched lower to the ground and Kevin pointed.

"There. See it?"

A blur swept past the window.

"Seriously guys, let's just go," Tyler pleaded.

The boys were still looking at the window, so when a figure came out of the door it caught them by surprise. The dark creature stood staring at them, breathing heavily, its hands clutching the railings in a posture of defiance. It was covered in dark hair with matted long tresses running down its back and it stood completely naked, its genitalia dangled obscenely from its nest of pubic hair.

The creature roared.

Phil and Kevin screamed and ran as fast as they could.

Tyler watched them go and shook his head at the beast man. He slumped back to the house to tell Mum.

"It will all clear up in a day or two," Tyler's mum said, passing the bean salad.

Tyler dished a measly spoonful onto his plate, knowing he wouldn't be chastised about his lack of vegetables.

"It won't," Tyler said. "They're not going to be able to play here anymore, are they?"

"Well, Phil's dad said probably not." What he'd actually said was a lot less polite; Tyler had heard when she'd held the phone away from her ear. It certainly accounted for Phil's colourful language. "But you never know, Kevin's mum is very understanding. Her husband is an alco-hol-ic." She whispered the last word as if it wasn't suitable to be uttered at dinner.

"At least that's normal."

"Hardly."

"More than we are."

"Now Tyler, your father is entitled to express himself in whatever way he sees fit."

"Couldn't he do it with clothes on?"

Tyler's mum sighed and spooned more beans onto her plate.

"It's two afternoons a week," Tyler continued, "couldn't he put clothes on then? It's not a big ask. Even his loincloth would be better."

"Tyler, you know your father lost his conception of time long ago. His world is governed by the seasons, not our weekly schedules."

"Well couldn't we signal to him to put some clothes on when we have friends over?"

"I don't think he has clothes anymore."

It was pointless arguing. His mother supported, no, *encouraged* his dad's crazy way of life.

"I mean, what your father is doing is actually very brave, going back to nature. People shouldn't be so scared of embracing their bestial natures. I'd do it, if I didn't have the shackles of motherhood to contend with. No offence."

Tyler seriously doubted that. For all her talk she was too addicted to hot baths and Freeview to live in a state of nature. And he had to wonder if perhaps she preferred dad down at the bottom of the garden.

Tyler carried the bucket slowly down the garden path. He could hear the planks of wood shaking as his father jumped up and down in excitement. When Tyler emerged from the thicket his father leapt from the tree house in one mighty motion to land at Tyler's feet, panting. If he'd had a tail it would have been wagging.

Tyler tipped the bucket up and a slab of raw steak fell to the ground. Like an animal, his father tore at it with his teeth, ripped with his fingernails that were sharp points and scooped it up into his mouth. Blood dripped from his chin and Tyler saw that his hands and chest were still stained dark brown from the last time.

Tyler's mum insisted that his father should have at least one good meal a day. Before he'd given up the ability to speak, his father was adamant that he wanted to survive only on what he could catch. But pickings were slim in the suburbs; there were only so many squirrels to eat. Nobody wanted him to starve so they began to subsidise his diet. Tyler's father turned his nose up at their first offerings; conventional meals were thrown back up the garden path. The only thing he'd eat was raw meat. Most of the time his father would grab whatever meaty morsel Tyler brought him and scuttle away with it, burying it somewhere in the garden to allow it to rot and tenderise. He liked it best this way, unless he was really hungry.

Tyler hadn't wanted to take him his breakfast this morning. He was still angry about his display the previous day. Even animals could be trained to behave civilly and Tyler hadn't given up hope of tempting the wildness out of him. But as long as his mother allowed him to spend his days running around naked and nibbling squirrel cadavers he'd continue to take steps further back down the evolutionary scale.

Tyler remembered his father before the tree house. He used to wear a shirt and tie then, carry a briefcase. Tyler had never been inside, though it bore his name above the door. At first he'd been excited about it, even helped his father sketch ideas. But his father had become obsessed by it. He'd work into the night, building the rafters, laying cladding, varnishing it over and over. It became a monster of a project, becoming larger and more elaborate than any tree house Tyler had ever known. And his father approached it with more commitment than he had ever invested into anything before. He became consumed by the details.

Tyler watched him build whilst other facets of his life crumbled away. He began to work shirtless and it wasn't long before his flabby white torso was trans-formed into lean muscle. But it wasn't just his clothes being stripped away. He lost all interest in his day job, in his family and his responsibilities. And he didn't seem to mind. It meant he could spend more of his time making the tree house perfect.

His father began to use it as a den. Sometimes he wouldn't even come into the house at all and soon these days stretched into weeks. When the single mattress was put in, Tyler knew his dad had perma-nently moved out. At first it was as if nothing had really changed—he'd always been evasive presence in the house anyway—only now he was down the bottom of the garden. But Tyler and his mother soon forgot to visit him and the garden became overgrown, obscuring the tree house and separating him from their world. Before they knew it, left to his own devices, Tyler's father had degenerated.

Watching him now, Tyler thought he was witnessing a strange kind of devolution. The tree house wasn't an opportunity to live off the land; it was an oversized kennel that facilitated a transformation into something beastly. His father appeared hairier each time he saw him. And he smelt too. A lingering odour travelled with him, carrying a scent of earth, decay and faeces. He communicated only through a series of grunts. Tyler imagined a time in the future when he'd have a full pelt and his teeth would be sharp carnivorous points. Soon he wouldn't recognise anything human at all.

Tyler sat in the science lab. He held a test tube in one hand and a pipette in the other. Janie was recording the results in a neatly lined table that had taken longer to draw than the experiment so far. He'd arrived late to class and the only lab coats left were at the very back of the science cupboard. Janie had insisted he spend another five minutes wiping them down of any cobwebs that may have gathered on them. Tyler didn't care that they were behind their classmates. He didn't care that they'd probably fail this assessment. He didn't care about anything. His mind was preoccupied with thoughts of Kevin and Phil running screaming from his naked father. He'd expected to come to school to be greeted with gibes about his father being a flasher, or about him being the son of Tarzan, but both boys were absent. Too traumatised, probably, by the whole experience.

Tyler suspected his father had a mental problem. There was a counsellor at school and he often wondered what she would make of his father's unique living arrangements. He was pretty sure that mental patients needed to be kept in mental institutions, not a tree house at the bottom of the garden. Granddad hadn't gone to a tree house.

Janie looked up from her table. She blew particles of rubber off the page.

Aren't you going to start?" she asked.

Tyler placed the pipette into the test tube, extracting the chemical and depositing it on the slide that was already prepped with blood. He pushed the slide underneath the lens of the microscope and peered through the eyepiece without really seeing.

Tyler waited at the school gates for sight of his mother's beat-up camper. He looked at his wristwatch for the hundredth time. Surely she hadn't forgotten him. It was usually Phil's mum's turn but that was before his father had behaved, well, like an animal. For a moment Tyler had the dreadful thought that she'd finally sold the camper. She'd been threatening it for months, fed up with the guilt of running an automobile and the pollution it caused. He didn't like the van but before "Parent Share" she'd seriously considered buying a tandem. Perhaps this was the excuse she needed. Tyler sighed. If there was anything worse than a feral father it was a mother and son in matching fluorescent cycling jackets, bicycle helmets and ankle clips.

After forty minutes Tyler decided to walk home. It wasn't far really. Dusk was beginning to settle, triggering the streetlamps, which slowly flickered to light. As he got closer to home, he became aware of an abundance of posters pinned to lampposts and telegraph poles. Images of tabbies and terriers snapped in red-eyed poses dotted the neighbourhood. So many had disappeared in the last year, as if they'd been hunted to extinction. Tyler sighed and looked elsewhere. Though the sun hadn't completely set, Tyler could see the pale outline of the moon. It was full.

He let himself in the front door, kicking off his shoes in the hall, knowing his mother didn't like him to bring the outdoors in.

"Mum?"

There was no answer. She didn't appear to be in,

though the camper was in the drive and her handbag in the hall. He checked the rooms one by one, finding evidence of her here and there, a cup of coffee on the sideboard, her sketchbook open on the table. Tyler walked through to the kitchen and saw with surprise that the back door was wide open.

"Mum?" he called into the darkness.

He placed a tentative step outside; the grass was dewy and made his sock damp. He was about to wander into the garden's depths when he saw a pile of clothing on the ground, a bra laying casually on top in all its feminine effrontery.

And then he heard the noises.

It sounded not unlike his father's growling, a long, guttural exhalation of emotion. But as he listened harder, he could hear another sound, a voice not quite so wild, but uninhibited and familiar. The voices merged together, howling wildly into the night. The sounds became more urgent, quickening and Tyler realised with wide-eyed apprehension that he was listening to the bestial coupling of his parents.

He slammed the door in disgust.

Tyler heard humming in the kitchen the next morning.

"Morning, sleepy head," Tyler's mum called as he descended the stairs. He came down two at a time, hoping to speed up the breakfast process and get out of the door as quickly as possible.

"I made waffles." She smiled.

Tyler didn't want anything borne of this mood. "I'm not hungry."

She placed a plate in front of him regardless. "And how was school yesterday?"

"Fine, especially when you're the only one there gone five."

Tyler, we've been over this," she said, placing her fork down. "I've apologised."

Tyler thought back to the previous evening, to the sound of his mother eventually stumbling back to the house and her tentative knocking on his bedroom door. But he had successfully managed to barricade himself in and his monosyllabic responses had kept her at bay.

She resumed eating, "I was just a little preoccupied last night."

Tyler grabbed his lunch box; he didn't want to think about how she'd been preoccupied.

"Will you take your father his breakfast before you go? He'll be ravenous."

Can't you?"

Tyler's mother looked at herself in her pink flannel dressing gown and shook her head. "Not like this."

Tyler sighed. She was behaving like teenager. "You could leave your clothes by the door again."

"Tyler!"

"Well *I'm* not doing it," he continued. "If you want to pretend that this is normal, you can take it to him yourself."

"Tyler, he's your father."

But he isn't, is he?" Tyler yelled, "He's a beast."

Tyler's mum cupped a hand over her mouth to suppress a sob. She was an emotional time bomb at the moment and Tyler was happy to be the detonator. She sat down heavily at the kitchen table and let the tears fall.

The feeling of victory was fleeting. He didn't want to leave his mum like this.

"Mum, don't cry," Tyler began, "I didn't mean it."

He stroked her dressing gown. It reminded him of fur. "Forget I said anything. I'll take it."

Tyler placed his lunch box back down and grabbed the handle of the bucket instead. He pushed the door wide and hurried down the garden path. This was what he didn't like about women, how unfairly they used their feminine wiles to get what they wanted.

As usual, Tyler heard his father before he saw him, the sound of wood thumping and creaking as he jumped in excitement like a baboon. Tyler pushed through the wall of foliage and emptied the bucket onto the earth. His father leapt to the ground with cat-like dexterity. He began devouring the meat in voracious mouthfuls. Tyler sat beside him.

Once, before his father had gone completely feral, Tyler had found him at the bottom of the garden, hunched over a spider's web. Tyler watched him pick off the mummified remains of flies and pop the cocooned bodies into his mouth. After he'd picked the web clean, he'd move onto another one, snacking on the web coated corpses. He seemed slightly embarrassed when Tyler had asked what he was doing.

"They're perfectly nutritious Tyler," he'd said. But his expression was confused as if he knew something was wrong but couldn't help himself. As if he couldn't help any of it.

Now, watching him devour the meat, Tyler cried quietly, using his sleeves to wipe away his tears. The beast man paused and looked up from his food. He sidled closer to Tyler and sniffed his hair and patted his head. Then he placed an enormous hairy arm around Tyler's shoulders and pulled him into his great earthy body.

৯

Janie was in her lab coat already when Tyler got to class. She handed Tyler his with a smile, clearly proud of having braved the science cupboard on her own. She'd laid out the equipment as neatly as his mother would have and had set up the microscope.

"I thought we could make up for lost time," she said.

Tyler nodded and slipped the lab coat over his uniform. He was excited about the project, eager again to embrace the cold logic of science. He fingered a length of his father's coarse hair in his pocket. He'd taken it from him that morning when he had unexpectedly embraced him. If he could distract Janie, he could pop the hair onto the slide and look at it through the microscope. He wondered what he would discover. If the microscope could reveal the dappled intricacies of a blood cell, what would it be able to tell him about his father? He doubted that the magnification of his father's hair follicle would reveal a lot but he liked the idea of placing it under the lens and under the scrutiny of science. With science on his side perhaps he could uncover the mysteries of genetics, unravel the gene sequence and find some crucial missing link. If he could understand his father, maybe he could cure him.

Tyler thought back to the beast man's strange embrace that morning and of his mother's happy mood before he'd disrupted it. The way she engineered it so Tyler would see his father daily. Perhaps it wasn't the promise of breakfast that made the beast man so excited, that had him banging about on the wood planks but the opportunity to see his son. Despite the putrid odours, the tickle of matted hair and the blood on his skin, his father had embraced him. And Tyler had liked it. It was something they had never done before the tree house.

A spider, large and black as an inkblot, suddenly darted across the back of Janie's lab coat and into her hair. Without hesitation, Tyler dropped the pipette he was holding and seized the creature from Janie's tresses. Janie jumped at the unexpected contact and Tyler held the spider at arm's length by one twiggy leg.

Instinctively, he popped it in his mouth.

And as Tyler felt the squirming body on his tongue, tasted its juices as he chewed; he finally understood what his father had meant. He swallowed the writhing remains to Janie's screams of disgust, but it left an insatiable taste in his mouth, a new hunger and he suddenly realised that his father had built the tree house for him after all.

Time Keeping

———— ✍ ————

1
Monday
11:29 am

Time waits for no man. But Howard wasn't just *any* man and Time would wait if it had to. Howard didn't like to keep it waiting if he could help it. In fact, the only time he had kept Time waiting was June 5th 2006 and that was only for 5 minutes and 45 seconds while he, agitated and bewildered, ran through darkened streets back to his flat, then around his workshop hastily setting in motion the mechanisms to resume it once more.

He had lamented the loss of those 5 minutes and 45 seconds, but over the years he had managed to claw them back. A second here and there and, without too much bother, he had set to right the universal system of temporality. No one was any the wiser. Why should they be?

It was the first time Howard had ever been late for anything. He hated tardiness in people. He had given up public transport for that very reason and instead walked everywhere, reasoning that he alone possessed the only reliable record of time, his strides governed by the resounding tick of the second hand of his antique

83

wristwatch. Besides, he couldn't go too far and holidays were certainly out of the question. Who would keep Time then? It didn't bear thinking about.

No, that one was of the drawbacks of being Time's keeper. His life was localised, limited to the immediate proximity of his flat and nearby shops. He had devised a system that enabled him to leave for approximately two hours per day. This window allowed him the essential time needed to run errands, pick up parts at the hardware store and, occasionally, allowed him a little leisure. He'd usually arrive home at 11.30 am, half an hour earlier than he needed to be. Why risk being late? He didn't want another June 5th 2006 on his hands again.

But as he returned home from the hardware store one rainy January morning, he realised his compulsion to be home early was costing him an inordinate amount of his free time. Three and a half hours a week to be exact. That was approximately 14 hours a month, 168 hours a year. Normally he didn't mind at all, an occupational hazard, he would say. But on that particular day, as he walked along the grey concrete tributaries of the city reflecting on the somewhat unusual thing that had occurred 21 minutes and 41 seconds ago, he minded quite a lot. And he saw in that moment, as the rain began to fall in a misty shower, causing car lights to blink on almost simultaneously, that his role as guardian was quite an inconvenience.

The somewhat unusual thing was called Helen.

2
Monday (22 minutes earlier)
11:07 am

Helen glanced at the wall clock. 53 minutes until lunch. She wasn't sure how her uncle had managed to stave off boredom. The morning had been duller than expected. The highlight had involved sorting her uncle's orders for his suppliers, followed by dusting shelves of long outmoded DIY products, clearly no match for the swankier variety found in giant super-stores. And with no customers for two days now, she couldn't see how her uncle managed to keep his little store going all these years. If it were her business she would sell up.

The tinkling of the bell above the door signalled a customer. A sound so unfamiliar that Helen, crouched on the floor dusting a low cobweb-strewn shelf, bumped her head on the shelf above and let out a series of profanities.

This was very unusual for Howard. Howard liked routine. Along with the customary toll as the door swept open, Howard was sure he had heard a muffled "Mother fucker" along with other more colourful expressions. Even curiouser was that Mr. Tinton of Tinton's Hardware Store had vanished and in his stead a woman emerged from the adhesives aisle, a hand on her brow. She was dressed in a dusty blue overall, "Tinton's Hardware" emblazoned across her chest adding further mystery. Howard hovered in the doorway. His natural inclination was to leave.

"Can I help you?"

Howard turned to go.

"You're the first customer of the day and that's saying something, since it's midday."

Howard stopped. "Ten minutes past eleven."

"Sorry?"

"It's ten minutes past eleven. Eleven minutes past, now."

"You knew that without even looking at your watch," she said, genuinely impressed. Howard felt a rare feeling of pleasure.

"You're one of those people with a built in body clock, aren't you? That would sure be handy."

Howard usually disliked talking about his profession. It caused people embarrassment when they either pretended to know what he did or admitted ignorance. "I'm a horologist. I repair..."

"Clocks. Wow, that's amazing. Must be pretty time consuming though."

Helen smirked. Howard didn't. He hadn't allowed the time to develop a sense of humour.

"Yes. It takes a lot of patience."

So what kind of things do you fix?" Helen said with seriousness.

Howard disliked people assuming he only fixed. He also created. He wanted to tell her that he was a pioneer in timekeeping but that was a conversation for another occasion. He was running out of time.

"Clocks, wristwatches, pocket watches, timers. Anything that ticks."

Mr. Tinton emerged from the back, the curtain beads rattling as they disgorged his overly large form. "Couldn't fix me, then, could you boy?" Mr. Tinton insisted on calling him boy despite the fact Howard was in his forties. Howard didn't contradict him. People go to all kinds of lengths to trick Time.

Helen's joviality stopped so abruptly that Howard cursed Mr. Tinton despite the discount he gave him on bulk orders. She looked at her feet and Mr. Tinton put his arm around her, pulling her into his cushioned paunch.

"There, there, no more of that girl."

This was even more unusual. Howard inched his

way closer to the threshold.

"It's my heart, Howard. It's out of juice. Docs say it's got a few months left.

I'm sorry to hear that."

"No need to fret, I'm getting a new one. Going in for a transplant. New parts, I say. Spent my whole life fixing things, bout time I'm the one getting fixed."

"Just so, Mr. Tinton."

But I don't want you to be in any way inconvenienced. My niece, Helen here, has agreed to take over the business while I rest up. Helen, Howard is one of our most important customers. He orders a lot of specialist material through us."

Howard wondered if it was customary to shake hands now formal introductions had been made but the idea of contact made his palms suddenly clammy.

"Helen, do you know much about the business?"

Helen smiled. "Not yet, but I'm sure if everyone is as friendly as you, Howard, I'll pick it up in no time. You'll have to be a little patient with me."

Patience was his favourite virtue. But at its mention he became aware of not being aware of the time. It must be 11:19 am at least, he thought. He'd have to walk double speed to make it home for his 11:30 am curfew.

"Well, pleasure meeting you Helen. I must be going. Terribly sorry."

But you haven't bought anything."

The door clanged shut.

Got no time, that one." Mr Tinton said as he left.

3
Monday evening
10:32 pm

"Did you know that the Church regulated time for centuries? They had to calculate the time for Easter, you see, which changes annually in accordance with the lunar phases. Timekeeping was an exalted occupation. A divine art." Howard smiled.

"It's the mechanics of it all that interests me. I like that every bit is significant, every cog plays its part. Nothing is superfluous. Like a little communist state." He sipped his drink, trying to look debonair. "I loathe digital. Won't touch the stuff. When people call me asking, "do you repair digital watches?" I hang up. To replace all of those mechanisms with a tiny chip just seems wrong somehow. I like to see how things work, really examine them. And to watch it all come together, to witness this calculated release of power—the escapement, well that's really something." Howard smiled, the figure opposite him as engrossed.

"To be honest Helen, I like it because I'm the one winding the cogs."

Howard sighed. His reflection sighed back, a milk moustache prominent on his upper lip, an eager listener but a poor substitute for Helen.

4
Tuesday (the next day)
10:04 am

Howard had pondered it all night. How had he managed to lose time like that? As soon as he had left Tinton's Hardware Store he had pulled up his cuff to check the time. He was 3 minutes out. It had been 11:16 am. Helen was the cause. Her smile had transfixed Time.

Howard wasn't a fool. He had heard about women. His own knowledge had confirmed they were a mysterious breed. They could also be dangerous. Just look at June 5th 2006.

Howard decided it was best to find another hardware store. He had no time in his life for anything else and the risk Helen posed was too great. Yet his rational mind highlighted the difficulties of getting another supplier. Mr. Tinton had managed to source some unusual products over the years. And the time it would take to locate a new procurer and establish a relationship, all because a woman had been nice to him, seemed ridiculous.

Nevertheless, Howard couldn't shake the feeling of danger. He thought of himself as an intrepid sailor, tossed around in an angry current, helplessly drawn toward a siren's song. He would tie himself to the mast like Odysseus if he had to.

The bell tolled like an alarm in Howard's mind. Helen's bright face appeared from behind the counter and Howard wondered how he could have ever feared her.

"Morning, Howard. You're earlier today."

"Yes. A little. I have to pick up some-"

"Yes, my Uncle explained your order. I took the liberty of packing it in advance for you. I know that your time is precious."

Howard was touched but opened the bag to prevent saying so. "Seems to all be in order."

I was just about to pop out for coffee. Since you've got a few minutes spare, I wondered if you'd like to join me?"

Howard thought of Odysseus and felt the rope that bound him untangle and fall away.

"What about the shop?"

"Howard, *you* are our only customer. If I'm with you then technically I haven't even left."

V. H. Leslie

The coffee house smelt unfamiliar to him. Why queue for coffee when he could put the timer on his percolator at home? He had never been for a drink with a woman before and was painfully aware he would have to make small talk.

"I knew it wasn't midday yesterday," Helen said as they sat down with their oversized mugs.

"Sorry?"

When you came into the shop, I said it was midday."

"Yes."

"Well I knew it wasn't. Just wishful thinking, I suppose." Helen sipped her drink. Foam caressed her lips for a moment before dissolving. Howard wasn't sure why she was telling him this.

"Don't you ever count down to things?"

All the time.

"By 'counting down' though, you mean speeding up," said Howard. "You weren't counting down yesterday at all but accelerating time to what you wanted it to be."

"I suppose so, yes. Don't you ever do that?"

"No. Why wish for the future when you can enjoy the present?"

"Then you haven't been in love, have you Howard?"

Howard felt in dangerous territory again.

"Everything speeds up then," she continued. "You can't wait for the minutes to pass until you see them again. You don't know what I'm talking about, do you?"

Howard guzzled his coffee, burning his tongue in his effort to finish.

"I really must be going. I could walk you back to the shop if you...."

90

"No, I'm going to stay a little longer. I'm sorry if I embarrassed you."

Howard left.

5
Tuesday evening
11:14 pm

Helen perplexed Howard. He had never envisioned a woman in his life. He had experienced women of course, though he had paid for them. The first time on June 5th 2006 had been a rush and a revelation. A quick grope in an alley, her experienced hand with his zipper, before the wet release, like the energy exchange in a clock, followed sharply by shame as he realised he had not even entered her. She didn't seem to mind, favoured it in a way. He assumed he'd still have to pay. Now a seasoned customer, he knew he was paying for the secret embarrassment as well as the pleasure.

The first time had been an accident. But it stirred an appetite in him that had lain dormant for many years. If he went out now looking for an illicit encounter it took a bit more planning. That first time was before he had refined his guardianship of Time and regulated his system for breaks. With a bit of ingenuity he could take his two-hour reprieve at a different time of day. But two hours was still not long to cruise the streets on foot. He knew the local haunts of course, places where he was guaranteed anonymity as well as value for money. But the police moved women on from time to time and sometimes it was difficult to track them down. He had his favourites but tried not to see the same woman too often. Forming attachments made it harder. They were whores after all.

91

V. H. Leslie

Howard walked along the estuary. The silhouette of the foundry was clear in the distance and its metallic odour lapped off the river in greeting. As he approached the bridge he made out the hourglass figure he had been drawn to before. He liked Sharon, if that was really her name.

"Hello stranger." Her customary greeting echoed off the concrete underbelly of the bridge. Howard had never told her his name and he doubted whether she would remember anyway. Strangers suited them both better.

June 5th 2006 was etched in his memory for various reasons. It was the first time he had truly lost sense of temporal space. His conscious mind, preoccupied with minutes, seconds, and decimals, seemed to reset when the orgasm swept through his body. Time wound down and Howard floated in a sea of pleasure. He could hear his ragged breathing, at first distanced from his body then magnified in his head. His gasps regulated as his heartbeat slowed, like the reassuring ticking of a clock and when he opened his eyes he realised with horror that he was late.

Since the loss of 5 minutes and 45 seconds he had become much more cautious. As Sharon nibbled his ear, Howard wound his watch. Whores were more understanding than people gave them credit.

But this time, as Sharon pulled up her skirt, she asked, "Don't you ever want to take it slower?"

"Excuse me?"

"Don't get me wrong, I'm not complaining". It's just I like you. I feel like I'm taking your money and not really giving you much for it."

Howard was happy with their arrangement and said so.

1 minute and 47 seconds later Sharon counted her

payment as Howard caught his breath. He had even beaten his timer.

But later that night, as Howard lay in bed, the concurrent ticking of his clocks, his usual lullaby, only served to taunt him of his rushed intercourse with a prostitute. Perhaps Sharon was right. Maybe he should make some time for a woman, a woman who liked him for himself and not his money. He liked Helen. Maybe he should tell her about his workroom, maybe even let her in. Perhaps they could keep Time together?

6
Saturday (4 days later)
10:13 pm

"People ignore the importance of chronology, don't you think?" Helen was talking about a crime novel she had abandoned in the penultimate chapter. "I don't understand why stories have to hack at time so much, fancy flashbacks and leaps forward in the narrative is plain and simple cheating in my opinion. I gave up on this one for that very reason. You think you've solved the plot and BAM, a begrudged co-worker the protagonist slighted at high school emerges from the woodwork and is responsible for the whole spate of killings. There should be a law about it."

"A literary law," Howard laughed.

"Yes. Governed by me." She sipped her cocktail. "What do you like to read, Howard?"

Instruction manuals, *The History of Clepsydras, The Horologists' Guide to Antique Clocks.*

"I don't read much, I'm afraid. Not fiction, anyway." The first silence in their conversation filled the space between them and expanded above the noise of the

93

restaurant. "My work doesn't allow me much time," Howard said in an attempt to dispel the awkwardness.

"Oh yes. Tell me about your work?"

Howard remembered his prepared speech, rehearsed in front of the mirror, but it felt too artificial. "What do you want to know?"

"Well, if I'm honest, how do you make a living from it? When someone's watch breaks, they just buy a new one these days."

"I admit my work only caters for a limited few. I have my regulars, as with any trade, specialists and collectors. People who want to preserve heirlooms seek me out upon recommendations. The people I do business with appreciate my talents and are willing to pay well."

"That's really something, Howard. That's what I like about you. You're reliable, unlike a lot of men out there," the last part was muttered into her glass.

The waiter brought out their desserts.

"I know you're a patient man, Howard, I admire that in you, but I hope you're brave enough to seize the moment as well. After all, we don't know how much time we have left," she said licking chocolate mousse off her spoon.

Howard gulped.

"Bill please."

Howard led Helen along the corridors of his home. A timepiece of sorts hung on every wall. Some of them Helen didn't recognise as clocks.

"What's that?"

"A clepsydras. A water clock. It's one of the earliest forms of timekeeping. A relic. I'm a bit of a connoisseur, you see."

Time Keeping

"This whole place should be a museum."

Howard took it as a compliment. He fixed Helen a drink, slipping into his workroom while Helen was distracted with his eclectic collection of pocket watches.

"And the sound, doesn't it drive you mad? How do you get them all in unison?"

"Oh, just a bit of tinkering," Howard called as he finished up his maintenance of Time.

"What's in there?" Helen asked as he emerged.

"My workshop."

"Can I take a look?"

"No, it's not very tidy at the moment."

"Are you kidding? This whole place is immaculate. I don't mind, I'd love to see where it all happens."

Howard considered opening the door, letting her into to his secret world, but it was just too risky. Later, when she understood more about his job, then he would let her in.

"Perhaps later."

Helen pouted. "Well if you're not going to show me *that* room, perhaps you'll let me take a look at another?"

Howard led her to the bedroom. She sat on the bed and removed her stilettos.

Howard was duly nervous about the next few minutes of his life. Helen giggled as she drank wine. Howard downed his glass and filled up another. No time for that as Howard was pulled to the bed. Helen removed her dress and guided his hands. Howard thought of clock carriages and the way he tinkered with the insides to get them working. Sometimes that was all it took. But instead of the reassuring touch of metal, Howard's fingers delved into a fleshy dampness. To overcome his repulsion, he moved his fingers around

95

as if exploring the innards of a clock. A fleshy button, like the round smoothness of a pendulum, seemed to govern Helen's rhythmic movement and made her moan. Her oscillator. He felt around awkwardly, beginning to understand the strange mechanisms that made her tick. His fingers continued their prodding. He resisted the urge to put on his spectacles. She wasn't a prostitute, he reminded himself. He had to make her work.

Nothing.

After 26 minutes and 5 seconds of exploring, Helen's body came to a halt amid wordless exclamations Howard took for pleasure. Approximately 2 minutes later so did his. Afterwards, he lay entwined in Helen's arms and allowed the bliss of post coital slumber to wash over him. Lying in her arms, he felt Time slow down. He could hear his clocks running down, all of them in synchronised deceleration. They needed winding. Why hadn't he noticed it before? He wondered if Helen had.

Howard woke confused. Helen was gone.

7
Saturday (1 week later)
9:38 pm

Helen sat propped up in the armchair in Howard's study. Howard was hunched over his workstation tinkering with the carriage of a clock. They had been almost inseparable for a week now and Howard relished her company as he did his collection of hourglasses surrounding her. She looked beautiful amidst their reflective orbs, but he found he focused on her more than he did his creations.

96

"I made each one myself," he'd told her.

"The idea came from Ferdinand Magellan, a Portuguese explorer who sailed around the globe. He had eighteen hourglasses per ship to keep the exact time for his ship's logs. A page was entrusted to turn them at different intervals, an hour here, two hours there. What a responsibility! They had even fashioned some that were fitted to wooden frames so you could turn them simultaneously. I tried that once myself, but I thought it spoilt the look of them. So much more simplistic than clocks." He ran his hand over the curves of the glass bulbs.

"And I thought to myself, what an incredible thing that young man did, keeping guard of all that Time. It isn't the job of a page to keep Time, but a King.

Helen slumped in her chair. Howard didn't take it personally. It was late after all.

8
Monday (2 days later)
10:32 am

Howard smiled as he opened the door to Tinton's Hardware, the bell causing a melodious clamour. The word "clock" had derived from that little Celtic word for bell, which incidentally had also summoned the love of his life with its ringing.

"Morning, Mr. Tinton." Howard called.

"Morning yourself," Mr Tinton replied. Mr Tinton's usual friendly demeanour was elsewhere today. His eyes were circled with grey and Howard could detect a stale odour of alcohol on his breath. Best not to linger.

"Just my usual order, Mr. Tinton."

Mr Tinton was uncharacteristically slow in putting

the products in their brown paper packaging. Was he doing it on purpose? Perhaps he had taken Helen's resignation badly.

"For my accounts, Howard, I need to take down a few details, such as your address.

This was very unusual. Business had always been conducted without a need for personal invasion. Howard had always insisted on picking up his deliveries in person so he could check that the contents were to his specification. Mr. Tinton had accepted this as one of Howard's many eccentricities. Yet Mr. Tinton was poised, pen in hand.

"I'm afraid I don't have time today, Mr. Tinton. I must be getting off." He had to get back. He had Time *and* a woman to look after now. And though Helen watched him intently as he kept Time she wasn't ready for the responsibility of doing it herself. No, he had to get back.

"Then I can't give you your order."

Howard clenched his teeth. He would speak to Helen about her cantankerous old uncle. "Very well."

"Give my regards to Helen," Mr. Tinton called as the bell tolled.

Howard would not let Mr. Tinton's unusual behaviour dampen his mood. He thought of Helen sitting in his workroom, her bright smile waiting to greet him when he got home. He had been right to let her in. She watched him keep Time with keen interest and he had shown her his tricks to speed up the process. The first time he had let her into his workroom had been filled with trepidation. He worried that she wouldn't understand his Great Mission, that she would break something, but she had sat patiently in the russet armchair as Howard explained it all.

Hourglasses covered every surface. They ranged in height and width. He'd made most of them himself. The curtains were permanently shut as he worried about exposing his creations to sunlight.

He knew instinctively when to turn them now. Some needed to be turned more regularly than others. Turning his hourglasses had become a full time occupation. They each had their own separate rotation pattern. Some needed turning in 2-hour cycles, some in 4. Like balancing plates, he knew exactly when to give each one his attention. One hourglass could be turned up to 12 times in one day, another only 6. He had engineered it so that he had two hours free a day when the hourglasses could stand independently. Apart from 5th June 2006, the sand had never run out.

He experimented with the size of bulbs and the amount of sand. The sand itself presented the biggest problem. The quality of the grain determined its velocity through the glass chutes. Howard had tried all varieties of sand, ground eggshell and archaic components such as ground marble. But his most recent invention was his favourite. He congratulated himself on its ingenuity.

What had become his obsession had begun as an experiment. Soon he found he liked the pattern it created in his life. He found himself staying at home in order to keep the sand flowing. Time relied on him and him alone. There was some kind of grand purpose in the measurement of Time. He saw that he was a cog in a bigger mechanism, one that controlled the cycles of the moon and the pull of the tides, a great cosmic force that governed the lives of billions of creatures. And he was part of it.

But with Helen in his life now, he wanted more

free time. He wanted to refine his guardianship of Time, to make it more efficient. It would have been easier with clocks. Slave clocks were used in schools and other institutions when Howard was a boy. These clocks were wired to a main clock, which sent signals on the hour to keep them in time. If Howard could somehow engineer a way of synchronising his hourglasses to a master, perhaps he could keep time forever, without even lifting a finger.

9
Monday evening
10:35 pm

Helen lay next to him. He shivered as he snuggled into her body. She was less verbal during sex these days and Howard wondered if she was happy. He had heard that sex between married people became more routine as time went by. They weren't married, not yet, but that's where he wanted it to go. And he liked routine. He had hoped Helen liked his routine too but perhaps she was just pretending.

Still, he had reduced the 28 minutes and 5 seconds of their first night of lovemaking to a much more efficient 4 minutes and 10 seconds, and *that* still required an inordinate amount of restraint on Howard's part. He didn't understand why it had to be such a time consuming act. Perhaps that was the cause of her discontent. Or could it have been the talk about her uncle?

The smile on her face dispelled his thoughts.

჻

10
Thursday (two days later)
11:12 am

Howard did not want to return to Tinton's Hardware store until the disagreement between Helen and her uncle had abated. He had put it off for days but was fearfully low on supplies. Helen could not go so it was left to him.

The door rang with its usual greeting. The store was empty. Mr Tinton was nowhere to be seen.

"Mr. Tinton?" Howard walked through the aisles.

No one.

Perhaps Mr. Tinton had gone in for his operation. Yet that didn't explain why the shop was open. Howard had a vision of Helen's uncle lying on the floor, a hand clutching his chest. He had the sudden impulse of just picking up the goods he needed and leaving his money on the counter. But curiosity led him on. Breaking some kind of unwritten consumer code, he slipped behind the counter. He pulled aside the beaded curtain and peered into the darkness beyond.

"Mr. Tinton?"

He heard the sound of a dead bolt being pulled across the shop door behind him.

Howard rushed to the counter and saw Mr. Tinton standing in front of the door, a key in his palm.

"You're going to tell me where my niece is, you bastard."

Howard was stunned.

"Helen didn't tell you?"

"No, she didn't tell me. She hasn't told me anything for nearly two weeks, as you know."

Howard wondered if there was a back entrance.

"Unless you tell me where she is I'll keep you locked

in here. You always seem pretty intent on leaving at 11:20 am, I wonder what would happen if you had to spend an afternoon with me?"

That was not an option.

"And don't think you can fight your way out, Howard. I'm tougher than I look. Besides, I'll swallow the key in the time it takes you to get to me."

Howard considered what Mr Tinton said. He needed time to figure out what to do, to consider all his options, things that were suddenly in short supply.

"Now you tell me your address, Howard. I'm a patient man. I can wait."

Howard made it 11:17 am. Damn Tinton. Helen couldn't maintain Time yet. Not on her own. He was backed into a corner.

"And don't lie to me, Howard. "Cause if you do, I'll keep you here for the rest of your rotten life.""

11:19 am. If he complied with Mr. Tinton now, he still had time to run back to the flat to meet his curfew.

"The clock is ticking."

Howard told him his address.

Mr. Tinton was faster than he looked. By the time Howard had negotiated the counter, Mr Tinton was out the door and closing it behind him. Howard ran at it. His hand reached for the handle as Mr. Tinton attempted to lock it from the outside. Howard forced it open, pushing his shoulders into the gap and getting one arm through. The door was suddenly weightless and Howard thought Tinton must have fled when it was slammed heavily on his fingers. He let out a cry and clutched his hand. He heard the door lock with bitter finality.

❧

11
Thursday
11:55 am

Howard sat propped up against the counter cradling his throbbing hand. It was definitely broken. He hadn't even bothered looking for an escape route. He knew the old man had locked him in good and proper. He must have been planning it for days. Even if he had managed to escape he would never make it back in time.

His mind returned to Helen, the first night in his workroom. He sat her down and Howard and taken the hinge off a clock to show her how he would repair it.

"This is the pendulum, see. It's the easiest bit to repair in a clock and seems to get all the credit for making everything tick," he chuckled. "But see here, this bit is the main spring. Its job is just as important. You can touch it if you like." She didn't. "This is my favourite part. It's called the escapement. It transforms rotational movement into an oscillating motion. It does this by freeing one gear tooth on a mechanical wheel at each swing of the pendulum. This is where the magic happens. This is what makes it tick."

11:59 am. Howard was out of time.

6—CONTINUED
Saturday (12 days ago)
2.43 am

Howard woke confused. Helen was gone.

"Helen?" Howard called. He got out of bed and put on his dressing gown.

"Helen?"

The door to his workroom was open. He rushed

103

to it. He prayed she hadn't touched anything. Why couldn't she just be patient?

Helen sat in the chair in the corner of the room.

"Howard, I've discovered your secret."

"I said I'd show you this room another time."

"I'm sorry. Curiosity got the better of me. You're not mad are you?"

Everything seemed to be in place. Time seemed unscathed by her presence.

"This place is something else. These hourglasses are beautiful."

Howard smiled. Perhaps he was wrong to hide his mission from Helen. He moved to go to her, to wrap her in his arms.

"But why is the sand grey?"

Howard stopped in his tracks. How could he explain that his quest, his obsession came with a certain cost?

"It's almost like ash."

"It's a carbon compound," he agreed quickly. "It slows the sand down due to the size of the particles."

"Oh," she said picking up the hourglass closest to her, holding it to the light.

"No—" Howard began.

But she began to turn it over. Howard's universe was in jeopardy. He ran towards her and gripped her wrist. The hourglass was horizontal between them, the sand frozen in their symmetrical domes. Time suspended. And in that moment void of time Howard lost his grasp of the present. The smash of glass jolted him back into reality; time diffusing like the escaping sand. When he placed the hourglass back down and the trickle of sand resumed its steady flow as if it had never been interrupted, he saw a second stream, spouting from a fissure in the glass. Its progress slower because something red dripped with it. The globular

104

mixture dripped onto the carpet languorously. Howard couldn't take his eyes away from it because he knew what he would see. He stood there for approximately 25 minutes reflecting on the second time in his life Time had stopped, conscious all the while that Helen's inert body lay at his feet.

12
Thursday
11:59 am

Mr Tinton made his way up the flight of stairs to Howard's flat. He didn't knock but pounded at the door and when he realised he would get no answer he kicked it down.

He found her in a small, dark room that looked like a workroom. She sat unmoving in the corner.

"Helen?"

He pulled at the curtains and midday light poured into the room. Mr Tinton couldn't see for the sparkling light that rebounded off a multitude of glass surfaces. When the light settled down, Mr Tinton gasped.

Helen's body was interwoven with mechanical parts. Her arms bore wire-like tendons that were met at her shoulder blades in a series of cogs and bolts. Wires emerged from her spine and neck cavity, reaching into her jaw, hinged together with large screws. Her face was much the same apart from her mouth. The corners of her lips were stretched to reveal a grotesque smile, pinned artificially to her face.

Suddenly noise vibrated off of every surface in the room as a hundred clocks chimed midday. Then with mechanical slowness Helen's body began to move. The cogs in her shoulder turned with painful sluggishness and a pulley forced her arm into mid air. An intravenous tube ran from her forearm to the top of an hourglass attached to her hand. Mr Tinton watched its slow orbit as Helen turned the hourglass and placed it back down again. A thick red substance poured down the centre and into the base of the glass bulb.

With the glass turned, Helen's body resumed its stationary position, her artificial smile giving the impression of a macabre mannequin. She would be locked in position until the hourglass was full again.

Mr. Tinton moved to touch her but stopped when he realised her eyes followed his movement. She blinked. Her eyelashes fluttered in desperation. The whites of her eyes grew larger, imploring her uncle to set her free. She was alive!

Mr Tinton clutched his chest. His heart raced, beating faster as it broke.

Bleak Midwinter

It is cold.

The snow continues to fall, but it falls with less conviction now, drifting feebly in circular motions, resting occasionally on the windowpane as if to catch breath before being swept back into the flurry. The sky is still the grey-white of winter and colossal snow clouds hang dense and low and hostile.

The world outside is silent. Snow smothers the earth like an enormous blanket, a cold blanket, a vast emptiness stretching as far as the eye can see. If you were to shout out here, your words would be snatched away, hungrily absorbed into the void. The muffled syllables would lie dormant under the ice, waiting for a thaw that never comes.

I have wrapped Christina up as well as I can. A duvet unites us and a blanket covers her shoulders. She wears a tattered crown of green tissue paper over her woollen hat. She touches the window with a gloved finger as crystallized flakes pause on the glass to be admired.

"They're beautiful, mother."

I smile because I don't want to contradict her. Not today. This is the day of her Christmas wish.

"What do they feel like?" she asks.

V. H. Leslie

Cold, I reply.

I hand Christina her cocoa and try to avoid looking at the snowmen outside. They have the coal black eyes of the snowmen of my youth, the snowmen that my brothers and I would bring into being each year one compressed handful at a time. Inherently competitive, we'd try to outdo each other in building the perfect specimen. Ours stood taller and more fantastical than the traditional forms that converged on neighbouring lawns. Sometimes we'd sculpt extra arms or legs, two heads, maybe a tail, amalgamating animal appendages to our white figures like gods experimenting at the dawn of Creation.

The perfect snowman is a curious thing. Though each year mine surpassed the efforts of my brothers, some sense of male solidarity prevented me from winning. I didn't really mind. Partly because it was Christmas and partly because I enjoyed cultivating a semblance of life from something so frozen. We weren't the only ones subscribing to this mini-miracle. At the end of each snow day, every garden would have an extra Christmas guest. The populace suddenly doubled with the arrival of white men with carrots noses and twigs for arms, donned in last year's finery as new scarves lay wrapped and folded under the Christmas tree.

Fuelled by the long holidays our snow days never lost their novelty. Besides, the alternative was a list of chores Mother invented to occupy us. She didn't like the snow. It brought too much mess. She would plough the snow from the front door with Father's shovel but would venture no further, as if the act of clearing the porch should be enough of a welcome for visitors, though they'd have to negotiate the rest of the garden themselves if they were intent on stopping by. The snow formed a barrier she wouldn't cross, so that when we ran outdoors, away from the piling dishes, all she could do was shriek at us from the safety of the porch. Hence we welcomed the arctic breeze that buffeted the snow to our doors. We paid tribute with our white idols.

Sometimes there would only be a wet frosting of snow. Global warming, the adults told us, and we'd scrape the sludge from street corners and persevere—it's important to uphold traditions—but the snowmen became smaller, pitiful effigies that sagged on icy green lawns. Ironic that a time once warm could become so cold.

"Open it now, mummy," Christina demands.

We always open one present on Christmas Eve, a tradition we maintain though there will be no more tomorrow. This view of the world is her present and mine is folded in a piece of old patterned fabric tied with a shoelace. It rests on an old trunk with the other items we have brought up from below; blankets, a flask, rations. The room is bare save for these objects and a shovel by the window.

I hadn't counted on quite so many snowmen watching us with their coal black eyes. Though I'm eager to open my present I don't want an audience. I tell her I'll open it below and she places it to one side.

"Why can't we go outside?"

She knows the answer to this and despite the fact it's Christmas Eve, when one should be more tolerant, I'm disappointed in her.

It's too cold, I tell her again. It is too cold out there.

She's also disappointed.

I remind her how treacherous the snow can be. That it's safer to be inside with me, wrapped up against the cold.

V. H. Leslie

"What about the snowmen?"

I'm not sure what to say. It was so easy before to be rid of them before. They were only temporary guests then. Our child hearts pitied them when the warmer weather returned and they began to disappear. We'd try to preserve them, patching them up with icy slush until some child could stand their misery no longer and would kick their remains into oblivion. The objects of our affection became victim to all manner of tortures, condemned at the hands of those who would resurrect them the following year.

But now the snow doesn't stop and they don't leave.

Christina likes it up here above ground. After her cocoa she snuggles into me and watches the snowfall. Snow on snow. I want to take her downstairs to the bunker where it's warmer and safer. Where there are no windows to tempt her. But because it's her Christmas wish I let her stay and I stroke her hair as she watches the world outside.

After a while, her breathing becomes slower and deeper, the only sound in the otherwise silent night. I strain my ears beyond her gentle snoring to discern anything more. But the world is silent, as cushioned and cocooned as my daughter snuggled under blankets. I wonder how Christina would respond to the noise of before. Her ears probably deafened by too much solitude. Her breath is visible as it leaves her body and meets the cold air. Mine is too. Our exhalations like clouds of heat. The only sign we're alive—

There is a snowman at the window.

I freeze, mirroring the figure staring in with wide hollow eyes. They are drawn to the warmth, though I am not stupid enough to have lit any candles. We are the beacon, a warm nativity they want to be a part of. And where there is one, more will come.

I slowly untwine myself from my daughter, cautious not to wake her. I heap another blanket over her to compensate for my absence and sneak to the other side of the room, as I would have done if I'd been placing a stocking in her room. I grab what I need and edge toward the front door.

It's colder outside than I remember and the air nearly robs me of all breath. I move quickly, sinking into the snow with each crunching footfall, conscious all the while of the cold spreading inside.

The snowman hasn't moved and I make quick work of it. I lift the shovel and bring it down and down and down, again and again, as if I were obliterating him into icy particles, kicking his frosty remains into the wind. These snowmen are not like the snowmen of my youth. These men subsist in the cold and the ash, when everyone else has fortified themselves under-ground. And the winter has changed them. They have been sculpted and warped by the ash-snow, less men now, and more like the strange hybrids my brothers and I would construct from the snow. We should pity them really and perhaps we would if it wasn't for the fact they outnumber us, reminding us of what we could become if we let the cold get in.

I lug what's left of him, walking as far from the house as I dare, into the darkness. I can see Christina through the window as I make my way back. She looks so warm inside, no wonder he would want to come in from the cold. I wipe the bloodied shovel in the snow.

After I lock the door, I shake the ash-snow from my coat and hair. But the cold has gone much deeper. I can feel the ice travelling through my body, into my veins, my arteries, spreading around my heart and solidifying there like marble. I'll never thaw.

I place another blanket over Christina's shoulders and she wakes.

"Let's go back down," she mumbles. "It's cold."

And so we go back down below to wait out the winter.

The Blue Room

The room was entirely blue. The walls were deep cerulean and the carpet was the colour of cornflowers. The bedspread was lavender, covered in a patchwork quilt of turquoise and teal, dotted with forget-me-nots and irises. The furniture had been painted in varying shades of blue; the dressing table a baby blue with amethyst drawer knobs, while the wardrobe was almost navy, heavily lacquered so that you could see your outline in its panels. Even the dainty cups and saucers, sporting a chinoiserie design gleamed a cobalt blue.

In fact Gwen was hard pressed to find anything in the room that wasn't blue. She rummaged along the sideboard, flicking through the hotel literature, the list of local attractions, all printed on powder blue paper with the Hyde Hotel crest embossed in Royal blue ink. She was surprised to find such attention to detail in such a modestly priced hotel. She had expected magnolia walls, tired flat pack furniture and laminate fire safety notices pinned on the walls. But this felt more like some chic boutique hotel. She sat down on the bed, laughing at her good fortune. It was about time the universe relented a little.

Instinctively, she opened the bedside drawer,

expecting the customary plastic bound New Testament, but even the bible had not escaped the blue treatment, encased in a bright periwinkle jacket. It seemed appropriate, not only because it conformed to the décor of the room, but also because she knew that blue was the most sacrosanct of colours. The tour guide at the Scrovegni Chapel had said as much, when she and David had honeymooned in Italy all those years ago. She could still bring to mind Madonnas cloaked in blue, gazing out from canvases and frescoes. It was hard to imagine that this colour, extracted from lapis lazuli, had been such a revelation when it was first introduced to the Italian masters. They had never seen a blue of such vibrancy before. But lapis lazuli was extremely expensive, so rare that the Church claimed exclusive rights to it, even banning ordinary people from wearing the colour for a time.

Gwen sat down on the bed. It was hard to imagine a colour being outlawed. But then she thought about how much colour she used to wear before she was married. She'd even gone through a phase of having bright streaks of blue or pink in her hair. David was the eccentric. He preferred her to dress a little more conservatively and before she knew it her rainbow wardrobe was replaced with polyester skirts and white blouses. She rubbed the white material of her shirt between her fingers and with a sudden urgency began to undo the buttons.

She made her way to the bathroom, intent on continuing her inspection. A cursory glance confirmed her expectations: blue tiles, blue towels and a blue bathroom suite. Anywhere else, a blue bathroom suite would have been terribly outmoded. But somehow here, already immersed in so much blue, it seemed strangely elegant, stylish even. She cast her blouse on the floor and closing the bathroom door behind her, saw the crow for the first time.

It was actually a woman and a crow but the crow was so black against the blueness of the painting, in the blueness of the room, that it stood out. Though it was only a print, Gwen could see the heavy black brush-strokes, the suggestion of feathers, talons spread wide. But the crow appeared docile, immobile, allowing the woman to caress it, resting her long fingers against its black wing, administering a kiss, as you would on the forehead of a child.

It was a curious composition. And a curious place to hang a print, behind a door, where no one would see it unless the bathroom door was closed. And how unusual for the door to open outwards in the first place. The bathroom was rather cramped; a lot of old hotels in order to accommodate the modern demand for en suites had to be inventive with their use of space. It couldn't possibly be arranged so just to conceal a painting. Gwen leaned in close and saw "Picasso 1904" in the bottom right corner. It was not at all in the abstract style she associated with Picasso, or with his typical vibrant colour palette. It was so melancholically blue.

Suddenly exhausted, Gwen made her way to bed, but not before leaving the bathroom door wide open. She didn't want to look at this strange painting tonight; she didn't want to think about the crow bringing the blackness in, threatening to taint such an immaculately blue room.

Gwen woke to the scent of lavender, a memory of summer days and clear blue skies. She stretched remembering where she was. In the blue room. A room that even smelt of blue. She nestled deeper into the covers, feeling herself enveloped in blue seas, in gentle Mediterranean sunshine. Looking up, she saw how bright the ceiling was in the daylight. A Giotto ceiling like the one in the Scrovegni Chapel. The colour of heaven, except that this one wasn't dusted with gold stars.

She sat up and realised that she'd slept in her clothes. Her case was still by the door, and she was suddenly annoyed at herself for not unpacking the night before. All her clothes would be creased, not that she could remember what she'd brought anyway; she'd packed in such a hurry.

There was a typical lack of colour when she opened the case, so she opted for the least creased of her blouses and skirts and got dressed. It didn't seem to matter in the blue room, they gave a blue warmth to the muted, bland tones but stepping out into the hotel lobby she was suddenly aware of how washed out she looked. Invisible almost. But beyond the blue room, she saw that the rest of the hotel was fairly ordinary too. She had arrived the previous night in the dark and had barely taken in her surroundings. Now she saw that the décor was distinctly average: Artex magnolia walls, tired dado rails, worn carpets. The dining room was as uninspiring, except there'd been an attempt to brighten each of the tables with a vase of plastic red carnations.

Gwen sat down at a table next to the window, not that she could see much through the greying nets. At least the service was prompt, which was surprising considering how old the server was. He handed her a laminate menu.

"Good morning," Gwen said, the cheerfulness of the blue room was still with her despite her disappointment with the rest of the hotel. "I think I'll have the full English," she said after glancing through the options. "I'm famished."

The waiter stared. Gwen wondered if she should repeat her order. He was surely too old to be working still. She shifted under his gaze and looked about the room. She saw that the other patrons were staring too. Gwen smiled nervously.

"Tea or coffee?" the waiter said, recovering.

"Coffee, please," Gwen replied and the awkwardness lifted as the waiter took the menu back. The other guests seemed to be going about their business as if nothing had happened. Perhaps she'd imagined it. Perhaps it was normal being a little paranoid. It was the first time she'd been out without David in many years. The first time she'd ever stayed someplace on her own. She loosened the collar of her blouse, feeling suddenly hot. The aroma of fried food, the insipid magnolia room filled with even blander diners made her queasy. She longed for the calming influence of the blue room. Just thinking of its turquoise walls, its lavender sheets relaxed her; so that by the time her coffee arrived she was perfectly in charge of her nerves.

It was then that she realised, looking around the room at the diners tucking into their breakfasts, why they had all stared. The Hyde Hotel clearly attracted a certain type of person. Mostly on their own, its patrons were nondescript, plain types, dressed in unassuming clothes. Lacking colour. But Gwen wasn't one of them anymore. The blue room had leant her some of its colour and she couldn't help but stand out.

The sky was the colour of oyster. It reminded her of the woman in the Picasso painting with her sallow grey colouring. Strangely, as she walked through the busy streets, she couldn't help but seek out the blue tones of the city, in shop fronts, billboards, passing cars. Even the pavement beneath her feet possessed a bluish tincture in the drizzle. There was so much blue in the world, she'd never noticed it before. It was as if her eyes were suddenly open to a hidden palette, attuned to the blue in everything, and she felt its presence awakening something inside of her.

She made her way into a park, eager for a reprieve from the hustle and bustle and the feeling of sensory overload. She made her way along the tree-lined paths, past dog walkers and joggers, kids on bikes and scooters. She tried to see past the blue, to take in other colours but they were pale in comparison. She sat down on a bench and closed her eyes, but a blue mist swirled in her mind like a tempest.

When she opened her eyes again she noticed the woman on the bench opposite. She was hardly note-worthy, except for a blatant absence of blue; in fact a lack of any colour at all. Gwen stared more intently. Though the woman was dressed in beige and brown, she didn't seem to emit any colour at all. Not like the people she'd seen bustling through the city or the city itself, which radiated its presence in loud, blue tones. This woman was invisible.

In confirmation, a group of youths passed her by without notice, flanked by a couple of dog walkers who similarly ignored her. Even the dogs, yapping at the feet of passers-by, skirted past the woman as if there were nobody there. Perhaps there wasn't, at least nobody of any consequence. But Gwen could see her. She could see the way her shoulders hunched, the way she sat crumbled into the bench, a sense of sadness in her anonymity. How many invisible women were there in the world, sitting on park benches just like this one, their colour drained out of them by others, siphoned off so that they had none left for themselves? Slowly disappearing into a world that was too bright for them.

Gwen thought to go over. She had some blue now; perhaps she could lend her some of it. But as she made to move, a crow landed by the woman's feet, cawing loudly, undaunted by her presence. As if it were a rallying call, another flew down and another, until the woman was surrounded by a sombre black assembly. What were a flock of crows called? Was it a murder? How morbidly appropriate, Gwen thought as she watched them encircle their victim.

Back in the blue room, Gwen ran a bath. She wanted to be immersed in blue. As she sank into the water, she embraced the feeling of abandonment, of surrendering to the room, to its calming, sympathetic power. She hadn't expected to see Picasso's woman, but with the bathroom door open she could make out the painting's reflection in the veneer of the wardrobe. She thought about getting out of the bath and closing the bathroom door, but she could only see part of the painting and thankfully not the crow. It was just the woman. Seen through the navy panelling her appearance was almost ghostly, the tilt of her head seemed to imply supplication and her long hand was positioned as if in prayer.

Gwen felt tired. She sank deeper in the water, wondering idly how many people had drowned in their bathtubs, lulled into a watery sleep. She wondered if this had ever happened here at the Hyde, whether in all its history, some poor cleaning woman had discovered a pruned, blue corpse doing her morning rounds.

Gwen pushed the idea from her mind as she forced herself under. It is hard not to float she realised. It's an act of will to make yourself a dead weight. Lying against the bottom of the tub, Gwen opened her eyes and watched the bubbles stream up to the surface. It felt so good, this entirely blue world. She didn't see why she should come up at all.

A sudden screech pierced the water. Gwen bolted upright, already doubting whether she had heard anything at all. It had sounded like a shriek, an abrupt, short vocalisation, but the water was good at distorting things. Perhaps it had been a noise in a neighbouring room, or out on the corridor. The water had a way of cushioning sound, it could likely have been a bird at the window, cawing like the crows she'd seen in the park.

A blue woman walked past the doorway.

Gwen instinctively jerked backwards, water sluicing over the edge of the bathtub. She may have doubted the sound but there was no disputing this. A naked woman had just walked past the bathroom door. And this woman was now in her blue room.

Gwen froze as the realisation sank in. Should she call for help, alert the hotel staff somehow. But she was naked and vulnerable and she'd have to go through the blue room to get to the exit. Besides, Gwen had seen the grey blue hue of the woman's flesh, an intensity of tone that couldn't be down to the blue of the room alone.

Gwen didn't move. She listened hard but no sound came from the blue room, no footsteps, no opening of drawers or cupboards. It was as if no one was there.

Gwen stayed in the bath until the water was cold. Then she was finally roused by familiar sounds, of a television blaring from a neighbouring room, a trolley squeaking along the corridor outside. When she stepped out into the blue room she knew there would be nobody there. She'd already accepted that she had hallucinated the woman, that she had conjured her out of the blue mist in her mind.

Gwen sat down, wet and cold at the baby blue dressing table. She could barely see herself in the mirror through the condensation, so she wiped the glass gently with her fingertips, watching as cold droplets ran down the surface. She noticed the blue anaemic hue of her hands from so long in the water. Her lips too were a shade she recognised as the same unearthly pallor of the blue woman.

Gwen sat in the hotel restaurant, nursing a cup of coffee. The waiter hadn't stared so much this time, though she still noticed glances from other guests. At least she wasn't invisible any longer. She thought of the woman on the park bench, how even the crows had regarded her as an irrelevancy. Crows were scavengers weren't they? It was no coincidence that they conjured morbid associations; they sensed the nearness of death.

"Are you enjoying your stay?" the waiter asked, placing down the slice of cake she'd ordered. Despite his age, he still managed to sneak up on her.

"Very much so," Gwen replied, sitting taller, pleased to be engaged in conversation. "I have the most wonderful blue room. I wonder why the hotel doesn't boast about it more, it's a real selling point."

"Blue?"

"Yes," she said finishing her coffee. "Entirely blue".

The old man looked confused. H probably didn't get to the rooms very often, Gwen thought. He was probably confined to the restaurant and kitchen. Either that or he was likely going senile.

"My husband was a painter," Gwen found herself confessing. "He was always obsessed with colour."

"Hell," the old man said, as he reached for her cup with an unsteady hand.

"Pardon?"

"Blue is the colour of Hell, in some ancient mythology, I forget which one."

Gwen watched him knit his brows as he tried to remember. Shrugging, he turned away, the tray cluttering as he made his way back towards the kitchen.

Gwen couldn't sleep that night. She couldn't stop thinking about the blue woman. The daylight had helped her to rationalise what she'd seen—the steam had perhaps given the impression of things that were not there, things that her exhausted mind had clung to—but now it was night, it was harder to convince herself that the blue woman had been the product of an overactive imagination. She'd felt so real.

Gwen could almost see her now. Walking across the blue room, stepping into her dreams, naked and brash. How confident the blue woman had been, striding across the room. Not huddling along and creeping the way invisible women did.

It was very likely the Hyde Hotel was haunted. Of course it would be with so many people coming and going. Hotels often harbour intense emotions, emotions that can't always be played out at home. How many lovers had the hotel seen, those involved in illicit encounters, deceiving someone they loved back home? And how many lonely desperate people had arrived at its door? Home to them was nothing but a torment; the Hyde Hotel was a brief reprieve, a refuge while they figured out what to do next. The residue of all of this must have accumulated like dust along the banisters and behind the wardrobes. Perhaps sometimes in a certain light, in a blue light, you could see it swirling in the air like a mist.

Gwen stared at the ceiling. Like Giotto's, minus the stars. As close to heaven as that master could envisage. But all she could think of was the old man's words. Was this really just a well-decorated hell?

Hell or not, it was beautiful and Gwen found herself melting into the blue. As if she were back in the bath, she let herself sink down into it, she could feel it envelop her and hold her in its secure blue warmth. There was no need to keep her head up anymore.

She slept like a child. As one safely nestled beneath blankets, a lullaby sung close by. She half-woke with this feeling of security, of someone resting against her, holding her tight.

"David," she murmured, rolling into him. And in her half-sleep she had already forgiven him. It was so much harder being on your own. The warmth of another is sacred, like the colour blue. Though you're never aware that you agree to the terms of such an exchange, sometimes it is worth losing your colour for someone else. You don't mind as they shine brighter, siphoning off yours, you don't even object because they are at your side. That's the vampiric nature of love.

"David," she said again, moving towards him, needing to kiss him.

But the lips she touched were cold.

Opening her eyes, in the midnight blue room, Gwen saw the deathly pallor of those lips, and she realised it wasn't David but the blue woman at her side.

She recoiled, half expecting the blue woman to vanish before her eyes, but instead she sat up in bed,

125

bringing her knee up so Gwen could see her blue sex. Brash and bold, wanting to be seen. Gwen stumbled out of the bed falling against the floor and she ran from the blue room.

"I'd like another room please," Gwen asked. "I don't care what colour, red, green, pink. Anything but blue."
The concierge pursed his lips together. He glanced down at the register and shook his head. "I'm afraid we are fully booked."

"You don't understand, I can't go back in there."

The concierge was indifferent and Gwen was suddenly aware of her frantic, bedraggled appearance, the lateness of the hour. She folded her arms against her nightdress, smoothed down her hair.

It was then she realised there was a woman at her side, a woman that had a set of hotel keys already in her hand, a small suitcase at her feet. In her urgency, Gwen had jumped the queue. She felt a pang of guilt that she hadn't noticed the woman, that she hadn't even seen her. The woman hadn't objected and Gwen realised that she was probably used to being ignored.

Feeling admonished and foolish, Gwen stepped back from the desk, but not before the woman reached out for her.

"It was only a nightmare," she said in a small voice.

Gwen nodded, and slowly made her way back to the blue room.

It wasn't the blue of Giotto's ceiling that greeted her the next morning, but the blue black of Picasso's crow. Gwen could see the painting from where she lay and it was almost as if the tones of the canvas had seeped out into the room. Everything appeared to have taken on a black tinge, becoming a few shades darker. She got out of bed and began to dress.

She supposed she should have been thankful that David had given her a rudimentary appreciation of art, that she could comprehend this space that she now found herself in. It was hard not to absorb his passion. But she wondered about the passions of her own that she'd forfeited. Had she had some, before she'd gotten married? Or had she always been a blank slate? She rubbed her head, feeling a blue haze gathering there.

She made her way down to breakfast. It is easy to spot the invisible women when you were one yourself. The woman she'd seen by the concierge's desk the previous night was sat huddled in a corner, dressed blandly with her shoulders sagging. Trying to draw as little attention to herself as possible. Like the woman on the park bench, there was no colour about her at all. She was barely there.

Gwen made her way over. She had thought that she was gaining a little of her colour back, if only the colour the blue room had lent her for a time. But the reappearance of the blue woman had her doubting her perception. It had felt so easy when she'd first arrived in the blue room, immersed within its secure blue walls but now the blue was changing, getting darker and letting things in she didn't want to see.

She sat down opposite the woman, who recoiled slightly at seeing her.

"Do you mind if I join you?" Gwen asked, though she'd already made herself comfortable.

The young woman nodded, sipping her tea timidly.

"So what colour is yours?" Gwen asked.

127

"Excuse me?"

"Your Hell?"

"Sorry?"

"Your room, what colour's your room?"

"I'm not rightly sure," the woman replied. "Green, I think. I've only just arrived. I haven't taken much notice."

It was understandable; she'd arrived in the dead of night with only a tiny suitcase. She didn't look like a businesswoman and she had that nervous, hunched look Gwen was familiar with. What was she running away from?

"They have a lovely blue room," Gwen began, "the curtains are the colour of bluebells and the bedspread is cornflower with forget-me-nots on the coverlet. The lampshades are midnight blue and the ceiling is one of Giotto's own," she added, leaning in close, "minus the stars."

"Hmm," the woman smiled.

"But you can imagine those." Gwen felt the need to reach out to this woman, the way the woman had reached out to her the previous night. She took her hand and saw that she had a little colour after all. A band of bruised yellow imprints dotted her wrist. The woman snatched her hand away.

Gwen stood. "You can have the blue room when I'm gone."

Gwen ran a bath. She was sick of the blue room and its capacity for trickery, but it was the only place for her to go. Besides, she felt so exhausted with it all, she just wanted to sink into the water and stay there forever. Maybe, when she eventually resurfaced she'd be back in Italy with David, standing beneath the vault of the

Scrovegni Chapel, gazing up at the stars. But she knew that couldn't happen, so she might as well just stay beneath the water, immersed in her cold, blue world.

She forced her body under and watched as the bubbles raced to the surface. There was a multitude at first, but then they become more sporadic, until there was no air left in her lungs. She closed her eyes against the blue and welcomed the black instead.

A screech jolted her awake and opening her eyes she saw a black smudge dart across the surface of the water. She bolted upright, breathing hard, gulping in air while wiping the water from her eyes. In the blue haze, she'd thought she'd seen a bird fly out into the blue room. It would be a crow, she knew, sensing the nearness of death. Then she heard laughter, soft giggling and moaning. She stepped out of the water carefully, leaving a trail of wet footprints on the blue tiles, and following the sound made her way into the blue room.

There were at least a dozen blue women, rolling around naked on the bed and floor. Each in variety of erotic embraces, kissing and caressing one another and flaunting their blue nakedness for all to see. Was this the Hyde's past? Was this a ghostly echo of the lovers who had been here once, strangely resurrected for Gwen to see?

It was then that she noticed the suggestion of the man at the epicentre. In the middle of this swirling blue orgy, she could see him plain as day, painted black like the crow in the painting. Heavy brushstrokes obscuring his heart, the one he had pledged to her.

Gwen recoiled from the scene, from those young, willing, blue bodies. She had ignored them before, but here they were, all together, swirling around and around like the lovers in Blake's "Circle of the Lustful", condemned to some endless, purgatorial re-enactment. It wasn't the ghosts of the Hyde's past but the women—the models—that David had invited into their marriage, into their bed.

The room began to spin, with David at the centre of this crazed colour wheel. But the room wasn't blue any more; it was black. Gwen stumbled backwards, as the women seemed to take flight, encircling her like a murder of crows. They were crows, the lot of them, black-souled for what they had done to her. The blackness seemed almost absolute now and she knew with a feeling of clarity, that when she fell the crows would pick her corpse clean.

Gwen woke to a loud knocking.

"Room service," she heard and picking herself up from the floor, she managed to call, "Can you come back later?"

"I need to make up the room," the voice insisted.

Gwen made her way over to the door. Her body ached, not just from sleeping on the floor; it was as if she were only suddenly conscious of the tender feeling of her muscles and flesh.

"There's no need," she called through the door, "I'm going to check out." Though only just deciding, her body seemed to relax a little at the idea. She heard the cleaning trolley squeak past.

It was undoubtedly time for her to go, time to leave the blue room behind, but as she turned she saw that the room wasn't blue any longer.

It was magnolia, comprised of tired flat-pack furniture, worn carpet, dowdy soft furnishings and laminate fire safety notices.

Gwen rummaged along the sideboard, through the

cupboards and drawers. Where were the chinoiserie cups, the amethyst drawer knobs, where was Giotto's vault? But only a pitiable Artex ceiling gazed back.

Had she made it up, like Yves Klein when he made his famous blue? But at least his blue had been real. Her blue was nothing but a haze, a strange vapour that despite its subtleties and nuances had evaporated into thin air. The room was entirely different; nothing of her blue period remained, nothing except the Picasso painting.

It was just as it was, the woman leaning over the crow, planting a solemn kiss on its brow. But it didn't seem quite so morbid now. Gwen had interpreted it to be about the strange allurement of death, but now she saw there was gratitude in the kiss, it was the kind of kiss you would give before bidding someone farewell.

Gwen sighed, taking in the new room and sat down slowly at the dressing table, a dressing table that wasn't baby blue at all, but fake wood veneer. The sight in the mirror was even more startling, and though she wanted to withdraw from what she saw there, she knew she had to confront it, now that the blue haze had lifted.

In the stark light, she saw the black blue of herself, the marks he had left on her that made others stare. She wasn't thankful for these colours, though they made her see herself more clearly. And knowing then that she would eventually get her colour back, she watched as the crow that had been on her shoulder the whole time, flew away.

Ulterior Design

Daniel couldn't see beyond the impenetrable wall of brambles. In the distance he could make out serpentine vines gloating as they curled their forked shoots around tree limbs and branches, suffocating the very life that anchored them. Bursting from these curving stems were crimson buds. The edges of deep red petals rose to sharpened peaks so that they resembled the barbed briars from which they sprang. The blossoms were both familiar and strange, as if a number of exotic flowers had been fused to create the finest and most deadly hybrid. Long yellow stamen protruded from the centre of these plants, the tips such a vivid yellow you could anticipate the powdery pollen on your fingertips. Hovering around the nectar, butterflies in all manner of colors fluttered from one bud to the next like insincere lovers. Bees, too, crept from one sweetened platform to another. Exotic birds perched on thorny arbours, displayed wings that appeared to be gilded with gemstones, waiting to snap their beaks at the buzzing harvest that floated just out of reach. All about was movement and life and the incessant beating of wings.

Daniel disliked the wallpaper instantly.

The design was supposed to represent abundance

133

and plenitude. Flowers bloomed, berries swelled and in the world of the wallpaper life thrived and flourished as nature's everlasting cycle was interwoven with the pattern. The paper was alive. It moved and grew and shook as if some clever botanist had captured the vast array of flora and fauna between the fibres of the paper.

But the design was too complex. Daniel tried to trace a single stem but found himself knotted and entangled in the pattern. He wanted to get his garden shears and trim back the briars, curb the wayward undergrowth.

Worse still, it was predatory. Every inch of the paper spoke of danger. Insects fed rapaciously on the foliage and in turn were consumed by the birds that weaved between and even they seemed to be cowering in a state of vulnerability, as if they sensed a predator.

Daniel touched the wallpaper.

Hardly fitting for a nursery. Still, he had to relent on something. As far as wallpaper went, he didn't mind it *really*. He would have preferred painted walls, simple, unfussy, maybe a bold colour on one to add a bit of drama. Robyn had always liked red, he thought, why not red? But she insisted on the wallpaper. She said she craved pattern. That she couldn't imagine anything else. She'd had so little to do with the rest of the house that he had offered her this as an olive branch. More like a bed of thorns, he thought now. At least he didn't have to sleep in here.

The rest of the house was his vision. He had taken the barn back to its timbered skeleton to begin the transformation. Everything in his home was there through a process of deliberation and research. It was an extension of himself and everything within was carefully selected. But with the baby coming it was important that Robyn consider it her home, too. He had suggested she decorate the nursery. One wall. It was only one wall.

It was the colour, perhaps, that bothered him most. He could never understand why yellow had been elected the gender-neutral colour by would-be parents. And it wasn't even a conventional yellow, it was sulphurous, radiating heat like a greenhouse, allowing life to prosper with sickly, artificial radiance. It seemed to Daniel that it smoldered and smoked as if it could feel his gaze.

He felt his chest tighten as arms encircled him.

"Jesus!"

He jumped back.

"Sorry, I didn't mean to sneak up on you" Robyn said. "So, what do you think?"

He was slow to respond. "It's different."

"I think so too. Really unique." She held swatches against the wallpaper, looking for a complimentary tone. "Harry said our bedroom is going to take longer than expected so after dinner I thought we could move the futon in here."

"In here?" The idea of being in the same room with the paper filled him with dread. "He said that it would only take the morning."

"Harry says the paint you've chosen has been discontinued, so it's going to take a while longer to find a match."

"Oh."

"Besides, you can't have us inhaling all those paint fumes." She rubbed her stomach, which swelled over her jeans, her belly button marking the peak of a grotesque mound. She referred to herself as two people now, a club he was excluded from.

"You've got yellow on you," she said brushing his

135

shirtsleeve. He held the material between his fingers and saw a faint dusting.

He looked at the wallpaper.

"Just take a bit of getting used to," he managed.

She circled him with her arms again, "It'll grow on you."

That night he stroked Robyn's hair until she fell asleep. For him though sleep was evasive. His mind kept forming a mental list of things he still needed to do. The moon outside cast a pearly glow on the wallpaper. He could make out the silhouettes of the flowers and branches, the butterflies and bees but his eye became fixated on the silhouette of a solitary bird, slightly larger than the others, with three prominent tail feathers spread out like a hand of cards. Unlike the other birds, depicted in profile, this one seemed to look out of the landscape, head cocked as if listening.

The bird flew from its perch.

Daniel bolted upright in bed, fumbling with the bedside lamp. Light flooded the room and the wallpaper was lucidly clear in front of him.

The bird was gone.

He groped for his reading glasses; he needed clarity. He searched the paper and saw the bird on a lower branch, just off-centre. The same bird? He noticed the three tail feathers and the incline of its head. It looked the same.

"What's wrong, honey?"

He had imagined it. He was just stressed with the barn. Robyn moving in.

"Nothing, go back to sleep."

He looked one last time at the paper and turned off the light.

He woke to Robyn singing in the shower and the smell of coffee. He got up and approached the wallpaper. In the morning sunlight the yellow background shone brilliantly, the foliage shimmering as if sprinkled with dew. Daniel's eyes searched the pattern. The bird was where it had been the night before, nestled on the lower branch. That settled it. He must have imagined it moving.

But as he got ready for work he couldn't think of anything else. He had an important meeting with his investors but he couldn't seem to focus. Robyn brought him his coffee and nagged him again about finishing the crib. He tried to give the impression of listening.

Descending the stairs, he was greeted by the wall of glass installed the previous week. It was the single most expensive fitting in the barn and it ran the entire length of the property. Robyn had worried that she would feel exposed but Daniel relished this seamless connection with the outside. It afforded an excellent view of the woodland. An army of silvered trunks stretched back for miles without a pylon, road or house to obscure his precious view. It was the absence of these tokens of civilization that put such a premium on the house. But it was a price he'd been willing to pay.

As a seasoned city dweller, the novelty of country living had not lost any of its appeal yet even the view seemed to trouble him today. The day was damp and grey and heavy clouds hovering oppressively in the morning sky, threatening snow. There hadn't been snow since he'd moved into the barn, though he'd been warned the winters could be fierce and he realized now that he was ill prepared for such an eventuality. With only one road, he began to think he would have to have some kind of contingency plan. At least stock up on supplies.

He guzzled the dregs of his coffee and walked to the car, feeling an icy sharpness in the air. He started the engine and saw Robyn on the front porch waving frantically, his portfolio in her hands. He wound down his window and she ran outside barefoot.

"What would you do without me, eh?"

He smiled and kissed her.

"You'll be fine, knock em dead!"

He wished he could share her confidence. He smiled again and pulled out of the drive. He glanced back to see Robyn framed by the barn as wispy snowflakes began to descend around her.

He returned home full of optimism. The meeting had gone well, his drawings approved. The noise of the city had been a welcome relief to the silence of the country.

It was where he had studied and trained, the backdrop to all the important chapters of his life. But it was more than that; as an architect concrete and glass were his life fluid, the city an organism that fed and replenished him. Immersed by the city he shook off the ridiculousness of the night before. Maybe he was suffering from a kind of cabin fever.

He had the sense that he was on the right path, had faith in his own ability again. Starting out on your own is daunting enough he reasoned but when your home and your livelihood are one and the same it's perfectly normal to be a little on edge. And then of course having Robyn move in—

a black smudge shook the windscreen.

He swerved the car and slammed the brakes. The

car came to a halt. A red smear was arched across the glass. The road was empty so he got out to see what he had hit. He hadn't been concentrating but he had felt the impact.

At the side of the road he found what he'd half expected. Barely alive, a bloodied bird twitching its last spasms of life.

Daniel didn't want to leave it to a prolonged and painful death. He had never had to do this himself but he'd heard many stories of other people putting animals out of their misery, especially since moving to the country where road-kill was a common occurrence. Mr. Peters, his nearest neighbour, had recounted a time he had mown down a fox. The beast was still convulsing and baying beside the roadside, despite the fact its face was hanging off. The snout had been ripped from the head, held together by a thin fleshy filament, like a hinge on a door, and one of the eyes had rolled down the side of its cheek like a gruesome yoyo. Mr. Peters' description had made Daniel's stomach turn but he knew he had to do exactly what Mr. Peters had done.

He lifted his boot, aligning it with the bird's head, and turned his face away. He brought his foot down, stamped hard. There was a crunch, and blood splattered his polished shoes.

"Shit."

He imagined Mr. Peters was not quite so clumsy about it, but at least the bird was dead. He returned to the car, glad to see the glass wasn't even damaged.

He took off his blood stained shoes in the hallway. He was home before Robyn but her presence was everywhere. In the kitchen, her stuff spilled out of drawers. Piles of paper and books formed precarious towers on the work surfaces. Climbing the stairs he was following her trail to the nursery. Scarves and necklaces lined the hallway, cast aside carelessly, remnants of her early morning rush. As he opened the nursery door it was no better; worse, in fact, because now he was also confronted by the hideous wallpaper.

He hated it. It was everything she loved and he loathed. If he wanted to look at the landscape he could look out of his glass wall. There was something eerie about its contrived portrayal of nature, its blatant artifice.

He ran his hand over the surface of the paper. Despite the snow outside, the paper radiated warmth. As his hands glanced over the surface he imagined them heating up, as if warmed by a fire. He stopped when he reached the bird. He didn't want to touch it. Simply being there on the lower branch was evidence of what he'd thought happened last night.

The bird seemed to mock him from its newly found perch. Daniel wished he could crush this one under foot as well. What did he think would happen if he touched it, that it would fly away again? He reached out a tentative finger.

He heard Robyn's keys in the front door.

"Hi honey, you home?" she called.

Daniel looked back at the wallpaper. The bird had not moved. Of course it hadn't.

Daniel followed Robyn's voice downstairs into the living room. Within minutes of being home, she had filled the house with her verbal clutter. Daniel wanted to sweep her back out into the snow and enjoy the silence of the barn.

"...and then I went to the pharmacy for the indigestion but because of the baby I can't have the same prescription. And guess what, when I went to Stanley's café for a coffee all I could smell were eggs and I just had to leave before I puked over everyone. It was seriously close. Daniel, are you listening to me?"

Barely. He was fixated on the bottom left corner of the glass wall. From where he stood, he could see a black fissure running the length of the lower panel about a metre long. He prayed it was a blade of grass.

"Daniel, did you hear what I said about the midwife?"

He walked slowly to the panel of glass, fearing that any bounding movements would shatter it. It wasn't on the outside as he'd hoped. It was splintered inside, a long hairline crack. He placed his fingertips on the cold surface around the lesion. He needed to ascertain the damage but didn't want to touch the fracture.

"Daniel, what is it?"

"Robyn, for fuck's sake, can't you see what's happened?"

Robyn backed away, placing her hands on her protruding stomach as if the baby was likewise stung.

"There's a massive crack in the glass."

"Where?"

"Where? Are you blind? Here."

"I can hardly see it."

Daniel bit his cheek. Robyn was proving more frustrating than the breakage.

"It's a massive job, Robyn. We'll have to replace the entire window. I'll have to call the contractors back. It could take weeks, maybe a month. And if it breaks..."

"What happens if it breaks?"

"We'll get very cold."

"Shit. I'll get their number."

Daniel knelt on the floor. On the other side of the glass he saw a cluster of dark, bloody feathers and he thought of the dead bird.

When they made love he noticed that she watched the paper. Not the way he watched it, looking to see if the bird would move again, but as if she loved it. He felt strangely jealous. He couldn't understand its appeal when all he felt was repulsion. He had always known that Robyn and he had different tastes but he hadn't really thought that he'd have to live with them.

Her stuff spilled out everywhere. On top of his bedside cabinet, hairbrushes, beauty products and jewellery all seemed to encroach. He'd open drawers and find she'd rearranged the contents. Even his study had traces of her creeping in. Little reminders pinned to his notice board, address books and floral writing paper lying casually on his desk. The design was not that different from the wallpaper.

But though he despised the wallpaper, he found himself strangely drawn to it. Like road-kill, he thought, thinking again of the bird and the sick fascination it aroused in him. The wallpaper's pattern seemed to prod and poke his mind so that he couldn't settle. He would start at a singular root and attempt to follow it till its conclusion but somewhere in the middle he would become ensnared and feel the vines tightening in around him in a claustrophobic embrace. And at night the landscape appeared entirely different. He could see trees in the background that he couldn't see by day, a mighty forest reaching back into the distance. In the darkness, slender green stems metamorphosed into sharpened thorns, thick impassable briars that reached out ready to claw and scratch, their vertical silhouettes, the bars of some kind of organic prison.

He fancied he saw shadowy creatures lurk within the pattern, waiting for him to fall asleep so they could creep into his home. So he tried to stay awake, to keep vigilant but eventually his eyelids became too heavy and somewhere between sleep and reality he saw insects, centipedes and spiders, crawling out of the paper and onto the floor.

Daniel stared not at the woodland but at the crack in the glass. His eyes were circled with dark rings from lack of sleep but he was relieved to be able to focus on something other than the wallpaper. It had been a week since they had moved into the nursery and still the master bedroom was no nearer completion. The snow had stopped all progress. With roads blocked, the tradesmen couldn't get through and so the room was left in a state of stagnation. Paint tins and rollers spilled out of the room into the hallway adding to the feeling of clutter and procrastination.

The snow was falling softly and a white layer dusted the landscape. Daniel could see where the fields merged with the line of the trees that announced the beginning of the woodland. The trees stood as stark, black silhouettes against the whiteness of the snow. Not unlike the wallpaper by moonlight, he thought with a shiver. He wondered what wild creatures lurked out of sight.

Robyn had cheered at the news they were snowed in. She had put on the wood burner and made a stew to last them days. For Daniel the rustic idyll lost all its charm the moment he couldn't leave.

He didn't know what to do with himself. Half-finished jobs called imploringly but he was reluctant to attempt them only to answer to the tradesman when confronted by his inferior efforts. Besides, in his vision there was no room for mistakes. But the crib was something he could do. Half assembled, it had lain untouched for months in the workshop. He had started it just after hearing Robyn was pregnant, her suggestion so he'd feel involved in the pregnancy. But Robyn's ceaseless questions made him feel like he was making it for her, not the baby.

He decided to chop firewood for the log burner instead.

Icy gusts of wind greeted him outside. He pulled his scarf up and walked to the trees. He'd not ventured into his own land for some time now. He was always inside, designing and planning, or else in the city. He'd moved to the barn for the proximity to nature but had found he was actually more distanced from it. The snow crunched under his feet as he walked to the tree line. The forest stretched back like a deep, enclosing tunnel. Despite the trees having shed their leafy canopies, their skeletal awnings still loomed over him, forming a complicated network of branches. In one high branch he saw a birds nest. Against the starkness of the falling snow it was a sooty smudge in the tangle of trees.

Daniel gathered as much kindling as he could carry and returned to the house. His hands were as cold as the handle of the axe. He thought about the wallpaper again and was suddenly angry. This was his home. He was in charge here, no one else.

He placed a log onto the block and wielded his axe through the air. It split the wood it two with satisfying ease.

He slept soundly that night. The deep, satisfying sleep that only comes from being exhausted. It was a sharp shrill sound that woke him. Birdsong. He tried to ignore it but it came again.

Cuckoo.

He sat up and listened again. Sure enough, he heard the rise and fall of the cuckoo call. But it was the wrong time of year, wasn't it? He switched on the bedside light and saw snow mounting outside the window.

Cuckoo.

Robyn stirred beside him.

"You ok?" she asked groggily.

"Yeah, just damn cuckoos outside."

"At this time of year?"

As if to answer her question it came again. Daniel realized with growing frustration that she hadn't responded to the sound.

"Didn't you just hear it?"

"Hear what? Are you ok honey?" she sat up. She put her hand to his brow as if he was unwell.

He shrugged her off. "Are you telling me you couldn't hear it?"

Robyn looked back at him with concerned eyes. He was going mad, he thought. He was losing it. He jumped out of bed. Pulled on his trousers.

"Where are you going?"

He walked toward the garden. He didn't even put his shoes on but walked out into the fresh snow bare-foot. The sun was barely up, the morning dim and grey. As he approached the tree line he was suddenly aware of how frightening the forest was in the dark.

He reached for a stone. He didn't want to cross the periphery into the forest but his throw wouldn't reach otherwise. He crossed over. The trees overhead obscured his view of the sky and fallen branches and bracken scratched at his naked feet. His feet began to register the iciness of the snow and his toes deadened into numbness. He threw the stone at the nest. He remembered hearing that cuckoos lay their eggs in the nests of other birds, which then raise their offspring. Lazy parenting. The stone missed by a few inches. He aimed and tried again, this time dislodging it. He picked up another rock and hurled it. It hit the nest and this time both fell with speed to the earth below.

The water steamed from the tap. His feet were submerged in a shallow bath.

"What on earth were you thinking?" she said.

He decided not to answer. He wasn't entirely sure himself why he'd walked barefoot in the snow.

"Well your feet are going to blister," she concluded. He looked at his raw flesh and realised she was right. He could already see the skin swelling with angry sores beneath the surface.

"I used to sleepwalk as a child," he offered at last. He wasn't telling a complete lie and he knew it would pacify her. She opened the first aid box and unwound a length of bandage.

"You haven't been yourself lately, Daniel." She rubbed his shoulders. "Is it me?"

"What?" he replied startled.

"That I've moved in? I've disrupted your routine, your pattern? Perhaps it's me."

"No, no honey." He was surprised how quickly the lie sprang to his lips. "How could it ever be you? I wouldn't want it any other way. I think you're right, I haven't been myself for a while."

He looked at his feet now reddened with the mixture of steaming water and emergent blisters.

"Well you're not going to be up and about for a few days now. At least it'll give you a chance to rest up."

๑

Daniel was propped up on cushions in the living room. He could hear the welcome sounds of progress upstairs, of hammers and rollers and workmen, Robyn's footsteps on the stairs carrying trays of tea. He felt comforted by the noise and relieved that the house was moving closer to completion.

Robyn had left him two pills. They were yellow like the wallpaper. He had been taking them for the last few days now and the pain in his feet had diminished to a dull throb. He wasn't sure why they needed to be so yellow. He slipped one onto his tongue and swallowed.

The workmen filed out of the door just past five, Robyn in tow waving goodbyes. He couldn't wait until they left. Despite his sore feet he leapt up to climb the stairs to see if his bedroom was complete.

But as he hobbled upwards he saw with alarm that the entrance to his room was still littered with paint tins and rollers. He dragged himself along the landing, opened the door to the nursery. The entire room was papered yellow.

All four walls were covered. Vines twisting together, roping round the corners of the room so that Daniel was ensnared in the middle of an oppressive forest. He felt stifled. He was surrounded by the paper; caught in a grotesque, organic birdcage.

Robyn stood in the doorway. "Daniel?"

He glared at her.

She looked around the room. "I thought it would be a nice surprise."

"One wall. One fucking wall, Robyn."

She held her stomach as if summoning strength. "You said this was my room. I thought one wall looked stupid and the paper is so beautiful. It should have an entire room to itself."

Daniel turned around. It was everywhere, all around him. He was in the middle of a forest. He couldn't even run. The vines were upon him, tightening their grip. They swayed like fleshy tentacles. No, they were umbilical cords, a forest of umbilical cords, reaching out to suck him back into the blackness. Creeping closer, closer.

Darkness took him.

Back in the woodland, silver birches line the snow-laden path. They are pale ghostly figures that reach for him with spidery claws. He moves freely but as if in slow motion so that as he disentangles himself from their branches he seems to float. He looks down and sees his naked feet, pink and healthy against the gleaming whiteness. His feet are numb, as if to verify he curls his toes into the crisp snow. Nothing.

Glancing behind, Daniel sees the barn. Framed by the falling snow, it's like a modern huntsman's cottage nestled on the boundary of the forest. A black smear on the landscape. It is very far away. Up ahead, the path leads into darkening bracken. Birch trunks like street lamps serve to lighten the path for a distance, until black undergrowth swallows everything.

He can hear a soft murmur. The rustling of branches in the breeze and the crunch of twigs snapping underfoot only serve to mask the sound. But it's there. Constant, like the nagging feeling of something half-remembered half-forgotten. He strains his ears trying to ascertain its origin. He can identify it now, getting closer. It sounds like the beating of wings.

Looking down, there are two bloody stumps where

his feet used to be. His legs, like two fleshy islands, rise from glutinous red pools. He tries to move but a layer of ice grips his bloodied ankles. With increasing panic he tries to twist himself free. But he is trapped. T h e sound stops suddenly. He imagines the winged creatures perching in the boughs above him. He feels something swoop past him to land gracefully on an adjacent perch. He feels another bird swoop by, clipping his shoulder. And behind him he senses the branches are now encumbered with birds, circling him, looking down, waiting. The sound of beating wings is deafening. He covers his ears and crouches, awaiting the onslaught.

Put him out of his misery.

Daniel bolted upright in bed, his breathing fast and laboured. His body soaked with sweat. He pulled back the covers. His feet were fine, wrapped neatly in the starched bandage. Robyn rushed into the room.

"Are you ok?"

He looked around, adjusting. The wallpaper was still there in all its hideous glory.

"You've got a temperature, a mild fever," Robyn explained. "You fainted a few hours ago and you've been sleeping ever since. I think you've been having a nightmare."

Daniel nodded and Robyn passed him a glass of water.

"Take your pills, they'll help you relax."

His breathing steadied. It was just a dream. He wasn't in the forest. He was at home safe, tucked up in bed. Robyn was here and everything was ok.

He tried to rest his mind but the wallpaper stared at him with obstinate triumph. It was winning.

149

ॐ

The wind chased snowflakes past his window. Inside he felt like he was in a sauna with the wallpaper emitting its unnatural heat.

Robyn had prescribed him an afternoon of rest. Perhaps if he could just fall asleep he could escape the paper. He took his pills, hoping they would induce oblivion. But swallowing each yellow capsule he knew it would begin again like it had done in the forest. As he felt slumber slither near, he heard the beating of wings, distant at first, then louder. Getting closer. His eyes searched the paper, looking for the bird he knew would inevitably come.

As he had predicted, the cuckoo emerged from the foliage and landed on its perch. It tilted its head toward Daniel in greeting. Daniel wondered what to do. He would not take his eyes off it this time, even though he could feel the drowsiness of the pills kicking in.

The bird sprung into flight, its wings beating as fast as Daniel's heart as it flew the length of the paper. It flew the distance of the four walls, so that Daniel had to turn to follow it. It rested on a branch just above the futon and then repeated this again after a few moments, flying the distance of the paper in the opposite direction.

It was trying to get out.

It was trapped, like him, Daniel's fear melted like thawing snow. He watched its futile flight across the paper with increasing curiosity. Occasionally it disappeared back into the dense undergrowth but it always re-emerged, doubling its efforts in a desperate attempt to escape. He watched as it helplessly reared up, sticking out its breast in defiance, flapping its wings incessantly until it tired from the exertion. Daniel could not help but pity the bird, which he now saw was imprisoned in its glittering cage.

With one final effort it flew towards Daniel. He watched as it beat its wings forcibly against the paper, flapping back and forth. Its outline stretched the paper, like canvas around a frame. He could see the shape of its beak, just about piercing through, making tiny indentations in the paper. Eventually the cuckoo surrendered, reluctantly, and retired back into the mysterious coppice.

Daniel pulled back the covers, placing one painful foot before the other. He had to let it out. The pattern was killing it. He had to let it out of its misery.

Robyn lugged the crib into the hallway, forcing it through the doorframe. She knew she shouldn't be lifting in her condition but she was so excited about showing Daniel what she'd done. Kicking off her snow-caked boots she called to him.

No response. Probably sleeping, poor thing. She covered her handiwork with a white sheet. She'd show him later.

She crept up the stairs, not wanting to wake him, but as she rounded the corner she saw the devastated nursery and let out a cry. The paper had been torn. She approached horrified and saw that the entire room had been attacked. It resembled the forest mid-autumn, the carpet laden with paper strewn like a hundred glittering leaves. Under strips of shredded paper she saw Daniel slumped against a wall. He appeared to be sleeping, a length a paper clasped tightly in his hand. His fingertips were red and, at closer glance the wall-paper bore the faint traces of blood as if he had ripped

V. H. Leslie

the paper off in a violent frenzy with his bare hands before falling asleep in a nest of his own making.

Daniel woke to the sound of Robyn's voice. He could feel himself being shaken gently. He glanced past her and saw that the walls were different. In the corner of the room was a bin bag spilling over with the paper's patterned remains. The four walls surrounding him were ripped and torn.

Robyn followed his gaze. She looked disappointed.

"When I found you, you were talking about a cuckoo."

Daniel looked at her.

"You were saying something about other nests."

Daniel didn't know how to respond.

"You kept saying it over and over, like you were in a trance."

He shivered.

"When the snow clears a bit more we'll take you to the doctors. Perhaps they can recommend something."

Why couldn't she just come out and say it? That she thought he was loosing it. That he was going mad.

"I couldn't have done this."

She kissed him on the forehead, pushing two yellow pills towards him. He was little more than a disobedient child in her eyes. He saw now what kind of mother she would be. This is what letting her in had done. And now she thought she was in charge. Like the wallpaper. But he'd fixed that. He could fix everything.

৯

152

When Robyn got into bed that night he pretended to be asleep. As she snuggled up beside him he lay still. He felt her protruding bump against his back. He loathed the both of them. He wanted her to fall asleep. The bird wouldn't come out otherwise.

He had been trying to fathom it all day. Despite ripping the paper the bird had not escaped. He looked at his handiwork by the moonlight that filtered through the blinds. Great sections of the yellow wallpaper were missing. Big gaps. Big enough for the cuckoo to fly through. Perhaps they weren't big enough he thought. Perhaps he needed to chop through the briars and clear it a path. Perhaps the bird was waiting for nightfall, so it could make its escape undetected.

Daniel didn't take his eyes from the paper as the night wore on. Robyn snored softly beside him whilst his eyes flickered from gap to gap. With the whole room now containing tiny portals the cuckoo could emerge from any one of them.

He heard the distant humming of wings that signalled its approach. The remaining wallpaper, now ripped and torn, looked like an aged and haggard facsimile. The peeling sections swayed slightly as if they really were the branches and flowers they depicted. And with the pattern so disrupted, the paper seemed to be angry, the forest more foreboding than ever before. The undergrowth of the daytime was again transformed into a dark and menacing thicket of trees. The silhouettes of branches and twigs stretched into the room like menacing talons. Daniel was back in his forest now, walking barefoot along the snow-laden path. He saw himself ensnared by the trees, the trunks like the bars of a cage.

The bird suddenly flew into Daniel's sight, resting

on the rim of a torn section of paper, as if wondering whether to fly out or not. Daniel thought about stories he had heard of prisoners who developed a fear of freedom when their sentence was over. The cuckoo cast its head back and forth and, with a final decisive tilt, burst free of the paper.

It flew around the room in giddying circles. Daniel watched its excited flight above his head as it raced past him. He'd done it. He'd freed it.

The bird rested on his bedside table, as if in thanks. Daniel stretched out a finger to touch it. It arched its wings and flew towards the door. Daniel threw back the covers, suddenly anxious that the bird would fly off all together, but it hovered for a moment as if it wanted Daniel to follow.

He sprang out of bed, feeling a fire of pain in his feet. The bird was fast, so fast that when he turned the corner it was out of sight. But he could hear the beating of its wings and he followed the sound along the hallway, past Robyn's clutter on the stairs, the abandoned paint tins and rollers, down the stairs. He was racing now, the pain in his feet forgotten as he hurried after the bird.

He came upon it perched on the last banister, opposite the downstairs cupboard. As he approached he was surprised to find it didn't fly away. Was he supposed to open the cupboard door?

He gripped the handle and tugged and the contents of the cupboard collapsed out knocking him to the ground. He watched helplessly as rolls and rolls of the hideous wallpaper fell onto him in an avalanche of yellow.

He gasped. Where had all this paper come from? What was Robyn planning to do? Wallpaper the entire fucking house? How could he stand to live in the forest forever? He wouldn't be able to get out.

The cuckoo was gone but the mystical buzzing of its wings was somewhere in the living room. Hobbling after it, he saw it perched on a white object. A sheet, shrouding something. He pulled at the material.

What he unveiled was the finished crib. He sat down heavily. The crib had been his project. She had even ruined that. It wasn't to his specification. None of it was.

He felt an icy chill on his skin and became aware of the crack in the glass allowing cold air to slither through. In the darkness, he could see nothing of the outside world at all beyond the wall of glass, only his home reflected in its surface. It was the best view he had ever seen.

The bird flew over his head with more urgency than before. It reminded him of when it was looking for a way out of the paper. It circled him in large sweeping motions, getting faster and faster. With a decisive effort it flew into the window.

Shards of glass fell about him. Daniel shielded himself from bracing wind that swept into the room. Dragging his feet through splinters of glass and into the snow outside, he followed the bird further.

The cuckoo was perched on the handle of the axe. The blade glinted in the moonlight. Daniel freed it from its resting place and followed his bloody foot-prints back into the house. There was no need to follow the bird anymore. He knew where it would lead him. Climbing back up the stairs, his arms heavy with the weight of his weapon, he knew how he would fix this. He would chop down the briars and the trees that taunted him. He would be free.

Robyn screamed. She stood in the doorway of the nursery, her nightdress taut over her swollen stomach.

He could see the hideous form of the creature inside trying to get out. He pushed her aside and welded the axe at the paper. Great chunks of plaster came tumbling down with the shriek of metal against concrete. He aimed the axe again. The wounded paper yelled back in anger, its claws creeping closer and closer. He delivered another penetrating blow.

"Daniel?" she sobbed.

Put her out of her misery.

He'd paint the walls red.

The Cloud Cartographer

The plain stretched boundlessly into the distance, an uninterrupted path of white. Frontier land as untouched as virgin snow. The wind at this height blew unrestrained, buffeting the terrain, shaping it, creating a rolling appearance like the crests of waves ebbing and flowing against the horizon. It looked pure, solid from afar, but when up close, in the midst of it, you could see how insubstantial it was. Not even white but a medley of misty colours, grey or blue or pink. In a certain light, you could almost see the particles, the ground grainy underfoot as if you were seeing it drunk. If you looked at it too hard, at the hazy floor beneath your feet, your body would become conscious of the laws it defied and it was easy to imagine yourself plummeting back to earth. So you kept your eyes level with a point at the horizon and kept on walking.

Ahren had been cloudwalking for ninety days. He knew exactly as he recorded each day in his journal. It was more of a log really, containing details about the expedition so far, the terrain he'd covered and the distance he made each day, along with any meteorological data of significance. But he'd always conclude with a line or two of his personal musings, fragments of half-remembered poetry, his memories and regrets.

In such a lonely land, his thoughts were his only company.

Ahren looked up. Above, cirrostratus clouds had appeared like floating cotton and he squinted into the halo they'd formed around the sun. He was happy for the reprieve; the last fortnight had been especially fine and the lack of cloud cover above had left him terribly exposed. But though he was thankful, he watched the sky cautiously for if the halo began to shrink, it would bring rain. And rain was the worst variable on this cloudface.

Ahren needed to get further inland, where the terrain was more solid. He pulled the compass from his pocket and watched as the needle settled. He wrote the coordinates in his journal and began the slight ascent west.

Ahren had always been fascinated with the contours of the sky. He wanted to go up, up where the air was cleaner and purer, up where you could see stars, a mere myth to the people below his feet: the sky forever obscured by smog and dense cloudscapes of pollutants. The clouds that floated above Ahren—cirrus, altostratus, cumulonimbus—were the only reminders of what had existed before, and he was one of only a few privileged enough to see them.

Ahren had never known a time before the cloud-straits. They hung low and heavy, enormous masses clinging to the world like parasites, brushing the tips of mountain ranges, obscuring the sun. They lingered like floating tectonic plates constantly settling into new positions, the atmosphere shifting just like the ground below it. For Ahren they were platforms above the earth, a delicate bridge over the world below. But it was a rope bridge at best. You had to know where to step.

The Cloud Cartographer

Ahren carted his equipment on a small sledge. He didn't have much, just the essentials: his ration pack, a small portable stove, a first aid kit (including an oxy-pack and a couple of back up canisters) and a change of clothes. His outgear was state of the art, all-weather terrain, thermal lined, with the Company's name brandished across the front in illuminous lettering. Not that anyone could see it up here. It was his cartographical equipment that weighed the most though. Especially the density sensors and various mapping devices but they were crucial to his task. His task was relatively simple: he measured this undiscovered landscape and mapped it.

Ahren reached a reasonably safe spot and took some preliminary readings. When he was satisfied that the ground was stable, he sat down and opened his ration pack. Inside were a few protein bars and a selection of the Company's brand of liquefied meals. He selected one, opened, and drank without pleasure. There was a time when he studied the list of ingredients on each container in an attempt to determine what the pulp was, but the chemical names were always too obscure and despite whatever food it tried to resemble, it was always orange. Ahren pretended it was something else, some great feast, some culinary delight, and he would enter it later in his journal as pad thai or a cheeseburger and fries in the hope of wilfully deceiving his memory.

Often, if he were near the edge of a cloudface, he'd chuck the carton over when he was done. It somehow appeased a strange rebelliousness inside of him. If he wasn't near an edge, he sometimes chucked it anyway; the force of his throw could sometimes penetrate the surface of the cloud if it was a weak spot. Sometimes it could unsettle a whole cloudmass.

Ahren tried it now and it whistled through the air before thumping against the surface. He sighed and hauled himself to his feet to retrieve it. He wasn't going to litter the only unpolluted space on the planet. Below was different. Below was already messed up.

Ahren walked the rest of the day, only stopping when darkness began to descend. He took some more readings and pitched his tent, activating the synthetic cloudbase. He started the stove, warming his hands above it, and ate some more food from his ration pack.

It was very cold at night. Despite his thermal outgear and the stove, it was colder than anything Ahren had ever known. After his meagre meal, ham and eggs he decided, he retreated to his tent to record the day's activity.

Ahren was a creature of habit and he approached his task as mapmaker the same way every night. He began by entering all his data into the cartographical programme and watched as it constructed a topographical relief of the area he'd covered. Then, because he was slightly distrustful of technology, he unrolled a large sheet of paper and drew the map by hand. His drawing was much more topological, omitting many of the details of the computer projection in favour of aesthetics. This map was his backup, sketchily drawn like the ones leading to pirate treasure and included only the most significant features of the cloudmass— the valleys and peaks, the areas prone to flux and the places that were unstable. He always carried this on his person, folded into the inside pocket of his outgear. Then he'd write a brief summation of his day in his journal and pack his equipment away.

The Cloud Cartographer

It wasn't all work. Before he slept, Ahren would pour himself a scotch, a fine mature malt he'd told the Company was a medicinal necessity. Then he'd crawl out of the tent, his insulated sleeping bag wrapped around him, and watch the spectacle above. He loved the stars. They illuminated the otherwise absolute black, as no artificial light from below could penetrate the cloudstraits, and Ahren thought he could feel their light shining on him. He was comforted, enjoying the exclusive proximity to the heavens. Sometimes he traced patterns in their constellations and at other times he just let his mind drift, meditating on the composition of the universe or remembering snatches of poetry he'd read so avidly as a child. *I know that I shall meet my fate somewhere among the clouds above.* Before he became too drowsy he always retreated back inside his tent. He couldn't fall asleep outside where he could roll off in the night and plunge back down to earth. He had to stay grounded. So he finished the dregs of his whisky and went back inside.

"Do you think if there was a tree tall enough we could climb all the way to the clouds?" Lucy asked. They were perched in the highest branches of an old oak tree, looking up at the cloudstraits above.

"Like Jack and the Beanstalk?" Ahren replied, trying not to look down.

"Yeah."

"You'd need some magic beans."

"I've got some magic acorns." Lucy dug deep into her pocket and withdrew a handful.

"They're not magic."

"Yes they are. A fairy cast a spell on them."

Ahren sighed. It was pointless arguing with her.

161

"One day you won't need magic to go to the clouds," Ahren said with the certainty of a twelve year old boy, "we'll all be able to go. And live up there, and build cities up there in the sky."

Lucy smiled a partially toothless grin. "I'd like to go up to the clouds."

"Why?"

"To see what the angels see."

Ahren woke with a start. He lay still until the disorientation subsided and remembered where he was. Most days began like this, as if not only his body but his mind gravitated towards the world below. He unzipped the tent and stepped out into the clouds and began the day as any other—with a carton of Company-endorsed baby food (that he pretended were eggs and bacon) and a strong coffee. Imitation or not, he savoured his caffeine fix and packed up his belongings with no great speed. The cirrostratus clouds from the day before had grown in size and darkened in colour. If it was going to rain, it was better that he was here, in the middle of a fairly stable cloudmass, than walking on unpredictable terrain.

The problem with rain was that it rendered all terrain unpredictable. The cloudslide at the start of his journey had taught him that. He'd thought his position pretty secure—the readings were mostly stable—when the cloudmass below gave way and Ahren found himself running on a surface that seemed to collapse with every footfall. The Company had to send him more equipment to compensate for the kit that he lost to gravity.

Ahren called them aerial avalanches and they happened fairly frequently. Mostly near the edge of a cloudface but sometimes in the middle as precipitation and air pressures collided or mingled. Sometimes these air parcels became gaps or holes and often once they'd formed they released pressure, making the surface more stable. It was the forming of them that was precarious, marked by a distant rumble and the sudden appearance of a vacuum, sucking the ground out from under you. But much of the terrain was fairly solid, and after three months of cloudwalking, Ahren knew which straits were safe. That was what he was paid to discover. But there was always a level of unpredictability up here; it was what had attracted him to the job in the first place.

Ahren wasn't planning to go very far today with such ominous clouds nearby. He unrolled the map of the clouds he'd drawn and studied it for patterns. He saw the strait that he might recommend to the developers. With the world below crumbling, the Company could charge a fortune up here for unspoilt, virgin land. But Ahren wanted to be sure before he made any proposals; the clouds were in constant flux and he had to understand more about their extraordinary nature. Besides, he wasn't ready to share this land with anyone else yet. Or worse, to go back below.

When Ahren was a boy he had an atlas which he studied everyday. He'd make his sister Lucy test his knowledge of it, deriving boundless pleasure in accurately pointing out the source of the Nile or the location of Everest. Sometimes he asked Lucy questions, assuming that she'd assimilated some understanding of the world during these hours of play, but her responses were always a disappointment. He'd ask her easier questions but she found them just as hard. Lucy couldn't imagine the world like Ahren. She couldn't see it in a map. She tried but she found the visualising of it difficult. She understood what surrounded her, she could read the individual components—the trees, the warrens, the pond—but she couldn't see the bigger picture.

"If you ever get lost," Ahren had told her, "just climb up high and look down. Then you can see the way home."

Lucy had liked that answer and she'd begun to scale the nearby oaks. She knew the treetops like Ahren knew the ground. Ahren waited at the bottom, reading a collection of poetry from his father's study. He was clumsy in the trees and not too fond of heights.

Ahren and Lucy were fortunate to grow up knowing the natural world. Their father owned a vast quantity of woodland, an area coveted by developers and businessmen eager to accommodate ever-expanding population demands. It was only when Ahren and his father moved to the city and into one of a hundred tower blocks that he realised just how rare and fortunate a childhood it was. The city towers attained impossible heights, people stacked on top of one another as in some delicate card trick. It was a forest of concrete stretching up, up, up, brushing the cloudmass above.

Their father was a rarity too, though Ahren hadn't known it at the time. He was a landowner and would have rather died than give up that right. His forest was Lucy's and Ahren's playground. They had no idea how much others wanted it.

"Who's that?" Lucy called from her position in the boughs, pointing. But by the time Ahren had climbed up, whoever she'd seen was gone.

൭

The Cloud Cartographer

Ahren was walking again. He had a lot of ground to cover due to the delay of the previous day. In the end the cirrostratus clouds had dispersed after little more than a light drizzle and Ahren was reminded again of how powerless he was against the capriciousness of the sky.

He hadn't slept well. He had dreamt of Lucy again and woke up thrashing and flailing in his sleeping bag. When his breathing calmed, he thought he could discern a rustle outside his tent. He'd listened hard, surprised when he'd heard the sound again. Footsteps. The whispered hush of footsteps. Someone was circling his tent, he was sure of it. He grabbed his torch, fumbling for the switch. The inside of the tent was suddenly illuminated and he waited a moment, hoping that the light would scare whatever it was away. Then he stumbled to his feet and hesitantly unzipped the tent opening.

There was nothing there, of course. Absurd to think there would be. He must have imagined it, he told himself. Some sort of dream haze leftover.

But it had felt so real.

Ahren shined the torch over the cloudface a few times more before returning inside. The plains were empty. He was alone.

Walking now, he was annoyed that not only did he have to make up a day but that he had to do it on only a few hours sleep. It could have been an animal scavenging about, maybe. It was rare for them to be up this high but he'd sighted the occasional bird; sometimes they'd burst through weaker spots in the clouds beneath him. He was always impressed by their conviction, flying into a cloudmass at such speed with no certainty that the cloud was weak enough for them to pass through. It was either an incredible act of faith, or some suicidal impulse. Perhaps they could just read the clouds better than he could. Another time, Ahren had spotted a mountain fox on the edge of a cloudface, forced higher and higher in its search for food. They'd eyed each other for a moment before the fox disappeared into the cloudfog.

But the prowling around his tent hadn't sounded like an animal. It sounded more like human footsteps. Besides he thought he heard the soft ringing of a bell.

Irritable and tired, Ahren eventually settled down for the evening, pitching his tent perfunctorily. He was ravenous, but hungry for real food. The daily exertion and brutal temperatures cultivated an appetite that the contents of the ration pack were just not fit to satisfy. He wanted some meat, something with flavour and texture.

He was being punished, he thought, suffering the tasteless contents of another carton. This was his purgatory.

As if in confirmation, he heard a gentle ringing, far off in the distance.

Ahren paused mid mouthful, straining to hear the sound again. Was his mind playing tricks? Yet there it was again. A ringing, almost too low to hear, but it was there. He was sure of it. He listened hard and squinted into the distance. Was it possible something else occupied the clouds with him?

He put his food aside. "Hello?" Months of silence had rendered his voice hoarse and alien. He cleared his throat. "Is anyone there?" He felt instantly foolish. How could anyone be up here? This was frontier land, undiscovered territory. There was more probability that he'd encounter Gabriel and a host of angels, and for an atheist that was something.

He had to be the only one.

Ahren resumed eating, pausing occasionally to listen. Nothing.

He withdrew into the tent, taking one last tentative look around. If he were being tracked, he'd have no way of knowing: there are no footprints in the clouds.

Ahren woke to the sound of rain. Inside his tent it always sounded much louder like horses galloping, but despite its volume it still possessed a strange soothing lullaby quality. The rain always took him back to Lucy. Of endless play days inside when the weather was too wild to go out. Lucy would watch her breath cloud the glass, tracing the journey of wayward raindrops on the windowpane, while Ahren spun his globe faster and faster until he thought it would spin off its axis.

He wondered what she would make of this strange landscape, a world without words. Ahren tried not to adapt the language of below, *terrain, landscape, plain*. This new world demanded its own vocabulary, a more elevated language, and Ahren recorded his own coinages in the back of his journal. Perhaps, when the clouds were civilised, his words would define this new world.

When the rain subsided, Ahren spread the equipment over the sledge in the hope that it would dry. The ground was wet with the rain that would now descend on the people below, this time carrying the pollutants and poisons of the cloudstraits with it. The wind had not relented, whipping the cloudface into rolling vaporous peaks. Visibility was poor. He'd have to take it slow if he decided to trek today.

Ahren wrapped his scarf around his face and

pressed on. He preferred to be on the move. It felt like progress, though he knew in these conditions he could easily get turned around or lost in a cloudmist. He checked his compass often, preferring it to his more technical software. It felt like a more honest way to navigate the clouds. Ahren followed the quivering needle, aware that he was heading in the direction of the sound of bells he'd heard the previous night.

Ahren kept his head down, concentrating on the cloudsurface and compass. Cloud vapour streamed past him, wrapping him up in a blanket of white. He would have probably walked past it had he not lifted his head at that particular moment, thinking he heard the bells.

A line of prayer flags stretched into the distance, suspended on a length of rope that led into the cloud-mist. The colours were so bright they hurt Ahren's eyes. Ahren had seen them before on his way up to the clouds. They were comprised of five colours: blue, white, red, green and yellow. Each colour represented a different element and the order was important. He knew it started with the sky (blue) and ended with the earth (yellow) but he couldn't quite remember the significance of the colours in between, except for white. He knew what that stood for. The white flags were only discernible in the cloudmist because of the printed image on their surface, otherwise they would have disappeared into what they revered—the clouds.

The closest one to him was yellow and blown by the wind it looked like diamond or like the crude stars Lucy made out of tissue paper and glitter. As a whole they looked like a strange rainbow, stretching across the clouds like an absurd paper chain.

Ahren had never seen prayer flags in the clouds, though he'd seen many on his way up. They populated the mountains as abundantly as the people. Ahren hadn't expected so many people on this particular massif, though he knew that all the mountain ranges were prone to overpopulation—being the only pockets of affordable land left. It was his father's fault for telling him legends about the unspoilt mountains here. He'd read him and Lucy tales of Shangri-La. Tales of a mythical place, an impossible place hidden somewhere in the Himalayas. Ahren had imagined it nestled among snow-capped mountains, a beautiful lamasery amid a desert of ice and emptiness. An earthly paradise.

As a boy Ahren had tried to find it on his map and now that he was older he'd trekked the plains seeking it, before he finally came up here to the clouds.

Ahren had seen firsthand how densely populated the mountains were now, sprawling cities replacing green plateaus and paddy fields, tower-blocks upon tower-blocks stacked precariously on cliff faces, not like the images in his father's books.

Ahren was resigned to the fact that the landscape of Shangri-La existed only in his imagination. If it had ever existed at all there was no room for it now.

Ahren looked with dismay at the flags flapping above him in the wind and wondered whether he should take them down. They were not a welcome sight, despite their intentions of good will. Prayer flags were not offered to any higher being, they were a prayer to land. They were here to bless the cloudstraits.

And that could only mean that Ahren was not alone.

That evening was damp. The mist hadn't completely dispersed and it lingered in the air like guilt. Ahren warmed his hands by the stove, conscious that the

169

light was a beacon for whatever or whoever stalked him. Clouds above obscured the stars. He scanned the cloudsurface, staring into the darkness. He wasn't afraid of the dark but the unknown was a different matter. *Terra incognita.* Unknown land. *Terror incognito.*

He thought of how cartographers of the past had drawn maps to the edge of the world, a flat earth, before philosophers and astronomers said it was round. Then, if you sailed too far you would fall off the edge and into Hades or Hell or whatever underworld you subscribed to.

They'd said mapping the clouds would be impossible, but here Ahren was, sitting at the top of the world, the vast unknown stretched before him. He'd been in uncharted territory before, but armed with the tools of his trade he didn't need to fear it. But how could he possibly know what the clouds contained? For all he knew monsters could be lurking in the cloudfog.

Ahren stared into the light of the stove. It was far better to draw out whatever it was and face it, than let the unknown haunt him.

Ahren was pitched beneath the prayer flags. He'd thought about tearing them down, of getting rid of all signs that someone had been here first, but he was reluctant to pull out the pole they were connected to. It disappeared deep beneath the cloud surface. It was the fact it could possibly upset a cloudmass, he told himself, rather than his fear of disturbing some kind of spiritual balance.

Ahren tried to stay vigilant but the prayer flags soothed him. They flapped rhythmically in the wind, lulling him to sleep, spreading their blessings like a blanket around his shoulders. Ahren stared at the colours. Each of the flags was decorated with images of different sacred animals but the one that he was drawn to most was the horse. A wind horse: *lung ta*.

Lucy liked horses. Lots of little girls did. He imagined her now—how old would she be?—and the image his mind conjured was a grown woman with flowing charcoal hair. She was riding a wind horse through the clouds, dipping in and out of the swelling peaks, racing along the cloudstraits towards the sky with its stars shining like tiny diamonds. He could almost see her face, her eyes narrowed in concentration as she guided the horse toward a burgeoning cloudmass, so sure she could penetrate the surface of the cloud just like the birds. A rallying cry, the sound of hooves, the jingling of bells, and then she was bursting through, breaking against the cloudface like an enormous wave, an explosion of particles, foaming and frothing, filling the air with billowing clouddust as insubstantial as breath.

Ahren woke to a blurred world. He lay against the entrance of the tent in his outgear, the sleeping bag a nest underneath him. He was annoyed at himself; it was dangerous to fall asleep outside.

Snow was drifting from the underbelly of the clouds above. The suffocating grey—blue colour of cold. Ahren moved, his body stinging with pins and needles.

Something darted up ahead.

Ahren paused, unsure if he'd seen anything. His mind was fuzzy like the landscape as he waited for the cloudmist to pass. He strained his eyes.

There was nothing there.

Though he desperately wanted a coffee, he decided to forgo breakfast and began packing up. He'd tarried here under the auspicious prayer flags long enough.

Maybe it had been a mistake to stay here at all.

Again, a darting motion up ahead drew Ahren's attention. He shone his torch into the white haze, hoping it would penetrate the mist. He caught something running between the clouds.

He stood on weak legs, edging forwards but pushed back by the wind.

"Lucy?"

He waited a long time for a response but none came. When the cloudfog began to disperse he moved hastily on.

Ahren wished he were still dreaming when he discovered the body. He'd been alerted to it by a host of carrion birds, Himalayan vultures with white necks and tawny feathers making the cloudsurface ahead look dirty. They clung to their feast like a moving mantle, relinquishing their meal only when Ahren deliberately chased them away. Even then they took to the air lazily, unperturbed, and Ahren could still sense them above, circling him and the girl.

It was definitely a girl. Ahren could tell that much. A young woman, actually, by her size and shape. He stared down at the body; it was repellent to see so much of what made up a person but still he stared. The flesh of the face was entirely gone, as were the skin on the torso and the tops of the legs. What was left resembled the crude carvings of an unskilled butcher. Red and wet with glimpses of white bone gleaming beneath muscle and sinew.

"Jesus," Ahren said to the wind.

Around the hollow of her face was a mass of dark bloodied hair, blown into a halo by the wind.

Ahren put a hand to his forehead. How had she

172

gotten up here? Perhaps she'd put up the prayer flags. If so, it hadn't proven lucky for her. He couldn't see any traces of clothing. She wouldn't have been wearing outgear, that stuff was pretty costly. He touched the material he wore for reassurance and cast a glimpse up at the vultures above. Had she been stripped and left here?

Ahren didn't know what to do. It wasn't right for a body to be destroyed by scavengers. It needed a burial. But there were limitations in the clouds. He couldn't bury her up here. He thought about dragging her to the edge of a cloudmass and pushing her over the edge. But he didn't like the thought of her body hurtling toward earth, landing more broken than it was now, and who knew where she would end up? Yet while the body remained here it would only pollute the clouds. It would draw scavengers, and eventually maybe people, with questions. He wished she would just disappear.

The birds circling above waited for him to make a decision. They watched him move on before swooping down to resume their feast. There was nothing Ahren could do. He hoped the birds were swift about it.

I wandered lonely as a cloud.

Ahren walked the rest of the day in no discernable direction. His footsteps were not buoyed by the clouds as usual, but heavy and concrete. He couldn't get the image of the women from his mind. He wondered who she was. Her identity along with her flesh, were being picked clean by the vultures.

But more depressing was the fact the clouds didn't belong to just him anymore. Someone else had been here first. And though he had not known of her existence until that afternoon, the notion that he'd been alone all those months was a myth.

He should have been glad perhaps, had he ever really wanted to be alone?

In response he heard the tintinnabulation of bells.

And in the distance he saw a girl.

It had been a long time since he'd seen a child, a *real* child, not just the one that inhabited his dreams. It had been a long time since he'd seen *anyone* for that matter, besides the corpse a few miles back. Ahren sighed. When had the clouds become so populated?

He hoped she was a hallucination; that he had conjured a strange mirage out of cloudmist, but then the girl addressed him.

"What are you doing up here?"

Ahren was somewhat taken aback. He wanted to ask the same question but worried it would sound childish.

"Lucy?" he asked instead. The girl moved closer, out of the blur and shook her head.

"Are you the one who's been following me?"

She nodded.

"Why?"

"To see if you were real."

Ahren looked down at himself, half expecting his body to be grainy and blurred, made of the same transient substance as the clouds. He looked real enough.

"Are you satisfied?"

The girl nodded again, retreating back into the fog.

"Wait!" Ahren called, "Wait!"

He followed the ringing of bells, chasing behind like he was playing hide and seek. Except the girl was too swift and light-footed in the clouds. She disappeared ghost-like, only to reappear a few moments later with a smile and a wave of encouragement. She seemed to want Ahren to follow, though he had no idea where they were going. She was his only guide.

He considered turning around and finding his way back through the cloudmist to his equipment but this was the first person he'd seen on the clouds, apart from the dead young woman. Perhaps they were related? Still it had been impulsive and potentially dangerous abandoning all of his stuff and running after her. Maybe he'd been up on this cloudface too long. Maybe the altitude was affecting his sanity.

Out of the cloudmist came the façade of some kind of construction.

"What the..."

It was a cabin. It was comprised entirely of wood and had an aged look as if it had been there for a long time, though Ahren knew that was impossible. It appeared to be built on the clouds though Ahren couldn't see a cloudbase. Above the rafters hung the limp bodies of rabbits. A rocking chair on the porch was covered in the hide of some animal.

Suddenly the little girl was in front of him again. Closer than before. Ahren noticed she was wearing a fur coat with toggles at the front, a woollen hat on her head.

"Do you wanna come inside?"

What kind of strange fantasy world had he stumbled into? Ahren could see a wind turbine attached to the roof. It appeared to be a perfectly self-sufficient homestead and infinitely more comfortably than his tent. He stood dumbfounded.

The girl shrugged and went inside. Now that she had led him here she seemed disinterested in him. Ahren wondered why she had brought him. More alarmingly, Ahren wondered if she was alone, like him.

He couldn't bear the idea of a child alone in such an unremitting land. He climbed the steps and opened the door.

A cloud emerged. Ahren took it to be cloud vapour at first until he smelt tobacco. It was an aroma Ahren hadn't smelt for a long time. It surrounded a man drawing on a pipe. The lips that held it were entirely obscured by a heavy, yellowing white moustache. He had a long fur coat like the girl's. Ahren had the impression of some colonel from some long ago war.

The man stepped out of the smoke. He didn't say a word. Ahren was not one for words either, having exhausted them in his conversation with the girl. They stared at each other for a long time, both painfully sorry at discovering the other's existence. Their fantasy of isolation shattered.

"You'd better make yourself at home," the man said at last.

Ahren followed him into a warm interior. The smell of stew, mingled with tobacco suffused the room, which was aglow with candles. It was a basic room, though comfortably furnished. In the corner a bird sat on its perch. A bird of prey, maybe a falcon or a kite, though Ahren wasn't sure. It was tethered and hooded, though it hopped in agitation sensing an intruder. A bell tied around its leg rang with its every movement.

"I see you're a Company man." The man pointed at the branding across Ahren's outgear.

"I'm a cartographer. I work for whoever pays."

The man nodded and gestured towards the stove. Ahren sat down, removing his gloves and holding his hands to the flames.

"Been up here long?" Ahren asked.

"Since last November."

"Last November? But what about the cloudslide?"

176

"We were lucky. It passed us by."

Ahren made some calculations and began altering the contours of the map in his mind.

"If you don't mind me saying," the man began, pulling up a chair, "these clouds can't be mapped."

Ahren remembered all the people below who'd said the same thing. Only the Company believed it could be done. When you had enough money you were allowed to believe anything.

"Nearly mapped this entire cloudstrait," Ahren said, feeling a pride he hadn't felt in a long time.

"Not what I meant. It can be done, I'm sure. You're proof of that. But doesn't mean that it should." The man drew heavily on his pipe. "Too much change. Clouds don't want it."

How did this man know what the clouds wanted? Ahren remembered the prayer flags, the way they blessed the land. Were they to appease the clouds?

"Can't have too many folk coming up here," he continued. "Only room for a few. Best that this land stays undiscovered, if you ask me."

Ahren could understand why he wouldn't want to share this world with anyone else. Ahren didn't want to share it either. Maps brought developers, and developers meant people.

"I'm just doing my job."

"I'm sure you are."

Ahren sized up the man. Would this be something he thought worth fighting over? He was conscious of the map folded into the pocket of his outgear, close to his chest. He regretted leaving his equipment, anything he could use as a weapon. No-one knew he was here.

"Do you wanna see my pictures?" the girl said. She thrust a series of crayon drawings under Ahren's nose. Pictures of constellations, the stars connected like dot to dots.

The man pulled her back protectively, though she still held her arm out at Ahren.

Ahren took the pictures. They were drawn well, though not to scale.

"These are really good."

The girl beamed.

"Sally, the man's going to be on his way."

Ahren returned the pictures.

"I have more if you wanna look?"

Ahren looked towards the man and back at the girl.

"Sure."

The little girl grabbed Ahren's hand and led him to the other side of the room. Dozens of pictures crammed the walls, the constellations forming elaborate patterns.

"Don't you ever look down?" he asked

Sally shook her head. "Never."

Ahren tried to remember how long it had been since he had looked. It was always accompanied by an overwhelming feeling of vertigo. He felt it now. Here in this room, with these strange people, his eyes full of stars, he felt as if he were plummeting back down to earth.

"I draw pictures too," Ahren said at last.

"Will you draw me one?" Sally asked. Ahren remembered the map he'd drawn for Lucy. Nothing good had come of his drawings.

"Maybe."

Sally smiled and Ahren was reminded of how long it had been since he'd felt the warmth of another's company."

"Sally, time for bed," said the man.

Sally looked disappointed that her time with a

stranger was at an end, but she conceded.

"You can keep this one," she said, handing Ahren's one of her drawings before withdrawing to her bedroom.

The man poured Ahren a measure of whisky and busied himself at the stove. He dished up a bowlful of stew for Ahren. It smelt incredible. Ahren took the bowl gratefully, trying to dismiss images of carrion birds devouring the woman's corpse.

"How'd you come to be up here?" he asked between mouthfuls.

"Some folks need a little more space."

Ahren looked at the man again. It was likely he was a fugitive. Ahren wished again that he had some kind of weapon on him.

"How do you survive?"

"We have our own means," the man said, pointing toward the bird. It appeared asleep now, clutching its perch with strong talons. It was easily capable of hunting rabbits, maybe even bigger prey.

"And I have my nets."

"Nets?"

"Cast em over and see what I can catch."

Ahren couldn't help but be impressed with the ingenuity. They'd made a homestead in the most inhospitable place on earth. But it was built on insecure foundations; Ahren had done the calculations, the cloudslide could have unsettled more than they knew. But Ahren sensed that this man would rather be swept away into oblivion for a few good years in peace, than go back down below.

"Where's Sally's mother?" Ahren asked, tipping the bowl and fishing the dregs.

The man tapped his pipe against the table. He looked right at Ahren. "The only reason I've been hospitable," he said, "is because of that little girl. If it were up to me I'd have thrown you off the edge of this cloudface to see if you'd fly. I don't like Company men, and I'm sure as hell not going to share everything personal with a stranger."

Ahren found he couldn't make eye contact. "I found a body a few miles back. A young woman, from what I can tell."

"What are you implying?"

"How did she die?"

The man shrugged. "We all die."

"If a crime's been committed the authorities need to know."

"We're not on earth now, Company man. The law doesn't apply in the clouds. There's only one authority here. "

Ahren shifted uncomfortably. It sounded like a threat. "I thought I was alone up here," he said.

"We ain't never alone."

"There's more?"

He nodded.

Ahren's head hurt. The cabin felt too warm, too crowded, almost suffocating.

"Well thank you for your kindness," he said, standing. "I'll be on my way now."

The man nodded. He seemed relieved.

"Say thank you to Sally," Ahren gestured with the picture in his hand.

He walked out into the night, the sky decorated with real stars. The man stood in the doorway within a cloud of his own making.

"Sky burial," the man said.

"What?"

"It's how we dispose of the dead. Give them to the sky."

180

The Cloud Cartographer

"You knew her, didn't you?" Ahren pressed.

"There'll be nothing left in a few days," the man said, retreating inside. "She'll be part of the clouds then."

Ahren's father wasn't a particularly religious man, yet in his study, above the bookcase filled with Ahren's favourites poets—Yeats, Wordsworth, Dickinson—hung a huge map of the Garden of Eden. It didn't just depict the Garden of Eden but many other significant biblical locations as well: Mount Ararat, the resting place of Noah's Ark, the kingdom of the Queen of Sheba. Ahren had memorised the outline, drawn to the Tower of Babel, reaching higher and higher to the heavens. The architects then had not been driven by the need for space, but for the desire to touch the divine. At the time, Ahren couldn't understand it, though he marvelled at the enterprise.

Ahren had thought it was ridiculous to map a myth, yet here he was in the clouds. It was the only place Lucy could be. He recalled the prayer flags flapping in the wind and his own prayers scattered amongst the clouds. This was the only place left for him to find salvation.

The last time he had seen Lucy was the day of her eighth birthday. He should have known that she wouldn't find the treasure he'd hidden, though he'd drawn a map. The map that led her into the woods and away from the house. She didn't like maps but she was a willing playmate and wanted to please her brother. Ahren had waited at the trail's conclusion—land's end, with the locket he'd bought for her wrapped in a box with a blue ribbon. He waited until the sunlight was gone and returned home to the flashing lights of a parked police car.

They searched the woodland but could find no trace of her. Ahren told them they were looking in the wrong place. They needed to look up.

Ahren's father had sworn never to sell but after Lucy's disappearance, the land had become abhorrent to him, polluted in the way the cities were not. A reminder of innocence stolen—paradise lost.

It was what the developers had wanted all along.

Ahren was lost. He knew on this cloudface, without his equipment, that was tantamount to death. He'd tried following his hand drawn map but the cloudmist was too thick. He needed to find shelter. He considered making his way back to the cabin, throwing himself at the old man's mercy but then he remembered what he'd told Lucy. If you ever get lost climb up and look down, then you can see the way home.

Ahren made his way to the edge of a cloudmass and lay face down. He tried to peer through the cloud, pressing his face into it. He couldn't see much of the world below, only what the starlight permitted. He remembered all the trees he'd climbed after Lucy's disappearance, despite his aversion for heights. He remembered the one where he'd found a torn piece of her white blouse. She'd tried to climb up and away as well. He'd always thought if he just climbed high enough he'd be able to see her. He'd moved into the highest tower-blocks, scaled mountains and finally arrived here at the top of the world, but the view below was always a disappointment.

Lucy was gone.

He pictured the prayer flags, the white one representing the clouds, ready to wave it in surrender. He stared down at the emptiness below, feeling gravity's pull. He was at land's end, the edge of the world. His underworld was waiting to greet him. He could easily step off the map.

Instead he pulled out the map from inside his outgear. He unfolded it to look at the white expanse he had covered. This was what other's sought, a blueprint of the unknown. It would be worth a lot to the Company, and to others. It wouldn't be virgin land then, it would be crowded with people and tower-blocks.

The wind played with the paper, curling its edges. Ahren gripped it tighter.

Done with the Compass—
Done with the Chart

He ripped the map along its latitudinal and longitudinal lines. He scattered the pieces into the wind, an offering to the clouds to be blown like prayers above the heads of men.

He lay on his back and unfolded Sally's drawing. It was a mirror image of the constellations above. He traced the lines between the stars, imagining them connected by an enormously long string that spanned the galaxy like the contours on a map. It would take light years to follow the threads, to navigate his way through the cosmos. He could follow the stars as old explorers used to. Maybe the stars would lead him to her.

Above, a single star burst across the sky, shining beautifully bright as it expired. She was up there somewhere, Ahren knew, and once he found her he would finally have a place to rest.

In the distance he heard the sound of hooves and the whinnying of a horse, floating among the clouds.

Preservation

The kitchen spoke of indulgence and industry. The worktop was crowded with baked goods in varying sizes; muffins swelled in their concertinaed paper cases and cup cakes stood tall, waiting to be iced. The surface was cluttered with pastry cutters, spatulas and wooden spoons, all sprinkled with a thin film of flour.

Despite the surface debris, the kitchen was spick and span. The appliances shone from compulsive polishing and the windows gleamed from the scrubbing they had received earlier that morning. Dressed with gingham curtains, they framed a small but productive little garden containing a modest vegetable patch and three trees, one apple, one fig and one plum. Even the washing on the line blew in organised unison, whiter than they'd ever been thanks to a new wonder machine that washed and spun garments in record time, rendering the mangle redundant.

At the helm of this domestic enterprise stood Dulcie, stirring a sweet stew of figs that bubbled on the hob. She tapped her foot to a tune on the wireless, which was accompanied intermittently by the whir of the washing-machine cycle. A line of sterilised jars stood ready on the counter. More jars than the bubbling mixture could ever hope to fill.

185

Dulcie spooned in the mixture over the muslin cloth she'd placed in a bowl, watching as the juice strained through. Niles liked jam. She looked forward to summer's bounty, knowing that her few weeks of canning and bottling would appease him for the rest of the year. She left baskets under the boughs in case while she was doing the housework, a few eager specimens, too impatient to be picked, tumbled to the ground. Some found their way into the baskets. Others lay strewn on the lawn and at intervals Dulcie would retrieve them before the insects nestled in. She would select only the perfect ones for pies and crumbles, the remainder she'd stew. Waste not want not, was her motto. It was everyone's motto since the war.

Dulcie heard Niles pull into the driveway at six o'clock precisely. She finished wiping the work surface and removed her apron. She dusted herself down, sweeping away any telltale crumbs, evidence of her culinary endeavours. She checked her appearance in the hallway mirror and applied red lipstick.

"Something smells good," Niles said as he closed the door behind him.

"Dinner's nearly ready," Dulcie replied, turning her cheek for his kiss, "I hope you're hungry."

Niles followed Dulcie and the aroma of baking into the kitchen. He placed the hamper she had packed that morning on the kitchen table and went to the drinks cabinet to pour himself a whisky. Cake stands lined the work surface, displaying an assortment of sugary treats, and a neat row of jam jars stood in front, like a cookbook display. Dulcie stood beside her banquet, a vision no less sweet in her floral-print dress.

"You've certainly been busy," Niles said.

Dulcie smiled.

"Did you have a good time with the boys?" she asked.

"So so."

He swallowed the remainder of his drink in one gulp. A few rogue drops dripped onto his cricket whites. They were as bright as the laundry hanging on the line.

"Reggie's on form," he continued. "Scored a century, would you believe?"

"That's nice," Dulcie replied, opening the hamper. The pickle sandwiches she'd made had hardly been touched. The jar of onion chutney looked suspiciously full.

"Weren't the boys hungry?"

"There was a lot of food." He poured himself a second drink. "Bridget packed some as well."

If the uneaten food wasn't curious enough, the last statement confounded her. Bridget had no aptitude in the kitchen; the cricket team usually preferred Dulcie's offerings.

She unpacked the hamper slowly.

"Did you leave it in the car?" she asked. Niles must have forgotten about it. He was preoccupied enough these days. She hoped the others wouldn't think she hadn't prepared a picnic at all. What kind of wife would she be?

Niles didn't answer but finished his second drink even faster than the first. When he did speak his voice was hard and business-like.

"I said there was too much food." He went again to refill his glass but thought better of it, as if the conversation had ruined his thirst. He placed his glass down heavily on the worktop.

"I'm not hungry." He closed the kitchen door

behind him, leaving Dulcie alone amidst the feast. There were towers of cupcakes held together with vanilla icing, a sweet mortar, imploring to be eaten. The muffins and scones and sponge cakes all joined the plea. Dulcie packed them away in Tupperware. She had no appetite.

She picked up Niles' glass and wiped away the amber ring it left. Then she filled it with a generous measure of whisky. She couldn't understand how she made him so angry. Especially when she'd worked so hard to show him how much she cared. All her efforts, wasted.

She went to the pantry and found the jar she was looking for. She carefully removed the lid and poured a few drops into the whisky. Then, taking a cocktail mixer, she stirred Niles' nightcap. She placed it on a small tray with a cupcake, in case he was hungry after all.

Dulcie consulted her cookbook and rolled out the pastry. She didn't need to but found some comfort in it. She decided she would make him something sweet to counter the bitterness of the day before. Niles liked blackberry and apple pie. The berries had come from next-door's invasive hedgerow, a just penalty for trespassing on her property. She rolled the pastry over the pie tin, moulding it to shape, and spooned in the filling. Then she arranged the pastry top, sealing the edges of the pie together with swift pinches. Her hands moved deftly as she trimmed the edge with her knife, a ribbon of pastry coming away like apple peel. She brushed the top with milk and, using a fork, made tiny indentations around the perimeter of the pie, like the footprints birds left when it snowed.

She'd bake the pie for twenty minutes on a low heat, five minutes less than conventional cookbooks stated, so the pastry was still slightly doughy. She was reluctant to always follow the guidelines set by others and in this small way she felt marginally rebellious. Besides, her oven was a temperamental creature that, without patient surveillance, had a tendency to ruin things.

"Something smells good," Niles announced as he opened the front door. Dulcie waited while he removed his hat and coat, which she took from him and placed on the coat stand. He left his briefcase by the front door as usual, ready for the next day.

"Pie?" he guessed, sniffing the air theatrically.

Dulcie nodded. "Blackberry and apple. I picked them this morning."

Niles planted a kiss on her cheek. "You're my best girl."

Dulcie smiled but winced inside. She'd never liked that expression. She knew he meant it as a compliment but to her it implied there were others. Still, it wasn't worth fighting over so she swallowed her objections.

They sat at opposite ends of the table for dinner. Dulcie liked to make the table pretty; she'd arranged some tea roses in a vase and had lit candles. The smell of the pie had suffused around the house, eclipsing the aroma of other dishes. It was wholesome and comforting.

Niles talked about a new business merger. Dulcie didn't talk much; this was Niles' time to unwind from the pressures of his day. What he needed most was an avid listener and she was happy to comply. After dinner she brought out the apple and blackberry pie

189

and cut him a large slice; it said all she wanted to say, an apology on a plate.

Niles devoured it hungrily, as if he hadn't already had two courses, and Dulcie smiled because she had made the pie with love and Niles was eating it all up.

"Reggie says it if wasn't for their assets we'd—" he paused. His spoon hovered mid-air. He chewing decelerated and Dulcie could hear the cloying mouthfuls of the pastry against his palate as he hesitated. He finally spat out the offending mouthful.

"What are you trying to do, poison me?"

"I...I..."

He examined the regurgitated pie. "A maggot!"

Dulcie wasn't sure exactly what she was supposed to do about it but she picked up some serviettes anyway and rushed to his side.

"It's fine," he said as she tried to take the bowl away. "I said leave it." He tried to regain the dish but swept it out of her hands instead. It fell to the floor, breaking against the leg of a chair. He slammed the door behind him, treading the mushy remains into the carpet as he left.

"I thought maybe this weekend we could go for a picnic," Dulcie suggested at breakfast.

Niles didn't look up from the paper. "I'm playing in a cricket tournament this weekend with Reggie and some of the other chaps."

"Oh?" Dulcie poured Niles another cup of coffee.

"It's been arranged for weeks. I thought I'd mentioned it."

Niles' interest in cricket was a recent development. Sometimes the matches were further afield, which meant staying overnight. "Will you be gone the whole weekend?"

"Most probably."

Dulcie was about to object when Niles got up from the table. He'd only eaten half his boiled egg, the toast untouched. "Well, best be off."

Dulcie followed him into the hallway and tried to help him with his coat, but as usual he shrugged her off. He buttoned his coat up slowly, his good hand pushing the buttons through, while what remained of his left hand held the coat in place. He buttoned his coat all the way to the top. The scars that ran up to his collarbone were barely visible above the collar.

"Have a good day, sweetheart," he said.

Dulcie handed over a brown paper bag containing the corned beef sandwich she had made the night before. She'd sprinkled it with a few more drops from the jar that she stored in the pantry, disguising it between the processed meat and a thick layer of pickle. "Don't forget your lunch," she said smiling.

Dulcie had been lacing Niles' food and drink for months. Encouraged by the results she'd become bolder in her experimentation. She'd open a jar and sprinkle a little bit here, a little bit there.

It started when Niles joined the cricket club. He began to spend most weekends at the cricket ground. Boys only. Weekends were usually the time they spent together. Not that they'd go anywhere. They'd complete household jobs, tend the garden, but at least they'd share the same space and there was something comforting in that. Something close to normalcy. Now Niles treated home like a barracks, somewhere to lay his head, where he was duty bound to stay though he would much rather be elsewhere. And he had begun drinking again.

Dulcie resented his freedom. She was confined to the house all week, cooking and cleaning, looking forward to Niles' company in the evenings to break the monotony of her day. But he only wanted to sit alone in the lounge and drink his whisky. By denying her weekends too, she felt herself falling into an increasingly dark and lonely place. She began to wonder what her life would be like without him.

One night he returned home late and the dinner spoiled. In her desperation Dulcie opened the jar she had hidden in the dark recesses of the pantry. She'd poured the contents into his tea out of spite. She watched as he put the cup to his lips, aware all the while of what floated among the tealeaves. Over time, knowing he was consuming her concoction made her feel better. She began to increase the dose and for a while things had actually seemed all right.

When Niles left for work Dulcie gathered the jars from the pantry. The plums she had picked gleamed in the colander. Droplets of water lingered on their satiny skin. She boiled a large saucepan of water and immersed the jars to sterilise them.

A knock at the door startled her. She turned the heat down and removed her apron on her way to the door, opening it to a woman dressed in a flowing floral dress. Copious layers of fabric seemed to swell from below her breasts, accentuating her protruding stomach.

"Bridget, what a surprise, please, come in."

Bridget followed Dulcie into the kitchen and sat down at the table with a sigh.

"Won't you have a drink?"

"Oh, no, thank you Dulcie; it's just a flying visit. But I will rest my feet for a moment."

Dulcie tried not to look at Bridget's swollen stomach, though she sat there rubbing it with triumph. She was due any day but hadn't let it stop her paying house calls; her need for gossip was only surpassed by her desire to spread it. And she had just heard all the juicy details regarding Helen Graham's divorce. Dulcie listened patiently. She never had any news of her own to contribute.

"But the real reason I popped over was to invite you and Niles to our anniversary party next month. Our anniversary is actually in a week but we decided to postpone our little gathering for junior here," she rubbed her stomach again with a smile.

It was nice of Bridget to extend the invite, but Dulcie knew it was because Reggie wanted Niles there, to make it more bearable. It was always left to the wives to arrange, to be civil, though there was little friendship beneath the surface.

"It's hot in here," Bridget said, removing a silk scarf and wiping her brow with the back of her hand.

"Sorry." Dulcie turned her attention to the saucepan. The water was boiling now; urgent bubbles breaking the surface. She turned the dial, extinguished the heat and watched the sterile jars bob in the water.

The jars were very much like her womb in that respect. That's what Niles believed: that no life could be cultivated in such a place. It had nothing to do with the burns that ran down his torso to the top of his thighs. Nothing to do with his pink flesh, which, robbed of crucial layers, forever resembled raw meat. She sometimes fancied she could see the blood pulsing beneath the thin, taut layer of skin. Just a flesh wound, he'd say when people asked. Only skin deep.

V. H. Leslie

Bridget picked up a plum from the colander and bit into its flesh, wiping juice away from her chin. Bridget, garlanded in floral, surrounding by the plums and the apples and figs from Dulcie's garden was the image of fertility. Her engorged stomach was an offence.

For a moment, Dulcie considered flinging the boiling water at her, watching the water melting through her like acid, imagining it continuing all the way to the baby. Would it be scarred, too, emerging a monster like Niles? Or would it simply dissolve entirely?

"Dulcie?"

"We'd be delighted to come," she said.

"Good, good," Bridget replied, getting slowly to her feet. "Gives us a chance to wet the baby's head."

When Bridget left Dulcie took refuge in the pantry. She'd taken one of the sterilised jars with her and sat on the hard floor amid the jars of pickled onions and apple-sauce. Then in the dark space she allowed herself to cry. There were more tears than she expected. Bridget's visits, especially since her maternity, incited emotions that Dulcie usually managed to keep down. Still, waste not want not. She held the jar to her cheeks and let her tears drain into its depths. When she collected all that she could, she sealed the lid tight. Then she labelled and dated it and placed it on the shelf with the others.

Whenever Dulcie was at a loss she would consult her mother's recipe book. It was as weighty as a Bible and just as prescriptive, but with practice she had learnt that she could glean the message and adapt the recipe to suit her own devises. Her mother had done the same, and in the margins were her handwritten alterations, her substitutes for ingredients that were too expensive or had become difficult to acquire.

When Dulcie opened the book, she'd peer into the depths and hope for answers as well as gastronomic delights. Perhaps some of her mother's wisdom was hidden among the instructions or tagged on to a list of ingredients, needing to be baked, stewed or roasted before the answers became clear. They never did. But the process of cooking was therapy in itself. The war had taught her to keep busy. It had taught her to store things and to always be prepared. And it had taught her to make the most out of the little she had.

It had also made her independent. She'd worked in a timber factory; the lugging and heaving lumber had left her with more strength than she knew what to do with. Afterwards, when things returned to normal, she was surplus to requirements. When Niles returned he didn't like the calluses on her hands any more than the fact she could do things on her own. She could open the stiffest jars, while his palsied hand couldn't even grip the lid. It had taken him a while to restore her to how she was before. And she conformed because she had vowed to obey him.

She turned the pages of her mother's cookbook looking for inspiration. She no longer had to rely on the Ministry of Food's broadcasts to enthuse her about dried egg or parsnips flavoured with banana essence. There was no need for imitation and make-do anymore. She had a kitchen full of food. And she need never go without again. But there was still an emptiness inside that she couldn't fill. And she knew that Niles felt the same.

She put on her apron and rolled up her sleeves.

She could make the best out of anything. Perhaps if she made something really delicious it would compensate. What they both needed was comfort food.

Niles and Dulcie sat at opposite ends of the dining table. Dulcie had made a cottage pie, the mash potato crisp on top and fluffy beneath, just as Niles liked it. A cherry crumble was warming in the oven for pudding.

"Bridget popped by today."

"Oh."

"Yes, she invited us to their anniversary party next month. It'll be to celebrate the new baby as well, I expect."

Niles nodded.

"I thought I'd make a cake. Maybe date and walnut."

Niles smiled and reached for the runner beans.

"She mentioned that Helen Graham is getting a divorce."

Niles placed his fork down, the conversation instantly distasteful. "What on earth for?"

"She says it's Harold," Dulcie continued, spooning more carrots on her plate, "that he hasn't been the same since the war."

Niles shook his head. "What about the children?"

"I'm not sure. I suppose they'll stay with her."

"He fights for his country and that's what he gets?"

"Well, we don't know the full story. They may be deeply unhappy."

"That's not the point."

Dulcie placed her cutlery down now. "I think it is. What's the point in being unhappy?"

Niles wiped his mouth with his serviette.

"Why don't you ever talk about what happened out there?" she pressed.

Niles glanced back across the table. He stood up slowly, his plate only half touched, "Thank you for dinner," he said and he left the room.

Dulcie held back her tears until she'd cleared the plates. Then she opened the pantry door and sat alone in the dark with her jars.

Dulcie had been bottling her feelings for quite some time. The first time had been an accident. She'd been making damson jelly but it was her tears that were decanted into the jars instead of the compote and as she tightened the lid of the jar she felt strangely better. She'd kept it in the larder for the first few days before labelling it, and in doing so accepted it as part of her life, part of her provisions for the future.

Nowadays she kept a few jars back deliberately. If she ran out she would empty the contents of other preserves into the sink and watch the puree slip slowly away. An unavoidable waste but it was better than the alternative.

The alternative was talking, something neither she nor Niles were very good at—they hadn't had the practice. Two months married, that was all, before he was drafted overseas. All their talking had taken place on paper, filtered through the medium of letters, which never allowed either of them to say what they wanted. Dulcie had tried in the months after his return but Niles wasn't prepared to open up. They existed now in a kind of voluble silence, talking about everything but nothing really at all. At least nothing that mattered.

Dulcie had filled a lot of jars with her latent emotions. Though they appeared empty, each one was full to the brim with unhappiness. And she was getting low on space. She often wondered what Niles would make of the rows and rows of empty labelled jars if he ever ventured into the pantry but in all their years of marriage, he had never even opened the door. The kitchen was her domain, her sanctuary.

She wasn't sure why she labelled them; out of habit probably. She often wondered if they had an expiry date and she felt a curious dread that they might go to waste. This was partly the reason she began adding them surreptitiously to Niles' food and drink. She was filled with a strange compulsion to use them up.

She began by pouring her earliest emotional episodes into Niles' nightly whisky. When she opened them she expected a scent or a vapour, perhaps even a salty residue to coat the sides. But there was nothing but the customary pop as the air escaped. Despite the airtight seal, the tears had always evaporated. And yet she was convinced a magical part of herself resided in the depths of the jars. She could imagine her tears still preserved as fleshly as when they had been shed. Like a conjurer, she'd pour her invisible potion into Niles' nightcap, ready for his transformation.

It was barely noticeable at first. Gradually though, Niles became more compassionate. Sometimes he even hugged her. The physical contact between them had become so mechanical that she'd forgotten what it felt like to be held with affection. Sometimes he would bring up arguments from weeks before and reconsider Dulcie's point of view. Though never an outright apology, there would be some kind of acknowledgement of her feelings. These considerate moods were always short lived but she relished them as small recompenses for the pain he had caused her.

She wondered why tears on their own never had

any effect. She believed it was because she had let them ferment, that they had become more potent sealed away in the darkness of the pantry. The arguments they'd had when he'd returned from the war, when she'd begged him to talk to her, to confide in her, had only ended in frustration. Her tears merely enraged him. She soon realised that crying was a luxury, something to be done quietly at night into the pillow or when he left for work in the morning.

Dulcie wondered if depositing her feelings would perhaps trigger for Niles an outpouring of his own. She had never seen him cry, though he dreamt dark, anguished dreams. If Niles had his own method of storing away his feelings, it was just as good as hers.

But she was becoming addicted to these glimpses of the husband she'd known before the war distorted him, so much so that she used the tears indiscriminately; in his sandwiches, in his tea. Sometimes everything he consumed in one day was laced with her emotional discontent. But she felt she was only just breaking the surface and she didn't have many jars left. Not of tears anyway. She had plenty of other kinds of jars but she was a little afraid to open those.

Dulcie watched as Niles packed up the car with his cricket gear and overnight bag.

"Are you sure you won't stay?" Dulcie asked quietly.

Niles pulled down the boot of his Morris Oxford. "We've been over this. It's only a couple of days."

The knowledge he was leaving made her bolder. "I know. I just feel we haven't really been together for a long time."

"We're together everyday."

Dulcie sighed. She should have been happy that Niles was attempting to live a normal life. That he didn't allow his weakened hand to stop him playing. But she didn't want to be excluded.

"Perhaps I can come with you? I could ask Bridget. We could bring some food-"

"Maybe another time. This is just for us boys." He winked. "No girls allowed."

Before Dulcie could object he climbed into the front of the car—"See you tomorrow, sweetheart,"—and drove away.

When Dulcie was a child, her mother had taken her to a museum of curiosity. It had the usual attractions; five-legged animals, lambs with two heads, the tricks of taxidermists. But it had been the images of deformed foetuses conserved in jars had stayed with her.

She opened the pantry door and ran her fingers along the cold surfaces. That's what she had here; her own curiosity shop. She might as well charge admission. It was her own personal collection of bitterness, the only product of her unfruitful marriage. But the contents weren't dead like the embalmed embryos. There was life, real flavoursome life, harbouring in the depths of each one.

She was still angry about Niles' departure. It was the sixth one in two months. She wondered if Bridget minded Reggie being away constantly as well. If she could cope on her own.

Dulcie noticed that apart from a small reserve of tears, the entire contents of the pantry were compromised of anger. She decanted her anger in a similar fashion to her tears. She'd wait until Niles left for work and shut herself in the pantry. Then, holding a jar to her mouth, she would yell as loud for as long as she could and all her frustration and anger would pour inside. She'd seal the lid quickly, afraid of the substance deposited within.

Crying no longer sufficed. Nowadays she had to scream and shout and stamp to feel better. There was a whole row of jars filled only with profanities. She felt so much better shouting and screaming the forbidden words. The plosive syllables and sharp harsh fricatives burst into the jar, like fireworks before being muffled by a swiftly sealed lid. She could swear in the most inventive fashion now, and she ran her fingers fondly over the glass jars, her collection more colourful than any fruit from her garden. The labels didn't give too much away; they were purposefully euphemistic. *Bitter lemons. Sour grapes.* To write accurately what a jar contained would ruin the surprise if they were ever opened. Besides, great chefs never revealed their secret ingredients.

To make jam you need a lot of heat. Dulcie poured the halved plums into boiling water and stirred them until the skin peeled away from the flesh and coloured the water a deep puce. The fruit softened, attempting to stick to the bottom unless they were gently nudged back into the swirling mixture. She added lots of sugar, stirring continuously. She added more than she needed to, recollecting what sugar had been worth on the black market during the war. In those days it was illegal to ice a cake. Nowadays, if Dulcie had her way, she'd cover everything in sugar, compensating for a glucose deficiency she was sure affected her whole generation.

With no one to relieve her from her post, Dulcie stirred the pot gently, careful not to allow the sugar to burn. She had made a lot of jam in her life, invested a lot of time hunched over the stove. She was an expert at multitasking and had devised various rituals to make the passing of time more pleasant. Sometimes she'd sing, or dance the shuffle step, though her proximity to the stove allowed only a limited amount of movement. To tackle the heat she removed her shoes, stockings and her dress and laid them over the kitchen chair. She tended to her bubbling concoction in only her slip and apron.

She wasn't worried about being caught in such a state of undress; Niles wasn't due back until the evening. It was one of the only perks to her solitude. She liked the sense of freedom, the feeling of her bare feet on the linoleum, the unrestricted movement of her arms as she stirred the jam.

She wondered what Niles would make of the spectacle if he did come home early. No doubt he'd see it as further testament to her not knowing her place, his semi-naked wife dancing around her cauldron.

The heat in the kitchen intensified with her exertion. Perspiration gathered on her forehead and the back of her neck, trickling down her back. Her silk slip became soaked, clinging to her body as she moved.

At 220 Fahrenheit the mixture began to change consistency. Dulcie had been scolded many times, but never with jam. She had been taught to be cautious of its destructive qualities.

She thought of Niles. What temperatures can the human body endure? His left side had been the buffer that absorbed a metal egg of deadly flame and shrapnel. She thought that his body would probably look much the same if he had been submerged in her bubbling mixture. What *had* he endured? She placed her finger above the saucepan.

202

Preservation

There was a knock on the kitchen window. Dulcie turned the hob down and quickly slipped on her dress. She cursed under her breath, surprising herself that the words came so readily outside the pantry. She opened the kitchen door halfway to Bridget.

If Bridget was taken aback by Dulcie's flustered appearance and her unbuttoned dress, good manners had taught her not to show it.

"Afternoon Dulcie. I just wondered if I'd left my scarf here by any chance?"

"I haven't seen it," Dulcie replied. She was reluctant to let Bridget in but realised it would be more suspicious leaving her out on the doorstep.

"Would you like to come in?"

"Thanks, it won't take a minute." Bridget went straight to the kitchen table and rummaged amongst the jars. She held it high in triumph, ignoring Dulcie's shoes and stockings sprawled on the chair.

"Making jam?" she asked politely. Dulcie nodded. "Then I won't keep you. Besides, Reggie's taking me to lunch."

Dulcie paused. "Isn't he playing in the tournament?"

"Tournament? With me due any day? No dear, he's waiting on my beck and call. As it should be, don't you think?"

Dulcie managed a smile and Bridget said her goodbyes. Dulcie returned to her cooking which had begun to stick in her absence. She stirred it vigorously, annoyed that her attention had been diverted to something so distasteful. Namely the whereabouts of her husband. He never went anywhere without Reggie. Why would he lie? And what was he doing if he wasn't playing cricket? Dulcie stirred the jam in swifter motions. She knew Niles had his secrets, things

203

he didn't want to share with her, things he kept back. And though it was unpalatable, she could accept it. But he'd never deceived her. Would he? She'd felt it in her stomach the same way when he'd returned with the hamper full of uneaten food.

The jam began to thicken and congeal as it was supposed to. Dulcie stirred with increasingly forceful strokes. Her forearms ached from the exertion. When had he become so tired with her that he sought sweetness elsewhere? Why did she have to drug him to receive an ounce of affection? Why, when he was the one with all the scars, did he find her so repulsive? Why wasn't she his best girl anymore?

She stirred the jam with all her might. As if everything in the world depended on it. Perhaps she could cook something to make it better. A gâteau or a trifle, truffles or blancmange. But she didn't think she had the right recipe for this.

The pot spun off the hob with a crash.

Preservation is an art form. Like most women, Dulcie had inherited the knowledge from her mother, along with the recipe book and a set of ceramic-lidded jars. She hadn't thought much of this legacy at first and had looked at those empty jars with little expectation. With contempt, in fact, that her life was condemned to the kitchen.

But mother had known best. Over the years Dulcie had filled the jars with all manner of homemade creations: chutneys and relishes that had spiced up the most mundane offerings from her ration book; infused tonics and tinctures to protect her from disease; and jam. Lots of jam. Jam to sweeten it all. Jam, when there was no fruit in the grocers. Her pantry was always stocked and it had seen her through the worst of times.

Those little jars had contained some of her fondest memories. The jam that filled the Victoria Sponge she had made when Niles came courting. Elevated on her mother's cake stand, a showpiece of her domestic skills, the extra thick layer of raspberry jam had dripped temptingly onto the porcelain, a promise of the sweetness to come. And when they were newlyweds they had eaten nothing but piccalilli, often straight from the jar because they couldn't tear themselves away from one another. Those jars and the things they had contained had nourished them through their marriage.

Now there was nothing left to preserve.

The hospital had been a welcome respite for Niles. He liked the smell of it, the way the disinfectant tingled his nostrils. It wasn't like the syrupy sweetness of home. It was comforting in a different way. It spoke of cleanliness and repair. He liked being around people that looked like him. Even the ones who looked relatively normal carried their own scars. In the psychiatric wing no spoonful of sugar was needed to help swallow the medicine.

Now he was home. He entered the house by the front door. He was about to utter his customary greeting but the odour that welcomed him stopped the words in his mouth. It smelt like burning. He ran into the kitchen and towards the stove. He flustered with the dials and opened the oven only to be consumed by black smoke. He grabbed a tea towel, fanning the air and removed the charcoaled remains of a cake.

"Dulcie!"

The kitchen was unbearably hot. A saucepan lay

strewn on the floor, its contents pooled around it like congealed blood. Niles picked it up and returned it to the hob. The same sticky residue covered the work surfaces.

"Dulcie!"

He took stock of the kitchen. Cutlery cluttered all the work surfaces, dishes lay abandoned, mounds of dried-out pastry littered the floor and globules of jam ran off the walls. It was a battlefield.

"Dulcie?"

Though he'd turned off the oven, the kitchen was still hot. He opened the windows. Perhaps Dulcie couldn't stand the heat either and had fled. But straining his ears, he thought he could hear a soft whimpering. The muffled sound of crying was coming from the pantry. He walked slowly toward it and opened the door.

The room was cool and dark. He could make out a figure in the corner. He pulled the light cord and suddenly Dulcie was illuminated. Her unbuttoned dress, her wild hair, all were exposed under the yellow glare.

"Dulcie? Are you ok?"

She didn't answer.

"Have you seen the mess out there?" It was a stupid question.

She shrugged and he turned his gaze to pantry itself. He'd never been in here. He thought it would be bigger, this magical place of limitless food.

But it wasn't full at all. There was only row upon row of empty jars.

"What's this?"

Dulcie didn't reply. How could she explain that she'd been tipping away all the food to accommodate her own needs?

He saw that they were all labelled. He went to pick one up.

"Don't touch that!" Dulcie cried, and Niles' hand, the hand that had never regained the strength it once had, fumbled against the glass. The jar slipped from his grasp and torpedoed to the ground, exploding on impact. With the crash of the glass came a greater sound, a sound more horrific than anything Niles or Dulcie had ever heard. It contained everything that was black and bitter and, amplified by its duration in the jar, it reverberated off the wall of glass to produce a high-pitched wail. The other jars combusted. Small explosions of glass burst around Niles and Dulcie and they added their own shrieks to the cacophony.

Niles fell to his knees and crawled to Dulcie amongst the glass. He tried to cover his ears but the anger continued to rain down on him. And each anguished howl sounded so much like his wife and yet it was not her. The barrage of female voices, each one more desperate than the last, made him sink lower to the ground. It was a minefield of pain and suffering more intense than anything he had ever experienced, allowed to ferment within the bowels of his home.

Niles took Dulcie in his arms and there they clutched each other as the last of the profanities ricocheted through the air like shrapnel, holding each other, shielding themselves from the broken fragments of their marriage.

Niles had no training for this kind of ambush. He buried his head into Dulcie's shoulder and wept with her.

And eventually, when there were no more tears and silence finally reigned, they picked up the pieces.

Wordsmith

———— ✣ ————

Vernon looked up from the blank screen and out into the garden. It was the end of summer and the landscape was beginning to change into its russet attire. He was finding it harder these days. Writer's block of a kind no writer could ever know. Sometimes the words came swiftly, but at other times he would spend an age toying over *le mot juste*. He scanned the geraniums and the herb patch to see if any elusive words were hidden outside. He watched the tree at the bottom of the garden. Its branches swayed, moaning as the wind stirred its leaves.

A whoosh of air startled him and he ducked to avoid the flapping of wings. Poe landed on the keypad, dancing across the keys so that a line of letters trailed across the screen: *ljftsdfhajhghiodll.*

"Poe!"

"Cellar door! Cellar door!"

Vernon waved the parrot away and it flew across the room to its perch. It bobbed its head to avoid Vernon's glare.

He turned back to the screen and began to delete the letters. He paused. Maybe there was something here he could work with.

Vernon was a wordsmith. He crafted them from

all manner of things; from overheard conversations, from things he read, sometimes from just his imagination. He'd collect snippets here and there, stripping them back into tiny morphemic units and melting them down so it was only the base ore—morpheme, *ore*pheme—that remained, before forging them into shiny new ideas.

Some of his words were designed for practicality, to convey meaning in simple unambiguous ways. Words built with a purpose, explicit and unequivocal. These were resilient and hardwearing, built for longevity. Good. Solid. Words. Others were fashioned with more aesthetic concerns in mind, dancing on the tongue and satisfying the ear with euphonic harmonies: *languorous, alabaster, serendipity.* Then there were the superfluous; flimsy fickle words that said very little at all.

Vernon was more proud of some of his words than others. Some were an affront to good taste, expletives or taboo terms that somehow remained as necessary as the rest. Some he typed out without caring about their meaning. Meaning wasn't his concern. He was merely a manufacturer of words. He didn't need to believe in his product.

There had been a time when he was zealous and experimental, addicted to linguistic flourishes and the buzz it gave him—word-buzz, buzzword—but that was a long, long time ago. It had been a mistake to pour his heart and soul into his work when he could get away with any old creation. Besides the fashion, as it always did, changed. There was no need to be long-winded and elaborate any more. Monosyllabic words were the choice of today. This was the era of the sound bite, of saying what you wanted to say as concisely as possible. It suited Vernon just fine, anything to reduce his workload. He'd become sick of words long ago.

When he was done he sat back and inspected his handiwork. He turned on the printer. It whirred slowly to life, startling Poe who flew to his shoulder. Vernon clicked the appropriate icon and the page was slowly replicated. Poe leapt from his new perch and circled the room excitedly. Vernon retrieved the warm paper from the printer, running a finger over the font. Book Antiqua.

At the backdoor he put on his boots, careful not to dislodge the mud that already caked the sole. Felicity had always complained about cleaning up his muddy footprints. He walked out into the garden, welcomed by a chorus of chaffinches flying overhead. Birds had names he was especially proud of: *capercaillie, plover, needletail.* Perhaps it was because they were the closest to the tree, at liberty to rest in its boughs and nest in its leaves.

The garden was small but mature, the result of years of toil. Felicity's garden. It was a little overgrown now. Vernon ignored the wayward wisteria and the invasive hedgerows all but obscuring the fence. He passed the rhubarb patch he'd left untilled and he fed the chickens, absently—*idly, nonchalantly.* They clucked in sympathy.

When he reached the foot of the tree, Vernon knelt down in the earth and raked the soil with a small trowel until it was finely turned. Then he reached into his anorak and withdrew the sheet of paper he'd printed. He ripped it into pieces and scattered them onto the fresh earth. He secured the paper seedlings with more soil, pressing down firmly with his hands until each scrap was completely covered. He found the plastic watering can and baptised his offerings, hoping they'd take root.

V. H. Leslie

୭

Vernon wasn't much of a reader. Felicity had been the reader in their house. She'd loved stories. She'd happily spend an entire afternoon snuggled in her armchair with a good book. When the weather was fine she'd lie on a blanket on the lawn, waving to Vernon occasionally as she consumed another page-turner. When she became ill, Vernon read to her. She thought Vernon was capable of such an endeavour but he didn't know where to begin. She loved poetry too, everything from Coleridge to Cummings, from Dickinson to Duffy. The perfect words in the perfect order. Vernon could find the perfect words but he couldn't string them together. He was a wordsmith not Wordsworth.

Vernon stared at the computer screen. He hadn't touched the keypad for over an hour. His mind was outside in the garden. Where Felicity still walked and breathed and lay down in the wildflowers.

He'd met her in that very garden. She'd been a child then. He'd caught her crossing the stile, taking a short cut across his land to the fields beyond. She'd run away from home, she explained, to escape the prospect of boarding school. It was her intention to walk all the way to the port where she'd board a ship for the Indies or some other exotic location; somewhere where adventure stories were set. Vernon had let her feed the chickens and pick the wildflowers to make a bouquet. *Angel's trumpets* and *dogweed, buttonweeds* and *forget-me-nots*.

He hadn't meant to tell her about the tree but Vernon never received guests and he was encouraged by her curiosity. He told her what the Scandinavians called it, explaining how it was sustained by the waters of wisdom, which bubbled beneath the earth. He told her how it was revered by ancient cultures that sacrificed victims at its roots, and he told her about the snake and the apple, though she already knew that particular story. He picked a leaf or two from its boughs and blew them into the air to demonstrate its magic. It was with reluctance that he persuaded her to return home.

He hadn't expected her to come back. But years later there she was, crossing the stile again, this time intent on staying. Drawn back by a really good story.

Vernon fiddled with the printer, removing layers of plastic to retrieve the ink cartridge that was nearly empty. Poe watched him from across the room.

"Cellar door! Cellar door!"

Vernon ignored him. Usually he waited until the ink had run dry; it was such an onerous—*burdensome, tedious*—task that he put it off for as long as he could. But now he savoured these mundane chores as a way of escaping the present and taking his mind off Felicity. The cartridge came free with a satisfying click and Vernon withdrew his ink-stained hand.

At least it was easier than before, now that quill and ink were redundant. It had taken decades for the ink stains to wash out from where the quill rested against his fingertips. Technology had assisted his occupation no end. He remembered when Caxton first established his printing press. Such a wonderful invention. He'd marvelled at how his words would reach so many. Gone was the tedium of copying manuscript after manuscript.

Vernon was kept very busy.

He tried to move with the times as best he could but technology changed as rapidly as language. It was easy to get stuck in your ways when you'd been around as long as he had. Before he'd purchased his laptop, Vernon had persevered for nearly a century on his Remington Standard typewriter. He liked the way it punched out the words with mechanical certainty. But parts eventually became obsolete and Felicity had encouraged him to get a computer. It wasn't the same. He didn't like the way the cursor on the screen seemed to hover too close to the letters, making them appear tentative and uncertain, erasable with the mere touch of a button. As if they had never been there at all.

People were the same, Vernon thought. They could be erased as well.

He'd always known Felicity would die. It was inevitable. It had been selfish of him to allow her into his life in the first place. A life that was so clearly predetermined to be lived alone.

Poe flew from his perch and Vernon dropped the ink cartridge on the carpet. He stepped on it as he moved to avoid the bird.

"Poe!"

He picked up the cartridge quickly but already the ink had bled into the carpet fibres, an expanding unequivocal blot like a large full stop.

Vernon sat at the foot of the tree. He'd prepared a modest lunch of ham and pickle sandwiches and ate them beneath the boughs. He ate with relish—*relish-gusto, relish-pickle*—and smiled. He patted the ground where he had buried the day's offering. A lazy word, a suffix added to an earlier creation, but it was all he could manage.

Not all of his words took root and he wouldn't be surprised if this one languished in the ground. A lot died. Others lay in the earth for years, dormant, waiting for the right conditions to bring them up.

Words grew on Vernon's tree. Each seed he planted fed the ground and if they were strong enough they'd appear as new shoots on the uppermost branches. These word-saplings proudly pushed their heads into the world and, if they were lucky, they'd flourish and blossom. If the right wind took them, they were carried off into the air, circulating above the heads of man to be plucked and used when the time came.

Vernon took a bite of his sandwich and examined the tree, ignoring the large scar along its trunk. Some branches were entirely evergreen, the perpetual, hardy stuff of yesteryear. Dull, hard words that he'd constructed to endure; pronouns and determiners, propositions and conjunctions, the cement of all language, whereas the higher branches harboured nouns and adjectives, verbs and adverbs. Higher still were the new words, the most delicate of Vernon's creations. These words were vulnerable, subject to change or decay. They could be carried off by a fortunate breeze to decorate discourse or they could be swept into oblivion.

When his words died, he mourned them. Sometimes he'd find them, wretched and decayed, on street corners: *clanjamphry, pantofles, quisby*. He'd gather them up. Sometimes he buried them again in the hope they'd re-germinate, but they rarely did.

Sometimes he buried the same word over and over if he really wanted to give it the best start in life. He had his favourites, of course, and he'd write them again and again, hoping they'd stick when he sowed them into the earth: *cruciverbalist, curglaff, skookrum, petrichor*. Those he didn't like he barely scattered with soil: *rancid, biopsy, coarse, cancer*. But his efforts didn't seem to have any bearing. Some words were like para-

215

sites, drawing their power from weaker specimens. If a word was destined to exist it only needed to be planted once.

He'd tried sowing her name in the hope of bringing her back. Felicity. *Fliss. Bliss.* He'd created her name but had never fully appreciated the meaning of it until it was incarnate. A word made flesh. She had filled his life with joy, and now that she was gone he was bereft. It was a silly notion, he knew, her name still existed but no matter how often he replanted it he could not resurrect its owner.

Vernon woke to a gentle knocking. He reached instinctively for Felicity at his side but felt only the disappointment of an empty space, cold sheets. He stared into the darkness instead, willing morning to come, for time to hurry by. He saw his life stretched out before him like an endless ream of blank pages. How could he possibly fill them now, without her?

The knocking resumed, pounding against the door of his mind and his thoughts of Felicity. He sat up in bed. This wasn't a dream. He could hear the knocking, more insistent now, coming from the window.

Vernon thought of the stories Felicity loved. Of Catherine's ghost at Heathcliff's window, pleading to be let in. How he wanted that fiction, for Felicity to haunt him and share his ceaseless days.

Come in.

Vernon pulled the covers aside and went to the window. Opening the curtains he saw a solitary branch, driven by the wind, knocking against the pane. The tree had become so big; its limbs reached too far. Vernon opened the window and pushed at the nearest branches. Why couldn't it just leave him be?

Wordsmith

In the distance he noticed a dark shape nestled in its boughs. As his eyes became more accustomed to the dark he saw what it was. A raven. Harbinger of the dead. Vernon slammed the window shut and watched the raven fly away.

Vernon put on his boots with renewed resolve. He'd decided during the course of another unproductive day that enough was enough. He couldn't allow the world's lexicon to languish with his grief. He had words to create.

He stepped outside. He rarely left the house since Felicity's death but he needed to garner ideas. He had to know what was being spoken about in the streets. That was the only true reflection of language usage. Maybe it could provide the stimulus for a new word.

The town swarmed with people. It was market day. He wasn't prepared for such an overwhelming concentration of people. But the liveliest places often yielded some of the most creative and diverse specimens. He thought of Felicity weaving her way through the crowds and followed the memory of her to the front of the stalls.

He examined the wares: jars of chutneys and marmalades, homemade scones and fruitcakes, venison sausages and veal pies, ginger beer and local ales. Listening to the lexical assortment was just as appetising. Colloquial exchanges and witty repartee accompanied the monetary exchanges as goods were wrapped and bagged. Verbal quips as acquaintances and friends greeted each other, mock insults and bawdy wordplay from the youths who congregated on bikes by the post office. Vernon appreciated the goods on display but couldn't relish the taste and texture of

217

those words as he used to.

He retreated to a tearoom and ordered some refreshment. Tea for one. Opposite, a couple sat intertwined, holding hands as they sipped tea. Vernon cut his scone in half and tried not to think of himself as similarly cleaved. All of his best words were compounds: *bluebell, hummingbird, wordsmith.* Everything made more sense as a pair.

Vernon looked out of the window at the marketplace but saw instead the garden back home, the tree at the centre. He saw Felicity as she tended the vegetable patch, her apron grass-stained and fragrant.

He closed his eyes.

Felicity was sitting next to the fire, laying scrabble tiles across the board. They often played on a winter's evening. She was an easy opponent, laying her favourite words instead of the ones that scored well. She never complained about the unfair advantage he had, though she joked that he could cheat whenever he wanted, making up something new at whim.

Vernon opened his eyes and sipped his tea. On fine days such as this, they would have afternoon tea sitting beneath the tree, sipping from a flask while he read a story out loud. It was on a summer day, near the end, that she pushed the book aside and asked him to tell her a story of his own. He shook his head. Wasn't it enough that he'd named the earth and all of its creatures, everything beautiful it harboured? He had plenty of words for her and he pulled a batch from the tree and blew them into the air. She'd admired their beauty as they danced in the breeze, but it wasn't what she wanted.

Vernon pushed his tea aside and paid at the counter. He wanted to go back. He glanced at the lovers as he left the tearoom, their hands still entwined like the roots of his tree. He'd always underestimated the word *Love*. He'd cringe seeing it printed on Valentine's Day cards, small and inane, understated by over use. But no other word seemed to articulate the myriad of emotions he'd felt when she came into his life. Euphoria and bliss, grief and sorrow. There were many synonyms for other words. There were none for her.

Felicity.

When she died, Vernon took an axe to the tree to see if it wept as he did. It haemorrhaged words. They oozed to the ground in pools of sticky sap. They died soundlessly on the ground, while the wind spoke through the leaves, crying mercy.

Vernon felt better when he was back in the study. Felicity had painted the room green to remind him of the tree outside. It was celadon—*sage, olive*. He rummaged through the bookshelves. What he needed was to follow Felicity's example and get lost in a good book. Considering he was the father of language, he wasn't much of a reader. He'd never minded reading to Felicity, speaking the words he'd made rather than sowing them. Except strung together they expressed more than Vernon ever could. He'd wondered if he'd been too reticent, giving his words to the ground instead of her. Had he ever really told Felicity what she meant to him?

Vernon perused the shelves. Orwell's *Nineteen Eighty-four* lay atop a pile of poetry. He picked up the well-thumbed text, an imprint of Felicity still evident in the creased pages. It was the only text that had ever truly frightened him. It was one of Felicity's favourites; she was much better at facing the idea of destruction. Orwell had envisioned a world where language could be reduced down to its bare minimum, 'Newspeak' ironically denoting an end to new words. Adjectives and adverbs axed by the millions, a dystopian world made plain in only the plainest terms. Vernon thought briefly of his own attack on the tree but Orwell's vision was so much worse. Leaves and leaves would be lost. The tree would be pruned back to within an inch of its life, all linguistic beauty stripped away. Ungood. Doubleungood.

He placed the book down and walked instead to the side of the study where his dictionaries were housed. He ran his fingers fondly over their bindings. It was a formidable collection and he had become quite the aficionado. He admired other lexicographers, though he derived greater pleasure in seeing what they had omitted.

His words existed a long time before they were recorded by the first dictionaries. But the popularity of the dictionary proved that man wanted some control over Vernon's domain. Among them, Dr Jonson's tome was particularly renowned and Vernon spent many an hour amused by its content. Vernon had been prolific in the years that followed, creating hundreds more additions, delighting in the idea that Jonson would never catch them all.

Vernon wasn't the only inventor of language, but he'd been there from the beginning and that, he believed, made him the sole authority on the subject. He'd built the tower that brushed the heavens, his ambition to reach higher and higher no different really to the way a tree stretches its limbs to the sun. But it was not for him to build and it had been struck down. He was the architect of language now.

Vernon wasn't the only one making words. Many writers and philosophers dabbled in the creation of words. Where would we be without Milton's *pande-monium* or Thomas More's *absurdity*, Shakespeare's *radiance* and Sir Walter Scott's *glamour*? Vernon would marvel at the new shoots sprouting on the tree wondering if one day he could retire.

He would've liked that. He'd become so tired of words. He envied his own word seeds, pushed deep into the hush of the warm earth. Sometimes he longed to crawl into the ground beside Felicity and lie there in the silent depths.

Felicity lay still in the bed, a saline drip at her side. She breathed slowly, laboriously, a sound like the rustling of leaves. Vernon stood at the foot of the bed, watching. Waiting.

Poe flew across the room, landing on the covers, nudging the clasped hands of his mistress.

"Cellar door! Cellar door!"

"Poe!" Vernon reprimanded.

But Felicity's eyes fluttered open and she smiled at Vernon. "Don't be too hard on him," she whispered.

"Why can't he bloody say anything else?" Vernon asked. Despite Felicity's patient training, Poe had only retained the first thing she'd taught him, a reference to her favourite poem. Felicity had thought the bird would be the most suitable of companions, someone for Vernon to talk to when she was gone. All he wanted was for the bird to be silent.

"Cellar door! Cellar door!" Poe flew circles around the room before disappearing down the hallway.

Felicity held out her hand to Vernon. "Tell me a story."

Vernon sat down at her side, talking her hand in his. "I don't know any."

221

"Then I'll tell you one." But as she opened her mouth a green shoot emerged from her tongue. It grew steadily longer, higher and higher, reaching up in imitation of Babel. Vernon leapt back from the bed. Once it reached the ceiling it circled the room as Poe had done, licking the walls as it snaked around and around and around. It changed colour as it grew and hardened, becoming the coarse, thick trunk of a tree, sprouting limbs that expanded like the bars of a cage. Vernon ducked to avoid each spear-like stem and watched as they pierced the walls and windows. The glass smashed and the boughs ruptured the joists, the ceiling held aloft only by the enormous tree, like a precarious layer of a wedding cake set to topple. He glimpsed blue sky as the roof soared skyward.

"Felicity! Felicity!"

He could hardly see amid the debris. But there beneath the rubble he saw her sleeping form, the roots clutched around her like an enormous hand. The tree continued to grow up, up, up, whilst she lay entombed at its feet.

Vernon woke abruptly, startling Poe who flew from his perch. He was in his study, sat in his armchair, a pile of dictionaries on the floor before him. He stretched, listening to Poe's progress along the hallway.

"Cellar door! Cellar door!"

It was supposed to be the most euphonic combination of words in the English language but it had become something of an irritant. And it sounded like *celador*, Vernon thought, Spanish for keeper of the bedchamber. That was what he had become that last year, a guardian, a nurse, and their bedroom had been transformed into a *sickroom*, a compound he wished he'd never invented. He still slept in what had been her *sickbed*, and he thought how apt it was considering that he would never mend.

Poe burst back into the room and flew around excitedly.

"Cellar door! Cellar door!"

Vernon had built this house with his own two hands. He was too afraid to build upwards, he'd learnt his lesson there, but he'd built below. It did have a basement. A cellar.

"Cellar door."

Could it be, Vernon thought? He was ready to admit it was ridiculous but he was already heading in its direction, accompanied by the squawking parrot whose only purpose was to utter those two simple woods. Cellar. Door.

Vernon stood in front of a door long redundant. He tried it without success. It wasn't locked but it hadn't been opened for a very long time. He pushed against it with his shoulder, putting his weight behind it. The door moaned in opening and Vernon descended into the dark.

They'd hardly ever used the room except for storage. Felicity occasionally squirreled away a few jars of preserves or chutneys along with the usual junk but there was little else. Save perhaps for the roots of the tree, clawing into the foundations of the house, into the foundations of his life. Sustaining it all.

Vernon flicked on the light and a pale glow illuminated the underground room. Cold like a tomb—*crypt, sepulchre*. But it wasn't as empty as he'd imagined.

It was crowded with terracotta pots, the kind Felicity filled with begonias and tulips, gardenias and lavender. And the pots weren't empty either; they were full to the brim with rich black compost. Vernon shook his head in disbelief. What had Felicity been up to? It looked like a strange winter garden, waiting for the right conditions to bring up whatever lay buried.

Vernon reached for the nearest one and plunged his fingers into the moist earth. He was surprised when he felt something smooth. He pulled it out and wiped it free of soil. He stared in amazement at the letter E.

It was a scrabble tile.

Vernon upturned the pot and smacked the base until the compost fell free. He raked his fingers through the soil, looking for the letters hidden there. He wasn't used to pulling things from the earth. He lay out his unearthed treasures.

N N R
O V E

Nevermore? Vernon thought, remembering the refrain from Felicity's favourite poem. No, too many Ns. Vernon felt amongst the soil but there were no more letters. He rearranged the ones he had.

N O N V E R

He saw what the word was meant to be, but he felt compelled to examine it like this, jumbled up.

NON—a prefix meaning not, and,

VER—an abbreviated form, perhaps of verdant?

NON VER

He thought of the tree and of Felicity's garden. The tree replenished itself, generating new words when old ones died. Even though he'd taken an axe to it, the tree healed itself, continuing to get stronger. And Felicity's garden, though dormant through the winter, would blossom and thrive each spring. It was never the end.

Vernon picked up the letter V, the highest letter score amongst the tiles. Perhaps it wasn't a shortened form of verdant but Vernon.

NOT VERNON

He hadn't really been himself since Felicity's death. He lost more than just her; he'd lost who he was.

He upturned another pot. He felt in the caked earth for the letters he knew would be there. The same six letters as before. He laid these ones out in the order intended.

V E R N O N

A score of only 9 but it was his name and that made it invaluable. Felicity believed in husbandry, of preparing and cultivating the earth to ensure her garden would flourish each year. And she believed in her husband, sowing his name in each pot—

V E R N O N
V E R N O N
V E R N O N

—willing him to live. Hoping that his soul, in its grief, wouldn't stay beneath the earth with her.

Vernon typed without cease. Eventually he sat back to admire his handiwork. He turned the printer on and waited while it whirred into life. Poe circled the room excitedly as the page was slowly replicated. Vernon ran a finger over the typeface. Book Antiqua.

He put his boots on in the hallway, careful not to unsettle the mud that caked their soles, and walked out into the spring morning.

The chickens clucked at him though they'd already had their breakfast. He passed the vegetable patch and the flowerbeds, the ground tilled and ready for next year's crop.

The tree was healing well. The trunk still bore the scars from the axe edge, but now they only looked like the savage imitations of what lovers carve to tell the story of their love.

Tell me a story.

When Felicity had appeared all those years before, young and bold, crossing the stile, she had so many stories. She'd retell them with words he already knew, but from her lips they always sounded different. A new vocabulary. She breathed more than meaning into them.

Tell me a story.

Vernon ran his hands over the bark, over the wounds he'd inflicted. The leaves rustled above him, then hushed in anticipation. Straining. He unfolded the printed page. He would keep both their names alive with his words. He whispered into the crevice, into the hollow of the tree and filled up the void.

The Quiet Room

"**T**urn the music down," Terry said, standing on the threshold of his daughter's room. Some unspoken rule forbade him from going in, especially without permission. It was different for mums, he imagined; no part of the house was off limits to them, they could tidy and snoop in equal measure, unchallenged. But for dads, a teenage daughter's room was a minefield, a frightening place that only served as a reminder of how distant the days of childhood were. In truth, he preferred to stay outside.

His daughter, Ava, unaware of his presence, danced uninhibited to the music. The gap in the door allowed him to see more of her body than he would have liked, a body that had somehow grown overnight to replace the goofy child with pigtails and grazed knees. The clothes she wore seemed to belong to that younger Ava as well; too small and too tight, riding up to expose the body that had outgrown them, though Terry knew she'd bought them like that on purpose. Wearing as little as possible was the fashion these days and she was a dedicated follower, like all her friends. He should talk to her about that, about following the herd. But for now he just needed her to stop the music.

Terry rapped the door again. "Ava."

She was deaf to everything but the synthesized

227

wail reverberating from her speakers. Terry raised his voice, "Ava, I won't say it again..."

"Dad!" Ava replied. Her voice was louder than Terry's, amplified by embarrassment. "What are you doing up here?"

Terry was always amazed at how easily she could turn things around. Now he was in trouble for trespassing on her space. "Your music—"

"What?" Ava placed a hand behind her ear.

"It's too loud. Just turn it down."

She huffed as she walked to her stereo and turned it off.

"Happy now?" Her question was absurdly loud without the music to compete with.

"Yes," Terry said quietly. A poster of a very young looking man, tanned and shirtless, gazed back from above his daughter's bed. Terry pointed at it. "He'll catch a cold," he said, realizing as soon as he did how old he sounded.

Ava just raised her eyebrows, something she'd perfected to make Terry feel both chastised and insignificant. He wondered if she'd learnt it from Prue.

"You don't think maybe you have too many posters up?" Terry asked.

"It's *my* room, Dad."

It was *his* house, he wanted to say, therefore it was *his* room. But there was no sense in being pedantic. It was important for Ava to feel that she had a place. He supposed it was a good thing that Ava had become so territorial about her attic bedroom. The house had so many other good-sized bedrooms on the second floor, but she seemed to intent on having the smallest room, furthest from the nucleus of the house.

"It makes the room look a little crowded is all," he offered. He avoided what he really wanted to say, that he didn't like those half-naked men gazing down at his daughter. But there was no point rehashing an earlier argument; they'd already disagreed about poster-to-wall ratio and Terry had conceded. He couldn't start telling her what to do now.

Ava shrugged in a way that said she didn't care about his opinion. And why should she? He hadn't exerted any kind of influence on her life so far. Why should she listen to him now?

Terry realized he was hovering. "Dinner won't be long."

"Ok."

Terry looked around Ava's room one more time, trying not to be disappointed at how much it conformed to a typical adolescent space. As well as the posters of manufactured pop groups on the walls, piles of clothes and shoes crowded the floor. They'd only moved in a few weeks ago and already the room had the worn look of a teenage den. It wasn't just the room but Ava's choice of music he found so annoying. He worried about her taste. Those formative years when he'd been out of her life were responsible for shaping her in all kinds of ways. He couldn't expect to change her overnight. But he wished she would listen to something else.

He made his way back down the stairs, conscious of the volume creeping higher again. It was clear now why she'd been so keen to claim the attic bedroom; it was so she could make as much noise as she wanted.

Terry walked through the old house, waiting for the pizza delivery boy to arrive with their usual order. It was a big house, bigger than it needed to be for just the two of them. There had been few properties on the market so close to Ava's school and of those it was the

229

most affordable, though bigger and more expensive than he would have liked. Terry still wasn't accustomed to so much superfluous space. He walked through the house now, opening doors to rooms he wasn't sure how to use, how to fill, moving around the empty spaces before closing the doors once more. It was becoming a habit, a nightly tour. He tried not to think of it as some kind of vigil.

Though the house was old, the rooms lacked period features or individual characteristics. They were uniform, bare, gazing back at him with vacant expressions. All except the music room.

He hesitated on the threshold for a moment, drawn by what was on top of the piano. It was the first thing Ava had unpacked, the first thing she'd found a home for but Terry still wasn't used to seeing it. He just hadn't expected to bring Prue with them. The urn was much more plain than he would have expected for Prue. He would have imagined something more showy, more extravagant. But though simple in design, it still made him uneasy. He knew it was only ash and dust but it felt like he was facing an old adversary every time he saw it.

The sooner Ava decided where to scatter her mother's ashes the better. He'd tried to persuade Ava not to put it off, that doing it quickly would help her move on, but really it was because he hated Prue being in their home. The last time they had been under the same roof was thirteen years ago and, with the exception of Ava, he had no happy memories of that time.

Ava couldn't conceive of keeping the urn anywhere else. Prue liked the piano apparently and was especially keen on Liszt. The Prue Terry remembered didn't know the first thing about music, classical or otherwise. Prue's sister was the musical one.

Without looking at the urn, he walked towards the piano and pressed his finger to one of the shiny clean keys, cold beneath his touch. It let out a puff of dust. Terry pressed it again and imagined the effort inside as the mechanics attempted to conjure sound. A second silent exhalation was all he got.

Terry didn't know a thing about pianos but knew this one was busted. He would have thrown it out but for the fact the house was left so vacant, almost unusually so, that its presence seemed all the more engineered. It was almost a relief to find something from its past, even if it was broken. It was odd for a house of this age not to have more relics, Terry thought; old fireplaces, cornicing, fretwork banisters, any would have been typical of this period. The previous owners must have stripped it back to the bare essentials, purging it of its past with copious tins of magnolia. A blank slate.

Terry had moved a lot over the years and most of the homes he'd lived in had retained a few objects from the previous owners; mildewed white goods that were an inconvenience to take, unfashionable light fittings, the odd piece of furniture. And then there were the marks people didn't realize they left behind. Children's measurements on a doorframe, old photographs at the back of a drawer, a dent in the plasterboard from children play fighting too enthusiastically, or from grownups fighting for real. Terry liked to trace the narrative of the houses he lived in. The walls whispered their story through such scars.

But this house was silent.

Just like the piano. Terry pressed the key again, half expecting a clear shrill note to contradict him. But he only heard the click of the key as it moved and a whisper of air.

Terry sat on the stool. He wouldn't get rid of it. The piano was the only link to the building's past, a gift from the house. He spread his fingers over the keys, imagining himself a great pianist about to begin a concerto. He lifted his hands above the keyboard ready to bring them down in unison and glanced up at Prue's urn.

A shrill electric note echoed through the room.

Terry leapt back from the piano, stumbling over the fallen stool. He hadn't touched the keys and yet a sound filled the house, becoming a tune he began to comprehend- *The Flight of the Valkyries*, played on distant tinny notes. The new doorbell Ava had persuaded him to buy. Farcical, like the inside of a musical greeting card.

Terry rose quickly, closing the lid of the piano and hurrying to the front door.

Terry placed the pizzas and the dips on the table. He heard Ava bound down the stairs, surprised that she could hear the jingle of the doorbell over her music at the top of the house. She had a way of sensing food.

Ava piled her plate high, whereas Terry only took one slice at a time.

"You know we're going to have to eat real dinners sometime," Ava said with her mouthful.

"Why?"

"Because they're healthy. You're supposed to make sure I eat right."

"It feels right to me."

"Not for your cholesterol."

Terry, glancing at her plate, thought it a little hypocritical. "Well, what should I cook?"

"Pasta or fish. Vegetables and stuff."

Terry nodded, suitably admonished. He was

reminded of one of the last conversations he'd had with Prue, her concern that he spoilt Ava too much.

"What do you normally eat?" she said between noisy mouthfuls, "you know, when you were on your own?"

Terry was quite content with sardines on toast, or pub grub from the local. But he always ordered a takeaway when he had Ava. He saw her so sporadically, sometimes only every couple of weeks that it always felt like a victory. Prue had not made it easy, so he equated seeing his daughter with a kind of celebration. It still felt like that, even though he was well aware they were engaged in a complex renegotiation of their roles. He wasn't used to being a full time father yet. For him, seeing his daughter everyday had not lost its novelty. Though clearly pizza had.

She was still waiting for an answer.

"Oh, this and that," he said.

"Well, why don't we go shopping tomorrow? Get some healthy food in?"

Terry smiled; when Ava wasn't being moody or answering back she was actually a pretty nice kid.

"I'd like that."

"I can make my chili surprise."

"What's the surprise?"

"You'll see." Ava smiled. "It was Mum's favourite."

Terry swallowed hard on Ava's use of the past tense but washed it down with his beer. He wouldn't have imagined Prue liking chili, too much spice for her bland palate. He was beginning to realize how little he knew about his ex-wife. They'd been little more than strangers at the end.

Terry smiled, taking the good mood to try to connect with Ava. "So how are you finding it? The house I mean?"

"It's ok. I like my room. But it's not very homely."

"No?"

"It feels empty. Even with all our stuff."

Terry thought about the piano room, the only room that felt occupied.

"Who lived here before?" Ava asked.

"No-one, apparently. Not for the last twenty years at least. Just been sitting empty."

"About time we came along then," Ava smiled, helping herself to another slice.

Terry smiled too. When she wasn't in that room of hers he felt like she was actually listening to him. He wondered whether it was time to deliver some fatherly advice, to address the way she dressed, to talk about her tidying her room a little more frequently.

Upstairs, Ava's music blared suddenly. Terry couldn't make out the words but the tune was melancholic, lovesick. Not the kind of music he would have expected.

"Sorry Dad," Ava said, getting up from the table and heading toward the stairs, "I must have forgotten to turn it off."

Terry listened to her footsteps as she ran up the stairs and the music stopped as suddenly as it had started.

Terry decided it was time to unpack the boxes. He'd been so focused on making a home for Ava that he'd literally left his work wrapped up, concealed beneath bubble wrap. Ava was keen for them to fill the house, to get as close to normality as possible. Besides, she would soon be up for school and he couldn't spend another day roaming around the old house, waiting for her to come home.

He took the blade of a pair of scissors to the first taped box, opening it to a host of chinaware. The tiny porcelain cups rattled as he delved inside. He worked in antiques—at least that was what his shop's frontage had said, but it was really bric-a-brac. "Antiques" sounded better; it implied that the object in question was in some way important. Customers wanted to know when items were made, who owned them, and they attributed worth generally to how well those questions were answered. Terry had learnt very early on that you could sell anything if you gave it a story. And what people sought most were unique stories. What Terry tried to do was to offer the mundane, the forgotten, the overlooked a good narrative. He'd largely succeeded. He'd made some exceptional profits on some lesser-known treasures, partly because of his expertise in restoration but mostly due to the calibre of his stories. Making something out of nothing was his trade.

Terry had decided to make this room, one of the many indistinguishable reception rooms, his workshop. He doubted that it had ever been used for that purpose before. The house felt grand, and though it didn't provide many clues, he imagined it had been designed with only luxury in mind. The reception rooms would have been filled with occasional furniture, countless armchairs to nestle into, little mahogany writing desks for penning love letters or replying to dinner invitations. As he unwrapped dainty teacups and their saucers, vases and ornaments, he thought that it was very likely that once the house would have been filled with such knick-knacks. Except that now, as he arranged them carefully on the table, they looked out of place. Absence and neglect had filled the house so entirely that everything else seemed like an affront.

"Dad?"

It shocked him into nearly dropping the teacup in his hand. He placed it down carefully. "Ava, you made me jump."

"Sorry. What are you doing?" Framed by the doorway, dressed in her school uniform but still rubbing the sleep from her eyes, she looked more like a child than ever.

"I thought I'd start work today. Come in, come in. Take a look around." He used his best shop voice.

Ava entered the room, picking up bits and pieces that took her fancy. She seemed to like the things that opened and closed, playing with the hinges or the catches, mostly timepieces or ornate pillboxes. She was opening the front of a carriage clock when something in one of the cardboard boxes caught her eye.

"What's that?"

Terry pulled it out and dusted it down. It was a black box, decorated with brightly coloured images of birds in flight. "It's a music box," he said. "Look..." and as he opened it, it began a to play the notes of a lullaby.

"It's beautiful." Ava reached for it. She ran her fingers over the surface.

"It's black lacquer," Terry said, competing with the mechanical tune, "undoubtedly nineteenth century, though the origin is harder to pinpoint. I'd say European, though it looks Japanese. There was a lot of mock oriental stuff then."

"It's beautiful," Ava repeated, holding it up in the light. "Look, there's a girl here," she said, delighted at her discovery, "and another this side but with wings." She turned the box around. "Is she an angel?"

Terry put on his glasses and examined it more closely. "I'd forgotten about this piece. No, she's no angel, I think it's Philomela. You see the bird this side?"

He pointed, "The girl *is* the bird. She's transforming into it."

"Why?"

Terry shuffled in his chair. "Well, Philomela was very beautiful and her brother in-law wanted her very much. He engineered it so that she was alone in a cabin in the woods where he, er..." Terry searched for a euphemism. "Where he had his way with her. Then he cut out her tongue so she could never tell anyone what he'd done."

"Gruesome."

"Yes. But Philomela had a plan. She wove the story of his actions into a tapestry and sent it to her sister, who helped her escape. When the brother in-law pursued them, the gods took pity on them, transforming them into birds. Philomela was transformed into the nightingale, the bird with the sweetest voice. I suppose to compensate for a life of silence."

Ava smiled. Terry smiled too; he'd omitted the bit about Philomela's sister's revenge on her husband, how she had murdered their son and fed him to his unknowing father. Somehow infanticide seemed to tarnish the whole story.

Ava picked up the box. "Can I have it?"

Terry shrugged, "Well I'd say it would fetch at least £200."

"Really?"

"Shall we say... a clean bedroom and a hug?"

Ava pretended to think about it. "How about two hugs and I'll wash up instead."

Terry was so impressed with her bartering skills that he was more than happy to forfeit the clean bedroom. "Deal."

They shook on it.

Ava turned before she got to the door. "One thing

I don't get, why a tapestry? It seems like a lot of effort. Why not just write a letter?"

"A letter would have been expected. Only something more subtle would get past the guards. Sometimes we don't see the messages that are right in front of us."

Ava seemed satisfied with that answer and left Terry among his relics.

Terry spent the rest of the day in a frenzy of activity. He'd unpacked most of the boxes and sanded a few smaller pieces of furniture. The room smelt of varnish and woodworm treatment. Ava would be home from school soon and he was looking forward to showing her the progress he'd made.

He was repairing a Georgian chest when he first heard the tapping sound. He strained his ears, listening.

A dull repetitive tap. Terry walked about the room, checking the various timepieces that were scattered about. It wasn't a ticking. It was hardly noticeable but it was there, a quiet but indisputable tap, tap, tap.

He walked out into the hallway. The tapping louder now that he'd left the noise of his workshop behind. It was a noise that would drive him mad if he didn't discover the source.

The doorbell broke him from his reverie and for once he was glad to hear it. Any sound was better than that incessant tapping. He jogged to the door, imagining he had wings like the valkyries, excited to see Ava after a long day. Except it wasn't Ava.

Terry froze. For a moment he thought Prue had come back. That she'd somehow wangled her way back into the world of the living to take Ava from him. Then the woman removed her sunglasses and he could see a younger face, kinder eyes.

Philippa.

"Some Gothic mansion you got here," Prue's sister said, looking the place up and down. "I hope you've had a priest round to bless it."

Terry stood speechless. The resemblance had always been uncanny, though they were not twins. It was as if Prue was resurrected before him, but a younger version, closer to the woman he had married. He'd seen Philippa at the funeral of course, shocked then at how strong the resemblance had become over the years. They kept their distance. They always had.

"Come in," Terry said recovering. They leant in for an awkward kiss. "If you *dare*..." he added in an attempt to relieve the tension.

Philippa raised her eyebrows but followed him inside.

"It's big."

"More rooms than I know what to do with. We have a music room, don't you know."

"A haunted library as well, I suppose, and a madwoman in the attic."

"We definitely have one of those," Terry said, relieved to see Ava coming up the path.

"Aunty Philippa!" Ava ran the rest of the distance.

"Mad as a hatter," Philippa agreed as Ava bounded into her.

"Why don't you give Aunty Philippa the grand tour?" Terry said once the hugging was done.

"Sure," Ava said, straightening her uniform. "If you care to follow me."

Terry and Philippa exchanged glances and fell in step behind her.

"Nice piano," Philippa said, stopping at the music

room.

"It was here when we arrived," Terry explained. "The only thing the previous tenants left. But it's broken."

"May I?" Philippa asked, walking to it before Terry could object. She sat and pressed at the keys. Terry was reminded of the tapping noise he'd heard earlier, realizing that it had stopped in the interim.

"Silenced," Philippa said.

"Pardon?"

"I think it's been silenced. It's not broken. It's so people can practise without causing a racket. It can be reversed, I know a guy who could fix it."

"Really?" Ava exclaimed.

"I can teach you, if you like? I used to play," and she demonstrated with a silent flourish. "I'm a bit rusty but I'd be willing to share what I know. First things first," she said glancing at the urn, "let's get this piano to make some noise."

Terry found he could tolerate the quiet of the house in the daytime if it meant music in the evenings. Sitting in his workshop he listened to the snatches of melodies next door as Ava took her piano lesson. He could differentiate between them, Philippa's fluid cadenzas and Ava's hesitant and static playing. But Ava was improving. When Philippa left, Ava practiced on her own and he could make out the beginnings of tunes, the foundations of compositions he partially recognized.

It wasn't just the music that he looked forward to but the laughter. The house seemed alive with female voices. Sitting in his workshop he listened to his daughter's voice, laughing over the sound of the piano, and thought it was the most beautiful sound he had ever heard.

"Aunty Philippa said I need to practise more," Ava said at dinner.

"You play every day as it is," Terry replied, though he didn't mind Philippa's sudden involvement. In fact, he was surprised how naturally she slipped into their lives. It was important for Ava to have some familiarity, he reasoned. He helped himself to more of Ava's signature dish, the surprise being copious amounts of jalapenos. His mouth made an O shape as he tried to breath through the heat.

"But I want to get really good," Ava insisted. "I need to work on my tempo apparently and not rush the rests."

"Rests?'"

"The silent bits in between the playing. Aunty Philippa says silence is as important as the sound the notes make. She told me about this composer who wrote a composition of 4 minutes and 33 seconds of silence."

"I bet the audience wanted their money back."

"It was revolutionary."

"You can't compose silence," Terry said, pouring himself a glass of water. "It just exists. He didn't create anything that wasn't already there."

"But it wasn't there. Not until the composer closed the lid of the piano to mark the beginning of the movement. People listened more patiently than they would anywhere else because they were in a concert hall. Can you imagine how long four minutes of silence must have felt when you expected music?"

Terry thought of how quiet the house was in the daytime when he was alone in his workshop. But even then there were the sounds of sanding wood, the ticking of clocks.

"Except it wasn't silence," Ava continued. "People shifted in their seats, coughed. Some even walked out. That was the music he wanted the audience to listen to."

"Sounds a little lazy if you ask me," said Terry. "He wasn't the author of those sounds, he didn't plan that the man in the back row would cough, or that the lady at the front would tut."

"But he created the opportunity for those sounds, they never would have existed if he hadn't made the silence."

Terry looked at his daughter. He hadn't expected to have such a thought provoking conversation over dinner. Though still in her school uniform, she suddenly looked like a young woman and unmistakably like her mother.

That night Terry dreamt of the music room. It was full of people, dressed in black, sitting around the piano as if for a recital. Terry walked among them, noticing how still they all sat, their heads cast down. He saw instruments in their laps or at their feet. He tripped over a cello, the strings catching on his trousers, but it didn't make a sound. Nor did the cellist stoop to pick up the instrument. It was so quiet that even the sound of his footsteps seemed to have been silenced somehow. Terry stamped his foot, trying to make as much noise as he could, and when that failed he knocked over a set of cymbals, expecting the vibrations to shatter the silence. But nothing dented the stillness of the room. He tried to address the gathering but his voice faltered, the people didn't even look at him. Terry grabbed the nearest man by his lapels and shook him roughly, but the man merely stared back vacantly. Terry tried to scream into the man's face, pouring all his confusion and rage into one almighty cry, but no sound came and his throat became hoarse with the effort.

In the background he heard the piano.

Dissonant notes at first, but gradually they merged to form the beginnings of a melody. He avoided looking at what was on top of the piano but glanced across at the keyboard. The lid was down. To signify the beginning of the movement, he remembered. But how could that be? The melody began to gain speed, the volume creeping higher and higher, the playing becoming more crazed, more erratic, building toward an inevitable and deafening crescendo—

Terry sat bolt upright in bed.

He breathed deeply, trying to steady himself, fancying he could hear the sound of his racing heartbeat. As it slowed he was conscious of another sound. He strained his ears and thought he heard the same dissonant notes from his dream.

It was the piano.

It echoed through the corridors of the old house, drifting up the stairs, filling the rooms and recesses with its melancholic air.

Ava.

Terry pulled aside the covers and began down the stairs. He pushed his dream to the back of his mind as he followed the melody to the music room, opening the door with a thud.

The music stopped.

"Ava?"

Ava sat at the piano in her nightclothes. Her fingers were stretched out on the polished veneer of the piano lid. Had she closed it suddenly when he entered the room?

Terry walked towards her in the silence. She

opened her eyes slowly as if waking up. She looked around dazedly at her surroundings.

"It's ok," Terry soothed, placing his arm around her, gently bringing her to her feet. "You've had a bad dream. Let's get you back to bed."

As he closed the door, he looked one last time at the piano but saw only the urn.

Ava was quieter than normal the next day. She looked tired, as if she hadn't slept at all. There was no laughter during the piano lesson that evening either. Listening in his workshop, Terry could only hear Philippa's voice giving instructions between the playing. At the end of the lesson Terry walked Philippa to the door.

"Is everything ok with Ava?" she asked before she left. "She seemed a little subdued."

Terry shrugged. He wasn't ready to verbalize his concerns. "Teenagers," he offered.

Philippa looked at Terry for longer than was necessary before saying her goodbyes.

Walking back inside, Terry couldn't quieten his qualms. Ava had hardly uttered a word to him all day. Even at dinnertime, when she was usually so chatty. And she'd hardly touched her food. If something was on her mind he wanted her to be able to talk to him about it. He wondered if she could. She'd always had Prue befo...

Shhhhh!

He stopped in his tracks.

He was outside the music room. For a moment he thought he must have been speaking aloud, that Ava overhearing must have shushed him. But listening now, all he could hear was Ava's playing. He edged closer to the door. For a moment he was sure he heard two voices instead of one. Whispers, muffled by the sound of the piano. And in the background, a soft syllable. *Shhh. Shhh.*

Shhhhhhh!

Terry opened the door.

Ava sat at the piano. The lid was closed.

"Who were you talking to, Ava?"

Ava looked at her father bemused.

"Ava?"

Ava shook her head and made her way up the stairs to her bedroom.

The silent treatment continued for the rest of the week. Terry was reminded of Prue's sullen moods when they'd been together. She could go weeks without speaking to him if she wanted to. It was the worst kind of punishment. Terry hadn't expected Ava to inherit her mother's morose temperament; she'd always seemed so much more like him. Terry would have preferred Ava to shout at him, or skulk up to her bedroom and play her abysmal music as loud as her speakers would allow. But the house was as silent as his daughter.

The only exception was her piano lessons, when for a brief hour the house was filled with gentle refrains and familiar melodies. When Philippa left, Ava practised on her own, always the same song; the one he'd heard her play when sleepwalking. A sad, slow air that gradually built, stopping frustratingly short, just before the final crescendo. Terry wished she would play something else but she was as deaf to that request as she was to his pleas to open up.

The only time Ava said anything now, apart from the monosyllabic replies to his questions, was when she was alone at the piano. Listening at the door, Terry was sure he could hear whispers, hushed beneath the dark melody that had come to haunt him.

He resolved to speak to Philippa about it. Maybe she'd noticed something strange during their piano lessons. Seizing the next available opportunity, he took Philippa into his workroom and closed the door.

"Well, she follows instructions," Philippa assured him, "but she doesn't say any more than is absolutely necessary. Her playing though..."

"Yes, she's very good," Terry conceded. "Except that when she practises, she only plays the same tune over and over. It's driving me mad."

Philippa asked him if he could identify it. He hummed it instead, feeling a little self-conscious.

Philippa looked away. She shrugged after a few moments. "Sorry, I don't recognize it. Listen, I'm sure whatever this is will blow over. Ava is adjusting." She placed her hand on his arm. "She's been through an awful lot."

Terry leant in closer, "That's not all. When you're gone I hear her talking in the piano room. Talking to..."

Philippa nodded. "I don't think you need to worry about that. She's obviously not ready to let go of Prue just yet. At least she's talking."

"I suppose." But Terry couldn't see past how morbid it was.

"Besides, why do you think people visit grave-stones?" Philippa continued. "They offload. The dead have no choice but to listen."

When Ava went to school that day Terry went straight to the piano room. He needed to address the strange influence the urn was having on his daughter. Despite what Philippa said, there was something unnatural about the communication in the piano room.

He didn't give much credence to the supernatural, but he knew how stubborn Prue had been in life, and if anyone would flout the laws of death it would be her. He'd thought about replacing Prue's ashes with soil or something, wondering if getting rid of them would somehow restore normality. But it all seemed so underhand. He wanted to resolve this civilly, parent to parent. He'd practiced the words in his workroom but now, in the presence of Prue's urn, he was at a loss. He stared at the floor.

They'd managed to avoid each other pretty well over the years. When he picked up Ava he usually stayed in the car and honked the horn. But with death, a strange desire to see his ex-wife had overwhelmed him. He wanted to see what she'd become, to look down on the woman who had caused him so much misery. He remembered the last time he'd seen her in the Chapel of Rest; standing over her, he'd felt a strange sense of victory, one which hadn't involved the courts or social services. He'd won the right to his daughter just by waiting it out.

Prue had looked different, slightly bloated. He wasn't sure whether she'd put weight on over the years or if it was the effect of death. He'd read somewhere that a corpse had many of its fluids removed, to stop the natural bloating that sets in with rigor mortis and the body was pumped full of embalming fluid. He knew the dead were dressed up like this for the viewing public, a strange kind of charade; an attempt to stop the clock, to avoid the inevitable putrescence. Her face had been painted an unnatural shade, her skin alive with an artificial glow. He'd wanted to touch her cheek to see if it felt the same but he knew it would be cold and he didn't want to ruin the illusion.

He thought about how her body would have been doused in disinfectant and germicidal solutions. The body he had lain with, made love to in the back of his first car. The embalmer massaging the legs and arms the way he had once caressed them. The eyes posed shut with an eye cap. Worst of all was the mouth. The mouth he'd kissed. The mouth that whispered *I love you, I'm having a baby*, the mouth that had screamed at him a hundred times, or closed tightly in disappointment or anger when they'd exhausted words. All the things it had left unsaid, sown shut with ligature and a needle or stuck together with adhesive. He had known then, without any doubt, that Prue was gone. That the body before him was only an echo of her, the undertaker's artifice. In death the real face crumbles, the mouth rolls open, gawping in a way that Prue herself would have described as uncouth, expelling the soul with its final breath.

Back in his workroom, Terry finally began to relax. He wasn't sure if it was because he was surrounded by the tools of his trade, the reassuring ticking of the carriage clocks, or the silent narratives of the objects he'd resurrected, whatever it was, he felt consoled. He rummaged through his toolbox, forgetting what he was looking for but enjoying the sound of metal rattling. He wanted to make some noise. He felt like celebrating. He'd finally given Prue a piece of his mind after all these years.

He'd felt ridiculous at first, of course, speaking to the urn, saying the words aloud in the quiet room. It was absurd. But it was better than staying silent on the subject. It became easier when he imagined Prue in the Chapel of Rest. Then the words had poured out of him.

They gushed uncensored from his lips, thirteen years' worth of latent discontent suddenly given voice. He'd shouted and sworn, threatened to scatter her ashes to the corners of the earth unless she left their daughter alone. The dead have no choice but to listen and he left the room feeling as if he'd finally vanquished his demons. That by speaking his mind he'd performed some kind of exorcism, that the house would finally be free of its strange deathly silence.

The sudden blare of music startled him.

Terry put his hands to his ears, shocked at how loud it was. It thundered down from the attic, louder than anything he had heard before. It made his heart race, filling him with an urgency to make it stop.

He raced up the stairs, towards its source. It was too loud for any melody, for words. It was an alarm, a war cry, an enormous echoing din.

Bursting into Ava's room Terry made straight for the stereo and turned it off. He sat panting on her bed, listening to his relaxing heartbeat, savouring the new silence.

When he finally looked up, he received his second shock of the morning: Ava's bedroom was completely transformed. Her clothes were neatly folded, the debris that had previously crowded the carpet put away. Her desk was clear of make-up and CDs, and in their stead were a pile of schoolbooks and a neatly arranged pad of A4 paper.

Terry stood and turned. The room was immaculate, spotless. Apart from the work on her desk, there was nothing else in the room. Even her picture frames had been removed, the walls bare.

For a moment Terry wondered what Ava's room had been like when she lived with Prue. He'd never asked her. He imagined that Prue would've run a pretty tight ship. He doubted she'd be allowed posters on the walls, to leave clothes on the floor. Maybe these months living with him had been a rebellion against her mother. And if so, why had she reverted back?

Terry shook his head, bemused. He should've been glad that the images of bronzed hunks had been removed from his daughter's room, but it was all so sudden. And where had all of it gone?

Terry crouched, pulling aside the duvet to peer under Ava's bed, wondering if Prue had also snooped through their daughter's things. The space under the bed was pretty much empty as well, containing only the discarded rolled up posters and the music box.

Terry retrieved it and brushed it down, the black lacquer gleaming underneath the dust. He thought for a moment that maybe he shouldn't open it, that maybe it would contain something private, a diary or a keepsake. Maybe something that would explain her strange behaviour, he thought, justifying his desire to unclasp it.

Empty.

He waited for the mechanical notes to begin playing. He wound the spring and opened the box again, expecting the action to spur the steel mechanism inside. But no sound came. Terry opened and closed it a few more times, each time anticipating the tinny mechanical melody. But it was silent. He'd take it to his workshop and see if he could fix it, wondering all while why Ava hadn't told him it was broken.

Terry ordered pizza that night on purpose, hoping that it would incite Ava to criticize him about his cholesterol again. But she ate her slice in silence, cutting it into small neat pieces instead of picking it up with her hands like she used to. He wasn't sure whether to come clean about going into her room—she'd always been pretty protective about her private space—but she'd soon discover her music box gone and besides, any reaction was better than none.

"I went into your room today," Terry said, breaking the silence. "You left your music on."

Ava continued eating.

"Your room looks pretty tidy. I'm glad you took my advice." But he wasn't glad at all. He preferred it when it was a tip, when she played her music really loud and ate her food with noisy mouthfuls.

Ava glared at him but still she didn't say anything.

"Anyway, I've taken the music box." Terry knew she'd know now that he'd been snooping under her bed, but he didn't care. "You should have told me it was broken. I'll try and get it fixed, if that's what you want?"

Ava put her cutlery down and looked at him again. Her eyes were softer this time, almost imploring. It frustrated him more than her anger.

"Ava, for goodness' sake, what's wrong?" he said. He heard his words reverberating in his head. He waited a few moments for her to reply and when she didn't, he stood. "Talk to me!" he yelled, knocking his plate off the table in his rage. It fell to the floor, shattering into pieces.

Ava raised her hands to her ears, closing her eyes.

"Ava, I didn't mean to scare you."

But she was up from the table in a flash, running up the stairs to the attic.

Terry watched her go, then he stooped to pick up the shards of crockery. He wondered at Ava's reaction to the noise. For though his rage had been voluble, and he watched the plate shatter, he couldn't remember it

251

making a sound.

Terry gradually became accustomed to the silence. He went about his day as if his world had been muted. As if a strange cloud had descended over them, cushioning the usual sounds a household made. Ava withdrew into the silence, into the attic, only appearing for her piano lesson or for meals. He spent so little time with his daughter it was almost as if Prue had never died.

Terry sat in his workroom, listening, waiting for Ava's piano lesson to begin. Nothing happened for a while and then he heard Philippa's raised voice and footsteps on the stairs, heading to the attic. He headed to the music room, finding Philippa sat alone on the piano stool.

"What happened?"

"It's broken, I don't know how." She lifted the lid and pressed a key to demonstrate. "It's impossible, unless someone came in here and silenced it."

Terry sat down beside her, thinking about how his attempts to fix the music box had also failed.

"So Ava's still not talking," Philippa observed, "what's her problem anyway?"

Terry shrugged. He spread his fingers over the keys, pretending to be able to play. Without any sound it was easier to imagine the melody in his head, the melody Ava usually practiced. The imagined music distracted him from the alarm that was building up inside. Where was the sound going? Why did the house seem to prefer the quiet?

Philippa placed her hand on Terry's. He stopped moving his fingers in imaginary playing. He let it rest there under hers.

"You know," Philippa whispered, "before she took a vow of silence, Ava told me about why she wanted the attic room. She said that you hear things better at the top, that the acoustics are better the higher you are." She spoke the next words slowly. "The best seats in the house are in the gods."

Terry winced. They were Prue's words. Repeated often in mock enthusiasm when they couldn't afford the better seats, lower down. She believed them in the end, doggedly buying the seats the furthest from the stage.

"I lied the other day," Philippa said withdrawing her hand, "about the piece Ava plays all the time. I do recognize it. You do too. How could you have forgotten?"

Terry stared at the piano keys, hearing only silence.

And then he was sitting in the theatre, one sister on either side. He watched the orchestra pile in to murmurs from the auditorium. They were dressed in black formal wear, placing their instruments at their feet, or holding them in their laps. The conductor arrived and it became suddenly silent, the musicians and audience hushed. And then the tapping as the conductor counted them in.

They were in the gods of course. It had taken Prue ages to waddle up the stairs. But she couldn't be persuaded otherwise. Besides, they had no money then. She'd placed his hand against her stomach and he felt the baby inside swimming around to the music. At the interval, Philippa volunteered to help him get the ice cream. Prue was relieved to stay where she was.

They'd gone down together.

The theatre had a concave of private boxes. Relics from a time before, closed now for renovation. He

253

was helping to restore them; it was how they'd known about the production in the first place. He was proud of his work. Prue never seemed to want to listen but Philippa was so engrossed holding the pile of ice cream tubs. It would only take him a moment to show her the balustraded parapet, the gilded plasterwork.

He closed the door. The wallpaper was decorated with nightingales.

They just made it back in time for the second half. The ice cream was soft. Prue never said a word.

That night Terry dreamt of the quiet room. He was expecting it, almost hoping for it. He felt as if he were on the wave of Ava's melody, rising and falling, building up to a final, inevitable climax. He didn't want to fight against it any longer. He felt himself carried along by it, up the stairs to his daughter's room, sweeping him across the threshold into the cold, quiet space. The posters were back on the walls. They looked even more obscene than before. He didn't want to see their oiled male torsos, their wanton expressions leering down at his daughter. He ripped one off of the wall, standing back in surprise at what was exposed behind.

A huge gaping hole. An enormous black pit, audibly sucking the air out of the room. He pulled down another and saw a similar void. He tried to peer into the darkness but couldn't see anything, couldn't concentrate on anything but the noise. He removed the other posters, revealing similar vacuums, the sound deafening in the quiet room. Terry felt himself being dragged toward them, pulled toward the unknown.

Beyond the room, beyond the din, he could hear Ava's faint playing, the familiar melody barely a whisper. He latched onto its harmony and filled his mind with it, following its thread. He grabbed hold of the bedstead, then the desk, moving slowly through the room to the hallway, finally shutting the door behind him.

Silence.

He made his way down the stairs to the music room, this time prepared for the congregation inside. They were dressed in black as before, with their heads bent low as if in mourning. Terry didn't waste time trying to talk to them. He walked past them looking for the source of the silence. Ava was at the keyboard, her hands on the lid, her fingers dancing along the surface, playing her silent music. But this time Terry confronted what was on top. He could face Prue now that she was dead.

What he saw made him stagger. If he hadn't been condemned to silence, he would have screamed.

Lying on top of the piano was Prue's corpse. She looked almost as she did in the Chapel of Rest. Her eyes shut, her hands arranged demurely, but her legs wide open, revealing cheap stockings and a glimpse of her underwear. She looked like some slutty nightclub singer. Terry walked around the piano, an absurd bier, staring at the woman he had once loved.

He felt compelled to touch her cold skin, prepared to shatter the illusion. But just as he reached for her, she turned her head towards him and it wasn't Prue's face but Philippa's staring back, opening her lifeless eyes. And as he recoiled away from her she opened her mouth, ripping the embalmer's stitches from her lips and letting out the ear-piercing scream he couldn't make.

Terry woke with the scream in his mind. It was morning and glancing at his alarm clock he realized he had overslept. He wondered why Ava hadn't woken him, remembering then that Ava hadn't said a word to him for over a week. She had probably already left for school with nothing but the silence of the morning for company.

Terry put on his dressing gown and went up to her bedroom. He rapped a few times on the door and opened it, her absence confirming that she had already left. It was still a tidy, blank shell, an empty cocoon that had facilitated her startling change. Terry wanted to take a sledgehammer to it, to break the unnatural silence with the sound of wood splintering, of plaster falling. He recalled shredding the posters in his dream, the delight it had given him ripping them from the wall, and he remembered the actual posters rolled up under Ava's bed.

He fell to his knees, thrusting his arm into the darkness to retrieve them. He sat on Ava's bed and unrolled the first of them, revealing the image of a bronzed torso, progressing to well-defined shoulders, then a muscular neck with a prominent adam's apple. He stopped at the head, realizing, as he saw the model's mouth that he was reaching the end of the movement, that everything was beginning to make sense.

The pinup's mouth was scribbled out with black marker pen, the messy scrawl forming a blackened hole. Could Ava have taken the posters down to give him a message, hoping their absence would tell him something, then scribbling on them in case he still didn't see. Sometimes we don't see the messages that are right in front of us, Terry thought, remembering the day he gave Ava the music box. Remembering the story he'd told her about Philomela. How do you ask for help when you are bound to silence? Why not write a message? Too obvious, he remembered telling her, it

256

wouldn't get past the guards.

Terry shook his head. He could talk but he hadn't listened. Not really.

He got to his feet, straining his ears, listening now to the house below. You can hear everything better from the gods.

He heard a sound from the music room. He listened hard, but the silence itself seemed to be getting louder, sonorous, obscuring everything else. It was there underneath, barely a whisper.

Shhhhhh.

Terry raced down the stairs as he had in his dream, conscious that his footsteps on the floorboards emitted no sound. He pushed the door open as soundlessly and saw his daughter sitting at the piano. Her hands were on the piano lid, engaged in her silent practice.

Terry hurried to her side, turning her by the shoulders to face him. But her head flopped listlessly. Her eyes observed him vacantly.

"Ava? We have to leave. It's this house."

The silence buzzed around him like an angry swarm.

Shh. Shh. Shh. Shh. Shhhhhhh.

Terry stood, tried to pull her from the piano, but she was a dead weight.

"Ava, come on, we have to go!" He knew he was speaking, he could hear his voice in his head, but the sound he made was swallowed up, absorbed by the quiet of the room.

The silence was enveloping everything, feeding on the sounds they made, stealing them, leaving nothing behind in its wake. A blank slate. Terry tried again to wrench Ava from the piano, from this parasitic house, but silence closed in around them. His mind emptied, blackness swirled instead, accompanied by the sound of air being sucked away. *Shh. Shh. Shh. Shh.*

Terry put his hands to his ears, trying to stop the pain in his head. He reeled against it, falling into the piano, knocking the urn from its perch.

It all happened so slowly in the quiet room that it had the same blurred quality as his dreams. The urn rolled to its side, silently tumbling toward the ground, knocking against the piano lid on its way down and releasing an enormous cloud of ash.

The particles swirled into the air, caught in a whirlwind, and for a brief moment Prue stood before them. She looked at Terry and opened her mouth into an exaggerated smile.

The house, he realized, created the silence for other sounds. Sounds suppressed or obscured, dormant or tacit. Sounds long dead, buried deep in the heart, called back again to speak out, amplified by the vacuous silence of the room.

Ava had tried to warn him, though she'd been bound to silence in her role as dutiful daughter. She'd always been caught between two parents and Terry felt a sudden overwhelming sense of sadness for his daughter.

Prue stopped smiling. Her mouth opened wider and wider, her face collapsing into a yawning, swirling hole. Terry stared into the hollow and saw only the darkness at the heart. A low rumbling like distant thunder emerged from the pit of it, then a cacophonous melancholy strung out into the room. He'd been the author of those sounds he'd realized, of her anguish and grief. But it wasn't too late—

"Prue," he tried to say, but the words couldn't compete with the piercing discord. He placed his hands to his ears. The notes became louder and louder, starting to come together, flowing into the familiar melody. Climbing higher and higher, as if to the gods.

The crescendo surged into the room from her mouth, spiralling around as if in flight. The music broke against him like a wave, and in awe he opened his mouth dumbfounded and swallowed it all down.

The dead have no choice but to listen, but Prue always answered back. He should have known she'd want to have the last word.

The sound of the urn shattering broke Ava from her trance. She glanced at the shattered remains on the floor then looked toward her father.

"Dad? Dad?"

Terry could feel the ash in his throat, silted around his larynx. A cloud of ash and dust rested in his gullet. He reached for his voice but felt only his absence. Yet in his mind all he could hear was music.

Senbazuru

Paper, scissors, rock.

That's the way we've always made decisions. And settled arguments for that matter. Marriage is all about compromise after all; I put something forward, he puts something forward, and our hands do the rest. My husband jokes if only diplomacy were so easy. When we play we are back in the playground of St. Gabriel's again, with the Catholic sisters hurrying us in opposite directions towards the boys and girls dormitories and my husband is my darling childhood Teddy.

After all these years he knows how I play, my preference for paper, stretching out my hand as if holding it above a flame. I watch his calculated response, knowing his reaction in advance; his index and middle finger stretched into a V if he is being particularly stubborn or folded into a ball to satisfy me, letting me win.

Sometimes I let *him* win. When he suggested taking the job with the British consulate in Nagasaki I was eager to break the monotony of my daily existence and curious to see the world. Being married to a diplomat had lacked the excitement I thought customary with the role. I'd imagined life as a newlywed to be different. So I lay my hand submissively straight and gave in to destiny.

261

V. H. Leslie

Occasionally I won't use paper but maybe rock. Scissors are my least favourite (as they hurt paper the most) and I'll save it for only the most extreme situations. I register the hurt in Ted's face when I use one of these two, his faith in my constancy momentarily shaken by my desire to win.

It's hard living without him.

I live in a roundhouse. A tower, really. There are four windows, each presenting a different view of the surrounding landscape.

To the east, the sea, just beyond Nagasaki harbour. This is my favourite view. In constant transit, the ocean rolls by, grey and tumultuous one day, calm and tranquil the next. Some days it is spotted with the red sails of Japanese fishing boats or the rickety sampans of larger freighters.

The window to the south depicts a small Japanese garden where sometimes Hiroko takes me for a walk. It is comprised of neat, straight borders of jasmine and honeysuckle. In the middle, pebbles like pale flat eggs occupy the space that would have given way to lawn in England. It is the antithesis of my unruly garden back home. Now neglected, I imagine the profusion of wild hybrids and weeds have complete mastery over the box borders, and the wrought iron bench, speckled with rust, now completely submerged by green.

To the north, a road stretches into the distance to the town centre. In the morning the road is busy with people, rickshaws and carts taking goods to and from the port. At night it is usually quiet, save for the occasional beggar drunk on *sake*.

The west window depicts rolling green countryside and, further back, paddy fields tended by farmers,

262

who are only tiny specks from this distance.

If I turn in the middle of the room I can see out of all four windows. I am at the centre of the compass.

It must have been hard, furnishing such a room on account of its shape. The bed, just off centre, juts out into the rotund space like a small island. Some of the chairs have curved backs so they don't seem so anomalous against the curved walls. My desk seems to be the most incongruous object, its right angles at odds with the spherical nature of the room. But I wouldn't be without it.

My desk is positioned next to the east window so I can watch the boats. This is where I write my letters, though I don't receive many anymore. I *try* to write. Ted used to say that you could cure anything by writing but I can't seem to commit anything to paper. Sometimes I just like to think.

Hiroko brings me the British newspapers once a week. They are tied up in string. I keep these bits of string and tuck them away. I don't care much for the news. I'm more interested in the paper. I usually tear out a sheet or two from the correspondence pages, the most insubstantial part, and if Hiroko ever noticed them gone she'd be too embarrassed to question me. The Japanese don't talk about their problems. I always make sure I read the foreign affairs pages before I leave the pile for Hiroko to collect. The wife of a diplomat must be well informed.

The days are so repetitive here one can lose track of time. The dates on the newspapers are my only indication, though they are delayed of course. They tell me our anniversary is approaching.

I'm going to have to hurry.

§

Do you know that you can fold a piece of paper in half no more than eight times, no matter its original size? Ted used to like folding paper. Origami is very important to the Japanese. I remember the first one he gave me. We had been in Japan a few months and were guests at a party hosted by the Hammonds, a prominent English couple. Everyone wanted to talk to Ted. About whether war was really imminent. If expatriates should evacuate. Ted didn't really talk to me about the war, eager to protect me from the world. But I'd hear it eventually through the wives, along with rumours about corrupt officials and counterfeit money and public relations of an altogether different sort. Ever the diplomat, he gave them the company policy, the official lines. With the crowd placated and able to sip their imported gin with ease, conversation moved on to less contentious subjects. The hostess, relieved that her soirée wasn't overshadowed by Japanese foreign policies, gave the ladies a tour of her garden.

Like many immigrants she had attempted to embrace her new home not by adopting Japanese customs or traditions but through their modes of decoration. Nagasaki itself, with its history of being an open port when the rest of Japan was fearful of foreign intrusion, was imbued with western influences. A medley of European and Japanese architecture, it was Western and Eastern in equal measure. What's more, as foreigners tend to, we stuck together, colonizing a district of the city and making it as much like home as possible. British children were sent to European schools and British women took high tea at the Hilton on Wedgewood china. Ted used to say that the British art of hegemony was conversion through cricket and cucumber sandwiches.

But it worked both ways. Many of the guests were

Orientals who were perhaps more western in customs and dress than many Europeans. Whilst the English women experimented with kimono-inspired garments and fabrics, many of the Japanese women wore the latest Parisian fashions that the European women would have to wait until next season to acquire, when the ships arrived. Amid the joviality and cocktail music, a strange exchange of identity was being played out on Mrs Hammond's landscaped terrace.

When Ted eventually managed to extricate himself from all the questions, he found me standing beside a small water-feature of polished stones. We watched as it propelled water into a stream that coursed its way through the garden.

"Ted, tell me the truth," I asked. "Is there going to be a war?"

He produced a Yen note from the pocket of his tux and he began to fold it. I watched his hands move deftly with rehearsed practice. He ran his fingers along each crease with deliberate care and I wondered if he organized his thoughts as carefully. He placed the finished object in my palm.

"It's beautiful."

He told me to place it on the water. I didn't want to. It was too beautiful but he insisted.

"The crane is a symbol of prosperity and peace," he told me as I placed it on the stream. "But you can't stop the current of things to come, Elaine."

I watched as it bobbed uncertainly on the surface before being swept away.

Whenever Ted went away, which was becoming more and more frequent as the Kwantung Army swept through China, I would find a little origami crane in his stead. On my pillow when I woke, at the breakfast table, sometimes tucked into my purse, waiting until I paid a street vendor or when I took a rickshaw. I kept every one of them.

I make my own now.

I try to keep them as secret as possible, which is easy enough as Hiroko's jangling keys always announce her approach, long before the sound of her unlocking my door. I wouldn't want her to think I'm cultivating a strange habit. I am an Englishwoman after all.

After breakfast, I sit at my desk opposite the ocean and take out the segments of newspaper from the drawer. I'll fold the page once, then, using the edge of a book as a weight, I'll rip the paper until I have two equal rectangles. I repeat the action. Then I have four rectangles. The basis for four cranes.

You can make an origami crane fairly quickly but I tend to prolong the process, relishing each fold and crease. Twenty-eight folds to be exact. There is a lot of satisfaction to be had in their creation and doubly so knowing how much time I have invested in each one. Afterwards I'll attach them to the others with the string from the newspapers and hide them behind my clothes in the wardrobe.

I'll lick my fingers afterwards, rubbing the saliva into the creases of my fingertips to erase the newsprint ink.

The rainy season, or *baiu*, is nearly at an end. The days have been very humid. Hiroko brings me water for taking my pills in the evening but I dab most of it onto my brow and neck, relishing the coolness as the droplets trickle down my spine. The rain pours down in torrents but the mischievous wind blows it in all directions, and it hammers into the side of my tower.

All good fairytales begin with a princess in a tower waiting to be rescued. I feel more like the Lady of Shalott, waiting and watching the world below but unable to live in it.

I remember when I lived in England I used to visit my mother in her tower. Except, she wasn't really Mother by then. She looked the same but her mind was someplace else. Aided no doubt by the pharmaceutical concoction the doctors prescribed for her, sentencing her to a permanent state of oblivion. The staff would stand a little distance away but their presence was palpable in the small circular room. It wasn't the most conducive environment to form a relationship.

I know that trauma can often prompt a collapse of this sort. But Father didn't speak to me about such things. It wasn't proper. In fact, Mother left when I was so young it was easier for Father to tell me she was a princess in a tower. Every few months we would take the long journey by train to visit her. I would take my school projects for her to see. Father encouraged me; he hoped, I think, that something would bring her back to reality. But she would stare inanely at my crayon drawings and lightly rub the surface of the page until her fingertip was waxy and the colour faded and I felt as if I, too, were being erased.

The fact it looked like a fairytale tower gave credence to Father's lie. There were actually four of them, one tower on each corner of four crenulated grey walls, though the view from the roadside obscured the other three. I could only see the one perched beside the sea. If you looked closely there were stars interspersed in the masonry. Every time we visited, it seemed to snow. So much so that I can't remember the tower without a layer of white, like icing on a wedding cake.

V. H. Leslie

The town lay a little distance away, beyond the curve of hills, as if the inhabitants had deemed a buffer necessary. As if the tower's fortified walls were not sufficient to contain the sickness. The pinnacle of the town was literally the church spire, which rose to an impressive height out of the cluster of buildings, attempting to brush the heavens. I assumed my mother could see it from her window. But even if she couldn't, she would be able to hear the bells tolling, calling the congregation to worship or announcing the joining of those in matrimony.

The Lady of Shalott at least had her tapestry to keep her busy. I used to do a lot of needlepoint myself back in England but a lot of commodities are very difficult to acquire here, especially now. I have to content myself with my paper cranes.

She left them quite by chance. In the shade of the hibiscus, on a small ledge that serves as a border, I saw them glinting at me. The kind used for trimming bonsai trees. Sunlight reflected off their shiny surface and, magpie-like, I swooped. Hiroko was tending the wilted honeysuckle, examining the waterlogged roots, and did not see me. The rains had kept us indoors for so long that I took this brief reprieve to be a sign.

I intended to ask to borrow them. Yet asking posed a dilemma; what would I say I needed them for? I didn't want to explain the birds in my cupboard. But a pair of scissors would help my project along no end. What harm would it cause to pick them up?

They slipped easily into my pocket.

～

Ted always maintained that our wedding was hands down the best wedding he'd ever been to. It was, of course, an elaborate affair, full of pomp and ceremony.

Part way through the evening Ted grabbed me by the hand.

"Let's elope," he said.

"We're already married," I replied.

But I was already following him. We walked for miles, it seemed, my wedding gown trailing along the ground, snagged on brambles and ferns. He led me through the long grass and laid his jacket down for us to sit upon. Then he opened the champagne he'd been carrying and we watched the sun set over the English countryside.

There were no speeches. A diplomat's wedding with no speeches. My wedding gown still has the grass stains.

Not long now until our anniversary. I've worked out the date from the newspapers Hiroko brought me today, along with my pills. I didn't want to take them but there was no point arguing with her. She no longer waits until I swallow the pills so when she left I flung them at the window. I picked them up afterwards of course and tucked them behind a panel in the back of the wardrobe, stacking them up to form small cairns of tiny white rocks, which always topple when I close the door. Hiroko means well but I need to be fully alert if I want to finish what I've started.

The Japanese have their own customs but my favourite is a special tradition reserved for newlyweds. They believe that to give a couple one thousand paper cranes on their wedding day is to give a thousand years of good luck. These paper cranes are held together on lengths of string and hung up in the home. Senbazuru: a thousand paper cranes.

We are not so entirely different. In England paper marks your first year as a married couple. Everything of importance is made of paper.

This year will be paper too, despite so many years having passed like the pages in a book. I'm ready to finish the story. It will always be paper until he returns.

I've always been a dreamer. My head in the clouds, Ted liked to say. He was always the practical one. I suppose he had to be, in his line of work. He was able to marry his ideals with pragmatism as easily as he married me. But you have to be pragmatic to survive.

After the war broke out Ted was away a lot. His work was keeping him very busy back then. Many of the European families had started to evacuate. You needed a pass to get around town. Our European coterie that, months before, had been sipping champagne together in the warm evenings, was suddenly dispersed. The Germans and Austrians fared better but all foreigners were regarded with a kind of contempt, a disdain too strong to be fashioned overnight. In retrospect, perhaps it had always been there, hidden behind painted smiles and strained pleasantries.

Perhaps a kind of British stoicism prevented me from leaving, keeping me inside and ignorant of the dangers. Hiroko would venture to the market to get food and we would sit together silently in the evenings to eat whatever she had managed to acquire. It wasn't much. Usually a meat broth of sorts, though I had no idea, nor did I want to know, what animal or cut of meat flavoured the meal. The banquets of food Ted and I had been used to eating before faded into memory.

When they started rounding up foreigners and taking them away, I knew we had to get out.

Senbazuru

I had the most alarming dream last night. I remember turning in the centre of the room and looking out all four windows. I was the compass point, choosing which perspective I preferred. But the landscape was different. It was difficult to pinpoint exactly how at first, as the land outside was cloaked in snow. And the snow itself fell in heavy sheets against the panes, obscuring what lay beyond.

When the blizzard subsided I looked out of the south window, but instead of seeing the garden, I saw the road meandering towards the town. I rushed to the north window but instead of the road, I saw Hiroko tending the garden. I stood still for a moment trying to get my bearings, my compass was off; the views were inverted.

The view from the west window confirmed my suspicions. Instead of green fields, the empty ocean lay before me. But the sea was void of vessels, the harbour vacant. The west window however, was completely masked by snow. All I could see was a dark shadow, a tall silhouette like a column. A reflection of myself in the pane perhaps, but the image was so dark I couldn't make out any of my features.

I sat down at my desk, confused. I attempted to write a letter to Ted. He would know what to do. I was very cold. My breath formed little clouds, which floated on the air before dispersing. My fingers became so cold I could barely move my pen.

A butterfly landed on my finger. It stretched its wings. I remember thinking it such an oddity, to have a butterfly perched on my hand in the middle of winter. But when I looked closely I saw that it was a bird and I realized it was as white as the snow outside.

271

V. H. Leslie

It was paper.

It rested on my finger a moment then swept back its wings and flew away. It tried to fly out of the window but glanced against the glass. I would have opened it but I remembered that the windows couldn't be opened. It repeated this a few times but gave up after a while and lay on the sill defeated. When I touched it, it was dead. I unfolded it and unfolded it again, dissecting the creature until all that remained was limp paper.

I heard a noise then. It was very faint. I strained my ears to identify its source. It sounded like rustling and it was coming from the wardrobe.

I took a few tentative steps forward. The din in the wardrobe was getting louder. As I neared, the wardrobe doors suddenly burst open and a flock of paper birds flew out. They orbited the room and I watched their frantic flight in awe. But then a crane swooped to my arm. Another to my shoulder. One nestled into my hair—a makeshift nest. I swiped them away but another landed in its stead. They descended with more urgency. Their claws scratched at my skin, tearing flesh as I attempted to strike them off. They swarmed until there was no part of me left uncovered. I called Hiroko but I knew she couldn't come. I called, and the cranes flooded my mouth, scratching and scraping against my throat, muffling my cries with folds of paper. I tried to shake them off and they fell to the ground like confetti, leaving near-invisible marks behind. I ripped the remainder from my body, slashing and scratching at their wings, tearing the paper into shreds. The mutilated remains of a thousand paper cranes lay at my feet like a crisp first dusting of snow. I looked at my skin and could see the thread-like incisions of a thousand paper cuts; tiny, minute slits which paused pale a moment before smiling red.

໙

Hiroko has dressed my wounds. She registers her disappointment by not talking to me. Not that she's talked to me much since that last day in the market. She's never really been the same since. But her silence speaks a thousand words, as if she holds me responsible for the bloodied sheets. I'm not sure if she is angrier at having to care for me or for the theft of her scissors. I know she suspects I've taken them, how else to explain the curious marks on my body. But she'd never believe me if I told her about the paper birds.

The last time I saw Ted was around the time of Tanabata. The star festival. It's my favourite one. The Japanese believe that the Weaver Princess Vega and her lover Altair are separated by the Milky Way. But on this day they fly across the universe and are united in the heavens. The Japanese celebrate by writing poems on strips of paper and attaching them to bamboo poles to bring good fortune. It doesn't snow in July, but all that paper and Nagasaki is clothed in white.

That last time, though, we didn't feel like celebrating. No one did. We sat in the dining room and Ted went to the drinks cabinet only to find it empty. I asked Hiroko to fetch the liquor, which was locked with our valuables in the basement. There had been a lot of attacks on foreigners and foreign sympathizers, often fuelled by alcohol. It seemed best to keep it out of sight.

I waited until the jangling of keys subsided and went to him. I hadn't seen him for so long. I had almost expected him to be arrested, knowing all that he knew, but somehow he had managed to escape capture. He wouldn't tell me how. He looked small in his clothes, which were snagged and dirty.

Hiroko returned with a few bottles and Ted poured himself a large scotch and sat down heavily.

"In the next few days all foreigners will be taken to POW camps."

The statement occupied the room. He swallowed the dregs of his drink and poured another.

"We should have escaped sooner."

I asked if it was too late.

"We don't have the right paperwork," he said. "We would never make it past the check points."

"Surely you know someone we could bribe?" I had asked.

"Wake up Elaine, it would never be enough."

I knew he was right. We had lived like kings before the war and Japanese resentment ran deep. Prices had inflated anyway, but foreigners had to pay ridiculous prices for simple commodities. Even Hiroko wasn't exempt, the street vendors charging her exorbitant amounts knowing she served a *gaijin* mistress. One time she had returned with bruises on her face and arms.

"Is there no other money?" I asked.

I could see him weighing something in his mind. And I noted the reluctance in his eyes as he told me about a great quantity of counterfeit money the embassy had seized before the war began. It should have been destroyed. Only a handful of officials even knew it existed.

"To buy our freedom?" I asked.

Ted rounded on me. His eyes were fierce. "Do you know the risk if we are found out?"

We made the decision the same way we always did. I knew he would try to win this one. He thought we stood a better chance of survival in a prisoner of war camp. I knew that he would play scissors before our hands even began to move. He would hope I'd play my usual hand, and be the submissive wife he was used to. But I wanted to escape, to go home. I wanted England's green fields.

I rolled my hand into a fist, unmoving as a rock.

People often claim money doesn't grow on trees, but of course it does. Someone turns trees into pulp, then flattens it and stamps it with the head of some official. Who prints what onto those virgin notes is no concern of mine. But it matters to everyone else. Everything of importance is made of paper.

Marriage licence.

Money.

Travel permit.

Paper says who you are and what you've done.

Our sentence was printed on paper.

It's our anniversary today. I've worked out the date from last week's paper and though I can't be sure, it feels like the right time.

I go to my wardrobe and carefully take out the paper construction I've assembled. It hangs from a coat hanger, which I suspend from the wardrobe door as I close it. I sit back on the bed and admire my handi-work. I'm sure Ted would like it.

The lengths of string are attached to the wooden frame, each with fifty cranes attached, which flap and float. The string is thick and coarse, and a length of bamboo would be much more suitable than a coat hanger, but needs must. As it is, the paper cranes weigh

275

down on the coat hanger like a heavy robe and from afar my creation resembles a white fur coat, the kind I imagine a Tsarina of imperial Russia to wear. A coat fit for a princess.

I pull the small silver scissors from my pocket. I've sharpened them on a rock from the garden. It, too, found its way into my pocket. My beautiful paper cranes bob up and down on the string, caught like fish in a net, fighting against a current stronger than they can contend with.

In fairy tales the princess is always rescued. But what if your prince can't come? What if your prince is discovered face down in a paddy field. His body broken and bloodied, misshapen by bamboo sticks and rocks. Unrecognizable, save for the paper crane crushed in his palm. You have to be pragmatic to survive.

I stand in the middle of the compass. I can see the stars out of the windows. Their brightness is reflected in the glassy surface of the ocean. Like Altair and Vega, we'll meet again in the heavens. They are bright tonight, the stars, almost white. I watch them and realize they are falling. The stars are falling like snowflakes. But it doesn't snow this time of year, not in Japan.

I turn to my favourite view- the east.

Rock: I throw the stone through the east window. The image of Nagasaki harbour shatters. The room is filled with icy air and I shield my eyes from the torrent of snow.

As the snowflakes settle around me I see in the distance a tower I have known all along was there. The dark silhouette from my dream. I can see it clearly now, reaching up into the heavens. And I can hear the bells. The bells tolling as they did on my wedding day. In the garden I watch Hiroko tending the wilted honeysuckle, except it isn't Hiroko. Never was Hiroko. Easier to think it is though than to remember she never returned that day from market. Everything is unfolding. I look back out of the east window but all I see is west.

Scissors: I like the sound they make as the blades touch; Snip! Snip! Snip! I hold my garment of a thousand paper cranes and I cut the strings.

The cranes burst free from their shackles and soar into the air. The string falls to the ground. The cranes swarm around the room in unison and then, as in my dream, rest upon me. But the paper doesn't hurt this time. Their claws scratch against me but I feel no pain. One rests in my palm. Its wings open and close like that of a butterfly. Then it flies away.

Paper: the cranes have begun to move, their wings beating, beating, beating. And suddenly I am weightless. They lift me up by my dress and I let them, remembering being carried in the arms of my prince. Teddy's arms on our wedding day, across the threshold. My robe of a thousand paper cranes carries me over the broken glass, over the years, and out of the window I fly.

Acknowledgements

The title for this collection was taken from one of the short stories within its pages. "Skein and Bone", first published in *Black Static*, is about the beautiful layers we wear to construct an idea of selfhood and belonging. It is about how we fashion an image of ourselves, an image often informed by society and tradition, to better cope with our place in the world, or as a means to ascend to the place where we want to be. I came to realize when collating the stories for this collection that many of my narratives draw on this thread. Whether it is putting on a dress or a name, my characters engage in a various forms of fashioning or self-deception, in order to cope with a reality that for them is unsatisfactory. But you can't hide behind beautiful wallpaper or a pantry full of empty jars or even among the clouds forever. You have to come down to earth eventually.

I have a lot of people to thank who have helped in various stages of the production of this work. To Mitch Larney and Ray Cluley for looking at many of these stories in draft form and to early readers, Alison Moore, Adam Nevill, Stephen Volk and Conrad Williams. I'd also like to thank Tom Stammers and Duncan Leslie for listening to so many half-formed ideas and for helping me develop the geneses of many stories. To the editors who published my stories and who continue to champion speculative fiction for the benefit of us all: Andy Cox, Johnny Mains, Paula

279

V. H. Leslie

Guran, Michael Wilson, Rosalie Parker, James Everington, Steve Haynes and Joe Mynhardt. I'd also like to thank Vince Haig for producing the startlingly beautiful cover art and for taking such pains in creating this image, which, rather fittingly, involved photographing dressmaker's dummies in a deserted old house.

My short story "Skein and Bone" is also about inheritance and tradition and I'd be remiss not to mention these elements in my own work and the dressmaking impetus behind this story in particular. My mother was a seamstress and my childhood was spent unraveling yards of fabric, rummaging in tins of buttons and wrapping myself up in ribbons and lace, as if I were a mummy. It seemed that my mother could make anything out of the contents of her haberdashery chest. She could conjure fancy dress costumes or props for school projects at the drop of a hat. And despite the last-minute nature of some of my requests, whatever she produced was beautifully made with an attention to the construction that verged on obsessive.

Though I haven't really inherited her gift with the needle and thread, she did instill in me a need to make things. And to try to make those things as well as I possibly could. She was also a wonderful story-teller and with the same verve that she approached eleventh-hour costumes or alterations, she could craft stories at whim to appease my brother and I, who, like most children, were desperate to put off bedtime. Though I suspect now, it was the calibre of her stories that made us reluctant to sleep. This collection is dedicated to her memory, to her capacity to create beautiful things, oftentimes out of seemingly very little.

Finally, I'd like to thank Michael Kelly for his editorial input and for being such an enthusiastic supporter of my work over the years.

280

About the Author

V. H. Leslie's stories have appeared in a range of speculative publications, including *Black Static, Interzone, Shadows & Tall Trees, Weird Fiction Review* and *Strange Tales IV* and have been reprinted in a range of "Year's Best" anthologies. She is a Hawthornden Fellow and was recently awarded a place at the Saari Institute in Finland, where she'll be working on a novel concerning various strands of Nordic myth and folklore. She was the winner of the Lightship First Chapter Prize 2013 and is a finalist for the Shirley Jackson Award in the category of novelette. This year will also see the release of her novella *Bodies of Water* from Salt Publishing. When Victoria isn't writing, she is drawing or etching and is a member of the Omega Printmakers.

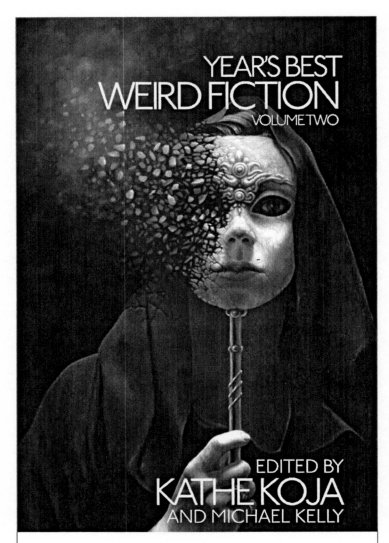

YEAR'S BEST
WEIRD FICTION
VOLUME TWO

EDITED BY
KATHE KOJA
AND MICHAEL KELLY

Year's Best Weird Fiction, Volume Two

Forthcoming Oct. 2015   www.undertowbooks.com

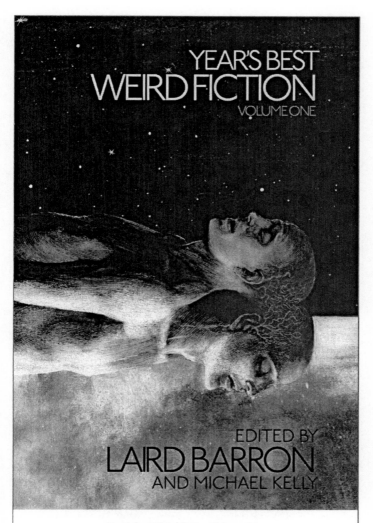

YEAR'S BEST
WEIRD FICTION
VOLUME ONE

EDITED BY
LAIRD BARRON
AND MICHAEL KELLY

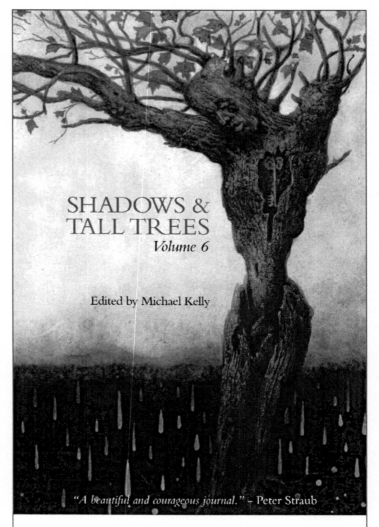

SHADOWS &
TALL TREES
Volume 6

Edited by Michael Kelly

"A beautiful and courageous journal." – Peter Straub

Shadows & Tall Trees, Volume 6
(Shirley Jackson Award Nominee, Edited Anthology)

"A beautiful and courageous volume."
—Peter Straub, author of *Ghost Story*

March 2014   www.undertowbooks.com

Lightning Source UK Ltd.
Milton Keynes UK
UKOW02f0718151015

260584UK00002B/30/P